MISTAKEN IDENTITY

Jack Dillon Dublin Tale 8
Second Edition

MISTAKEN IDENTITY

Jack Dillon Dublin Tale 8
Second Edition

Mike Faricy

Library of Congress Control Number: 2023920385
paperback ISBN: 978-1-962080-75-0
e-Book ISBN: 978-1-962080-76-7

MJF Publishing books may be purchased for education, Business, or promotional use. For information on bulk purchases, please contact the author directly at mikefaricyauthor@gmail.com

Published by

MJF Publishing
https://www.mikefaricybooks.com

ACKNOWLEDGMENTS

I would like to thank the following people for their help & support: Special thanks to Nick, Roy, Julie, Mittie, and Toui for their hard work, cheerful patience and positive feedback. I would like to thank family and friends for their encouragement and unqualified support. Special thanks to Maggie, Jcd, Schatz, Pat, Λv, Emily and Pat, for not rolling their eyes, at least when I was there. Most of all, to my wife, Teresa, whose belief, support and inspiration has, from day one, never waned.

"A criminal, you know, is always better concealed in Dublin than anywhere else."

ONE

T he voice on the loudspeaker said, "Ladies and gentlemen, as we start our descent, please make sure your seat backs and tray tables are in their full upright position. Make sure your seat belt is securely fastened, and all carry-on luggage is stowed underneath the seat in front of you or in the overhead bins. Thank you."

Kate Murray reached over and squeezed Megan Gaffney's hand. This was it. An eight-hour flight that seemed to have taken eight days was almost over. They'd watched movies, eaten two meals, drank wine, and never slept. Now, finally, they were descending into Dublin airport.

They didn't just smile. They grinned at one another. After two years of Kate waitressing in a St. Paul bar and Megan working a checkout lane in the grocery store, they were here. Add to that graduating last week after four years at the U of M. And they'd pulled it all off, the celebratory trip to Ireland. They held hands as the plane descended over the ocean, passed a small island just off the left side of the aircraft, and flew over a housing estate where all the houses appeared to be white with reddish roofs. Suddenly, they were just feet off the ground with the runway directly below them.

The plane seemed to skip for a second or two and began to slow as the engines roared. A moment later, a voice came over the intercom. "Ladies and gentlemen, on behalf of Delta Airlines, we'd like to welcome you to Dublin Airport. The local time is seven forty-five am, and the temperature is sixty-six degrees Fahrenheit, 18 degrees Celsius. For your safety and comfort, please remain seated with your seat belt fastened until the captain turns off the Fasten Seat Belt sign."

"Oh, we made it, Megan. After everyone said we'd never be able to do it."

"Well-earned, Kate. I can't wait. I've got the maps in my suitcase. We'll get the car and be on our way. As soon as the plane stops, let's grab our stuff and hurry off."

They weren't about to hurry. Since they were flying coach, they were seated in the back of the plane. Not so amazingly, once the plane stopped and the fasten seatbelt sign was turned off, everyone stood in the aisle. And that was all they did. No one moved. After fifteen minutes, they could detect some movement up in the next section. Eventually, it was their turn to pull bags from the overhead compartment and exit the plane. They walked along a mile or two of hallways with large black and white pictures of famous Irish people they didn't recognize. They were on the second floor of the concourse, and occasionally they passed windows that looked down onto departure gates filled with people flying out of Dublin.

A sign ahead signaled a ladies' room. They nodded at one another and hurried in, only to wait in line. The passport control area was huge, with a very short line, until they realized the short line was for people with EU passports. The non-EU passport line, meaning the rest of the world, wound back and forth for a mile or two and didn't appear to be moving very fast, if at all.

Forty-five minutes later, they stood nervously in front of a uniformed woman seated behind thick glass. "Passports," she said.

They placed their passports on the counter and smiled nervously.

She paged through the blank pages of both passports before looking up at the girls. "Purpose of your trip?"

"We're going to visit where our families came from," Kate said.

"We're Irish, Westmeath and Cork," Megan added with a smile.

"You were born here?"

"No, in Minnesota. St. Paul."

"So, you're American, which is why you have American passports."

"Well yeah, but my name is Kathleen, and she's Megan."

The officer didn't seem to be impressed. "How long are you staying?"

"One week," they replied in unison.

That seemed to bring a smile to the officer's face. She stamped both passports and pushed them back across the counter. "Enjoy your stay and drive carefully."

"We will," Kate said.

"Thank you," Megan said. They grabbed their passports and hurried to baggage claim.

It took over an hour by the time they had their luggage, exchanged dollars for euros, and signed the paperwork for their red Nissan Micra rental car. But finally, they were driving out of Dublin airport. Kate was behind the wheel, thankful for her father's insistence they pay the extra cost for an automatic transmission on the car rental.

"We follow this Swords Road to a stoplight and take a right onto Old Airport Road. That brings us to the M50 that's like the interstate at home, and we take that to the M4 and Westmeath," Megan said.

"This driving on the wrong side is weird," Kate said.

"I think that stoplight up ahead is the Old Airport Road," Megan said.

Kate stopped at the red light. After a minute, a green arrow flashed, but the red light remained on. Three seconds later, a horn honked, and then another.

"I think we're supposed to go," Megan said.

"But the light is still red," Kate said. More horns honked behind them. "I don't know," Kate said. As she began to make a right-hand turn, the green arrow turned yellow, and two cars suddenly screeched around her, leaning on the horn as they sped past. The woman driving the second car gave them the finger as she passed.

"Welcome to Ireland," Megan said, and they both laughed.

TWO

arshal Jack Dillon, and Detective Inspector Paddy Suel, both with An Garda Síochána Special Branch, sat next to Eric Bergman from the US Embassy. All three men occupied the last bench in the rear of the courtroom in Dublin's Criminal Courts of Justice building. They'd been in the courtroom for the past two and a half days at the request of the prosecution. Dillon and Suel had been the arresting officers in the Sands brothers drug case. Bergman was representing the US Embassy since the two brothers were Americans. Mercifully, none of the three had been called to testify, which, on the one hand was good, but on the other, made for two and a half very long, boring days. Not a complaint from any of the three.

At 11:38 am, according to the large clock on the courtroom wall, both Sands brothers were found guilty of possession with intent to sell and led out of the courtroom without uttering a word. Under Irish law, they were liable for a prison sentence of no more than 14 years. The prosecuting solicitor, a somewhat unpleasant blonde woman, named Caoilfhoinn O Tighearnaigh, packed her briefcase, flashed a quick smile in the direction of the three men, and walked out of the courtroom.

"You're welcome," Bergman said just under his breath as she walked past and stepped into the hallway.

"What are you on about? It's probably more excitement than the likes of you have seen in the last month," Suel said. Both he and Dillon laughed.

"What do you think the Sands brothers will get?" Dillon asked.

"Their sentence?" Suel said. "Hard to say. First-time offenders over here, but Keylin Tierney, that's Caoilfhoinn O Tighearnaigh to the likes of you two, had their histories back in the States entered into the records if you caught it yesterday. They've both done time. I'd say it's possible they'll get a minimum of five years here, but the full fourteen may be more like it. Thirty kilos of coke in their possession and an unwillingness to cooperate, hell, they'll be locked up in Mountjoy for a good long while. Be interesting to see how the lads fair after keeping their mouths shut."

"Whoever it is they're protecting, they'll run into his rivals in the Joy. Oh, to be a fly on the wall," Dillon said.

"Idiots came over here, thinking it would be an easy mark. They'll have plenty of time to examine their mistakes."

"Mistake number one was traveling with the girlfriends," Dillon said. "They're back in the States?"

"Yeah, they will be later today. They'll be met this afternoon, the moment they step off the plane in New

York. DEA took them into custody last night and quietly put them on a flight this morning." Bergman looked at his watch. "Right now, they've been over the Atlantic for about ninety minutes. They're theoretically looking at five years, but after their cooperation, there's a good chance that will be reduced to maybe two to three years probation, maybe some community service. Hell of a stupid move for a couple of college girls. Nice looking girls too, a blonde and a redhead. One can only hope they'll learn. I'm told the father of one has political connections. So, I'm sure he's been on the phone," Bergman said.

"Hell of a stupid move for anyone," Suel said and shook his head. "The world at their fingertips and they shit the bed."

"I'll never understand the attraction to bad guys that some women seem to have. It's like a phase or something they seem to go through."

"They're young, dumb, looking for some excitement, or maybe just doing something to piss their mothers off. Used to be, in my day, they were wearing short skirts or leaving the condom wrapper where their mother would find it. A simpler time, I guess. It all looks like so much child's play compared to what those two young ladies are going to be dealing with," Suel said.

"A week of parties and being stupid and they're going to pay for it for the rest of their lives. Think of all the job opportunities that just went out the window. It's a damn shame," Bergman said.

"It's damn stupid is what it is. Job opportunities are the least of their problems. They'll be fair game for pals of these two guilty knackers."

"Enough," Dillon said, rising to his feet. "Eric, you got time to join us for lunch? We can grab something just around the corner in Phoenix Park."

Bergman looked at his watch. "I can. You thinking the Tea Rooms?"

Dillon shook his head. "No. You know where the Phoenix Cafe is?"

"At the far end of the park, near the Ashtown Demesne?"

"Yeah. It's one of those rare, lovely afternoons in Dublin, not a cloud in the sky, or at least there wasn't an hour ago. There's an outdoor courtyard in the back. First one there grabs a table. You coming, Paddy?"

Suel nodded as he stood. "If memory serves, Dillon, you owe me a meal or two. You best follow me and stay close, so you're able to pay when the time comes."

"I'll see you two over there," Bergman said and headed out the door.

THREE

Megan folded the map resting on her lap in half and looked up just in time to see the sign announcing the town of Mullingar in thirty kilometers. "I don't get it. We were driving on the M4 for most of the way, and now, all of a sudden, it changed to the N4. I wonder what the difference is. It all looks the same to me."

"Thirty kilometers? How many miles is that?"

"I think about twenty, but I'm not sure."

"Let's stop and ask directions to the B&B when we get to the town. I don't know about you, but I'm getting tired. A little nap might do the trick. Maybe close my eyes for a half-hour."

"A nap? Kate, it took us twelve hours to get over here, and now you want to go to sleep?"

"Thirty minutes, Megan. I'll do a power nap. Otherwise, I'll be absolutely worthless. Besides, we can still do stuff today. It's just a little after noon."

Fifteen minutes later, Kate pulled to a stop in front of a two-story, white stucco building that looked at least two hundred years old. She was parked between two picnic tables. The sign above the door read 'The Swordsman Pub.' "I'm just going to get directions to the B&B. Be back in a minute," she said.

"I don't think this is for cars, Kate. They've got those picnic tables and chairs laid out. Maybe pull into the parking lot over there and let me go in with you. I need to stretch and use the bathroom."

"Yeah, now that you mention it."

The inside of The Swordsman was dark, nearly empty, with wooden tables and paneling that confirmed at least a century, if not two, of existence. Two men sat at the bar, five stools apart from one another. Neither one looked at the other, nor at Kate or Megan for that matter. They simply sat and stared at their half-finished pints, either asleep or deep in thought.

The back of the bar was filled with at least a hundred different bottles of liquor. The only name the girls recognized on the beer taps was Budweiser. The dark-haired woman behind the bar was wrapping black napkins around a knife, fork, and spoon and placing them in a small bucket. She smiled as the girls approached and said, "What can I get you, ladies?"

"Directions," Kate said. "We're looking for McGovern's Guest House. Have you heard of it? It's a B&B."

"Oh yeah, I know it. You're only about ten minutes away. Were you planning to check-in."

"Yeah, just for the night," Megan said.

"Well, they'll let you drop off your bags. But they're pretty strict about no check-ins until three. Whoever was there last night has to be out by noon, and they clean the room, make the beds with fresh sheets, and place clean towels in the bath. Mrs. Brady runs it. She's pretty strict. I suppose you could call her, see if you could drop your bags off."

"Three o'clock?" Kate said.

"Sorry, but like I said, she runs a tight ship, which is a good thing. But only three hours to clean the rooms and the bathrooms, you can see her point. Why don't you grab a table and have some lunch? My name's Megan, by the way," she said and held out her hand to shake.

"That's my name, too. Without the 'H'," Megan said, shaking hands.

"Same here. Grab a table and have some lunch. Best to get your order in before the noontime crowd arrives."

"I'm Kate," she said, holding out her hand.

"Let me guess; you're Americans, and you're coming from Dublin."

"Right on both counts. We needed to flee the city. A moving target is harder to hit," Kate joked.

A man sitting across the way, alone in a booth, listened to the conversation. After Kate's moving target comment, he pulled his cellphone from his pocket and hit the speed dial button. After two rings, someone answered. "Yeah Toby, what'd ya got?"

"Brennan, you're never gonna guess what just fell into my lap."

"I don't know, based on the disgusting muppet you are, I'd guess it was a bowl of stew," he said and laughed.

"Very funny. Not. What if I told you I know where to find the two bitches what turned on the Sands brothers and gave the Guards all that information? Showed the coppers where your thirty kilos were hidden."

"The first thing I'd say is you're one stupid bastard if you're thinking I'm finding this the least bit funny. The next thing I'd say is you better get your ass in gear because, when I get my hands on the likes of you for making a joke of it, you're gonna wish you was dead."

"Stop yelling and listen to me for a minute. For fuck's sake. I'm sitting down here at the Swordsman, minding me own business. When who should walk in but two American bitches."

"You stupid bastard. Have you any idea how many Americans come into this country every day? God save me, there'll probably be a dozen just in the Swordsman tonight."

"Oh really, Americans? A blonde and a redhead? And they just told Megan behind the bar that they had to get out of Dublin on account of a moving target is harder to hit. Said they left this morning, which means they was waiting around for the Sands brothers' trial to end before they hightailed it out of town. Probably left so you and your ilk wouldn't find 'em."

"A blonde and a redhead, you say?"

"Yeah, and most definitely American. I put their ages at maybe twenty-two, twenty-three. You ever meet 'em, Brennan?"

"No, but Kevin told me a little about them. Describe them to me."

"Describe 'em? Blonde and a redhead. Shoulder length hair on the both of them. Both about the same height. The blonde's a little heavier, but you'd never call her fat. The redhead's got the tighter ass. Blonde has the bigger boobs. Nice big ones, Brennan. Both wearing jeans and nice tops. Maybe looking like they've been on the run for a couple of days. You know, the hair ain't quite done up. Tops are a little wrinkled."

"Toby, that sure as hell sounds like them."

"You ready for the best part? They introduced themselves to the woman working the bar. Know what their names are?"

"Don't fecking tell me."

"Exactly. Megan and Kate. The one named Megan said it's spelled without the 'H.'"

"Oh, sweet Jesus. They drinking or what?"

"They both just went into the loo. Brennan, I bet they're in there doing a line of coke. Probably some of the stuff what belongs to you."

"You keep an eye on them. They go anywhere, you follow. Got it?"

"Yeah, I guess I can do that. What do want me—"

"I'm heading out there now. Be there in a bit."

"Don't get the Guards after you, Brennan. They got speed traps set up all along the way."

"Don't you worry none about me. You just stay on their ass, and I'll make it worth your while. I'm heading out now."

"Drive careful," Toby said, but Brennan had already hung up.

FOUR

Dillon walked up the street to his car. He pulled out of his parking place on Conyngham Road, drove past the Criminal Courts of Justice building, and turned onto Chesterfield Avenue in Phoenix Park. Suel had stopped at the light a few cars behind him. The park was the largest urban park in Europe, dating all the way back to the seventeenth century. Among other things, along with being home to the headquarters for An Garda Síochána, it was home to a large herd of fallow deer.

Once in the park, it was a long, straight shot along Chesterfield Avenue. He passed the Wellington Monument, the Phoenix Tea Rooms, and the Dublin Zoo. He had to stop and let a car pass at the roundabout encircling the Phoenix Park Monument just opposite the entrance to the American Ambassador's residence before turning off Chesterfield and onto the road leading to the Phoenix Park Cafe. He parked close to the entrance, climbed out of his car, and waited for Paddy Suel to join him.

Once Suel climbed out of his car, Dillon glanced across the field and down the road looking for Bergman but didn't see his car. "I don't see Bergman. We might as well go in and get lunch, hopefully, he'll be able to join us."

"He probably stopped at the Ambassador's Residence to raid the refrigerator, so he doesn't have to pay for a meal. Not that I'm worried about paying. Good thing, too, 'cause I'm fecking famished. Starving as a matter of fact," Suel said.

"Well then, let's get you fed."

They walked into the Phoenix Park Cafe and stood in line. The food was served cafeteria style. Grab a tray, slide it along the rail, and point to whatever you want. Dillion grabbed a panini sandwich and a decaf coffee. Suel smiled at him, pointed at a salad, a slice of quiche, a pot of tea, and a slice of yellow cake with what looked like strawberry jam drizzled over it.

"You sure you got enough?"

Suel flashed a quick smile across the counter, nodded towards Dillon, and said, "He's paying for me."

The woman glanced at Dillon just to make sure.

"Yeah, against my better judgement, I'll pay for both of us."

"Let me find us a table while you settle up," Suel said and carried his tray out to the courtyard.

Dillon had about two bites left in his sandwich when Bergman sat down. He had a small salad and a mug of coffee on his tray.

"Sorry I'm late, fellas. Ended up stopping at the Ambassador's Residence for what I thought would be just a moment and, well, you know how that goes."

"Sure you don't want more than just that salad? Dillon's buying," Suel said.

For a moment, Bergman seemed to be considering the offer then shook his head. "No, I better not. I grabbed a chocolate brownie just out of the oven over at the residence."

"See, what'd I tell you?" Suel said to Dillon.

"What?"

"Ignore him, Eric. You have to do anything else regarding the Sands brothers?"

"No, basically, we filed paperwork in support of the prosecution. Nothing more than a formality in this case. I guess the only thing that was kind of surprising is that they even had passports in the first place. We've already sent both passports on to the State Department. Given their criminal records, neither one should have been able to hold a passport. Either someone at state was asleep at the switch or paid off, both slim chances. More likely, the passports are fake, but that sort of begs the question. With all the technology involved, if they were fakes, they were damn good. State's on it, and they'll find out."

"And the girlfriends?"

"Like I said, they'll be escorted off the plane and in the custody of the DEA. You guys find any connection with the Sands brothers prior to the girls coming over here?"

Dillon and Suel shook their heads. Suel took a large bite of his panini and wiped some sauce off his chin.

Dillon said, "Both girls are from wealthy families. They've known one another since nursery school. Apparently, they came over here to party for a couple of weeks and ended up with a lot more than they bargained for."

Bergman shook his head. "Too bad, they were both nice looking and supposedly smart, but they were in way over their heads."

"Like we were saying before, Eric. Some pretty serious probation and a record that's going to disqualify them from a lot of future job opportunities. If they ended up having to do a chunk of time in some rehab facility, it wouldn't surprise me."

"They're lucky they aren't going to be locked up over on North Circular Road," Suel said and took another bite of his panini.

"You mean the Dochas Centre?"

Suel nodded and continued chewing.

"Sex and coke seemed to be the main items on their agenda," Dillon said. The only thing that saved them is they somehow knew the Sands brothers kept the stash in paint cans. The girls had no idea there were thirty kilos there, but then again, they were so high they didn't know their own names when they were arrested."

Suel popped the last of the panini into his mouth and licked his fingers. "They showed us the empty paint can with the coke hidden inside. We were looking at maybe forty different paint cans—"

"Forty-five to be exact," Dillon said.

"Yeah, and the cans looked brand new. No paint spilled around the edges or anything. I pick one up, and I can sense something solid inside the can. We open it up, and there's a neatly wrapped kilo. Open the next one, same thing. We get thirty kilos and an extra fifteen empty cans, probably just waiting for the next shipment. It was like something out of a movie," Suel said. He stabbed his fork into the slice of yellow cake, shoved a forkful into his mouth, and grinned.

"Yeah, well, finish up. God only knows you need sweetening, and we need to get back to work," Dillon said.

FIVE

The Swordsman was gradually filling up with the lunchtime crowd. Kate and Megan were seated in one of six booths. They had just finished their lunches. Kate pulled out her phone.

"Who are you possibly going to call from here?" Megan said.

"No one. I'm just going to send my mom a text message so she knows we arrived safe and sound and she can go on to worry about the next thing on her list." She ran her thumbs back and forth across the keys for a good minute then pressed send. "There, mission accomplished." She checked the time on her phone. It was only 1:15. "God, almost two more hours before we can even check-in. I'm ready to fall asleep just sitting here."

"I could go for a little cat nap, too. It's only about seven in the morning in our heads. I'd be able to sleep for another thirty minutes if I was home. We've been up for twenty-four hours straight. I think once we check into the B&B, we should close our eyes for an hour, just so we're fresh for the rest of the afternoon."

"You think if we went over there now, we could maybe sit on a couch or something and just nod off?"

A waitress stopped at their table, carrying a tray of beer glasses. She set two pint glasses filled with Guinness on the table. The glasses were topped with a creamy head of foam and sported Guinness labels on the side of the glass.

"We didn't order these," Kate said.

"Yeah, I know," the waitress said, and nodded over her shoulder. "Toby sent them over. He's that lad sitting in the corner booth wearing the U2 shirt. He's not hard on the eyes. Careful, now. I think he fancies the two of ya's." She turned and headed toward another table, where she delivered four more glasses.

Megan glanced over at the booth where the Toby person was sitting. He raised his glass in her direction and smiled. Megan smiled, raised her glass, and mouthed the words, 'Thank you.'

"Megan, don't. He'll think we want him to join us."

"I think it was nice of him to do that, and she was right. He's not hard on the eyes. Besides, we're going to be leaving in a couple of minutes anyway. We'll be out of here before he gets up the nerve to come over."

"Maybe you're leaving, but I'm not going 'til I finish this beer."

"It's not just beer. It's a Guinness, Kate. They're pints of Guinness."

"Oh, well, excuse me, miss know it all."

They clinked glasses, took a sip, and set the glasses on the table.

"What do you think, Kate?"

"I think it must be an acquired taste, and I haven't acquired it yet."

"Excuse me, I'm sorry to bother you. Would you mind if I sat down for just a moment? My name is Toby. I hope you don't think I was eavesdropping, but you mentioned you had family from out this way, and I'm a bit of a genealogist. I caught your accents. It sounded like you're not from around here." As he spoke, he pulled a chair out and sat down at the end of their booth. He wore blue jeans and a dark grey t-shirt with **U-2** in red letters across the front.

Kate moved her glass a bit closer as he spread his arms across the end of the table, more or less boxing them in. "Thank you for the beer," Kate said.

"Didn't know if you liked the Guinness or not. Even if you don't, you have to be able to tell your friends back in the States you tried it. You can't come to Ireland without having a pint of Guinness."

"I think it'll take some getting used to," Megan said.

"You know what the best-selling beer is here, um, besides Guinness? Go ahead, take a guess."

"I have no idea," Kate said.

"Me neither," Megan added and took another sip.

"Well, I'll tell you, and you may not believe it, but it's an American beer."

"Oh?"

"Yes, Ma'am. Budweiser. By far and away, the biggest selling beer. There's a bit of a generation gap that's developed. If you're over forty, you're more likely than not to be drinking the Guinness or maybe Murphy's if you're from down in Cork. But, if you're under the age of forty, then Budweiser is probably going to be your beer of choice."

"Really? Budweiser? There's kind of an anti-big brand movement at home. Of course, now there are so many of the small craft breweries popping up everywhere, we've all sorts of choices," Kate said.

"Yeah, and they make really good beers. We've got fourteen or fifteen of the small craft breweries just in our city alone, and we're not that big of a city."

"Where are you girls from?"

"A place called Minnesota," Megan said.

A blank look seemed to wash across Toby's face.

"It's in the middle of the States, up north against Canada. Lots of lakes and it gets pretty cold in the winter and really hot in the summer," Megan said.

"You ever hear of Rochester, Minnesota?" Kate said. "There's a famous hospital there, called the Mayo Clinic. Started by some English doctor and his sons in the early nineteen hundreds."

"Oh yeah, I've heard of it," Toby lied. "So, tell me about your families. I'm going to guess and say they were famine people who left Ireland. Our country had a population of about eight million and lost half of that over the course of five or six years because of the famine. Most Americans I meet, it's why their family left Ireland and went to the States."

They talked on for the next half-hour. Kate was fighting to keep her eyes open, and Megan eventually forced down the last four swallows of her Guinness. "Well, thanks for the beer, and it's been really nice to meet you, Toby. But we have to check into our B&B. We're still on US time, and we haven't slept for over twenty-four hours."

"Yeah, if I don't get moving, I'm going to fall asleep right here," Kate said.

Toby turned and waved at the waitress. "You said you're staying at the McGovern's Guest House, didn't you?"

"Yeah, we are," Kate said, too tired to recall if they'd actually told him that or not.

"Well, they're the devil for not letting you check in until three. I've had friends come to town, and they had to wait outside, in the rain no less, until three before they could go in. Don't get me wrong; it's a nice place once you can get in. But they're liable to not even answer the door until three, busy cleaning and arranging, I guess. It's just a little after two, now, so you might as well sit and relax here."

The waitress suddenly appeared with three more glasses, another large pint glass of Guinness along with two smaller glasses.

"Oh, perfect timing, darling, thank you." Toby grabbed the pint glass and set it in front of him while the waitress set the two smaller glasses in front of Kate and Megan.

"Oh, no, I don't think I can drink anymore," Megan said.

"Oh, not to worry. Those are half-pint glasses. Now usually, when a lad orders a pint of Guinness, he orders a half-pint for his lady. You say to the bartender you want a pint and a glass of Guinness, and that's what you get, my pint and your half-pint. You order like that, and everyone will be thinking you're pretty familiar with the way things are done over here." He raised his pint glass and held it there until they raised theirs and clinked glasses with him. He took a sip then nodded at some guy walking past.

"All right now, ladies. Drink up, and I've to get back to work. I have to drive right past the McGovern's Guest House, so let's finish these, and you can follow me to your B&B. We'll get you checked in, and you can rest up after your long flight."

"That would be great," Kate said and took a hearty sip. She felt like drinking down the entire glass just so she could finally leave, get checked into the B&B, and close her eyes.

SIX

Dillon and Suel parked in the lot behind the station and walked into the building together. Once Dillon entered the access code, Suel pulled the door open. They took the elevator up to the fourth floor and stepped into the hallway. Suel punched in the code on the steel door, and they entered the Special Branch office.

The office was a large, windowless room with too many desks and a break room at the far end. A number of phones were ringing, maybe half of the twenty desks were occupied. All the desks in the office had stacks of files on them. Someone stood in front of the copy machine cranking out multiple copies of a file. DCI McCabe was the head of Special Branch. His office was opposite the break room, and just now the door was open, which meant McCabe was at his desk.

Suel pulled out his chair and settled in behind his desk. Dillon walked towards his desk. Along with two stacks of files, there were two empty plates and three tea mugs scattered across his desk. The desk had been unoccupied prior to Dillon's arrival in Special Branch and was therefore still regarded as the collection point for used tea mugs, plates, and silverware. Nothing had changed when Dillon took up residence at the desk. He picked up the dishes and tea mugs and headed towards the break room.

As he passed the open door to McCabe' s office, a voice rang out. "Marshal Dillon, a moment of your time. Have DI Suel join us," McCabe called, making it almost sound like it was an invitation to share a glass of wine. Everyone within earshot knew better. Dillon placed the plates and tea mugs on top of the dishes already in the break room sink and headed to McCabe's office. Suel met him at the door. Dillon extended his hand, indicating Suel should enter first.

"Close the door," McCabe said without looking up.

Dillon pulled the door closed and took a seat next to Suel in one of the two chairs opposite McCabe's desk. McCabe continued reading for another minute or two before he closed the file on his desk and looked up.

"Gentlemen. The Sands brothers. A brief summation if you don't mind."

"Guilty as charged. Sentencing next week, probably five to ten in the Joy," Suel said.

McCabe leaned back in his chair and smiled. "And the American women?"

"The two American women were flown back to the States this morning. They should be landing later today, where they'll be escorted off the plane by the US DEA, Drug Enforcement Agency. Because of their cooperation with the prosecution, we're expecting suspended sentences, reduced to three years of probation. Not sure, but if they received a mandatory drug rehabilitation lasting four to six months, that wouldn't surprise me. In fact, it's fairly standard," Dillon said.

"They're lucky they cooperated. Otherwise, they'd be on their way to the Dochas Centre for at least the next two years. Which brings me to my next point, thirty kilos, that's a reasonably large bust. But we're picking up rumors that it was only part of the haul. We're hearing there's at least that amount still out there, somewhere."

"Any idea where? Or who else was involved?" Suel said.

"I'll give you the short answer, no," McCabe said. "That's part of the problem. We're not sure it's with anyone. The Sands brothers apparently had it hidden. The rumor is they purposely broke the shipment into different parts just in case. Low and behold, their worst fear was recognized. What I want the two of you to do is find out where the rest of that shipment is. The Sands brothers don't appear to have had the contacts or the funds to bankroll this undertaking. My thought is they were brought in by someone to act as the front. Logic would seem to suggest locals, but we currently have no evidence to confirm that. I want the remainder of that shipment in our possession and whoever bankrolled it locked in a dark hole for twenty or thirty years."

"You're aware, sir, the Sands brothers haven't cooperated in the least. They kept repeating their names and birth dates in response to any questions we asked," Dillon said.

"Let's see how they do once they settle in at Mountjoy and suddenly find themselves surrounded by a pack of hungry wolves."

"They're liable to have their own lot in the Joy with orders to protect them. Word will be out they didn't cooperate with us," Suel said.

McCabe smiled. "We're in the process of, shall we say, setting the record straight on that particular matter. Give it maybe twenty-four hours before you have a friendly chat with them at the Joy. They just might be ready to cooperate once they've been on the receiving end of some gangland justice."

SEVEN

Megan asked, "Didn't that girl at the Swordsman tell us this place was just ten minutes away? How long have we been driving?"

"Closer to twenty minutes," Kate said. "I don't know. Maybe she meant ten minutes once we got out of town."

"But the address said Mullingar, and we're not in the town anymore. I mean, look around. It's just farm fields and—"

"Oh, finally, he's turning onto this road. I hope we're close. I have to use the bathroom after those two beers," Kate said.

"Yeah, remind me to stick to wine for the rest of this trip. I have to go, too. Really bad."

They followed Toby's blue BMW down a gravel road for a mile before they turned and drove through a gate, entering a dilapidated farmhouse surrounded by a two-foot brick wall. The farmhouse was a small stucco structure with a sagging slate roof. The brick wall surrounded the entire lot. There was a gravel drive and weeds around the stucco structure instead of anything resembling a lawn. Pieces of lumber were scattered about.

A dead tree, devoid of leaves and bark, stood at the far corner of the structure. They followed Toby's car around the back. A stone building with straw hanging out an upper opening and rusted equipment scattered around in front came into view.

"What the hell is this place? It doesn't look like any of the pictures they had online," Kate said.

"It doesn't even look occupied. Look, Kate, that window next to the back door is broken."

Toby pulled next to the small structure, turned off his car, and got out. Kate pulled alongside Toby's car. "I'll look up McGovern's and get their address. This just doesn't look right." Toby knocked on Kate's window and signaled she should lower the window by circling his hand.

Kate lowered the window and said, "Toby, I don't think this is McGovern's Guest House. It doesn't look like it at all. This place looks like it's been abandoned."

"You're right. Which means it ought to work perfectly. You can scream all you want, and no one will ever hear you."

"What the hell," shouted Kate. She threw the car in reverse and floored it, tossing gravel and dust into the air. She skidded to a stop maybe thirty feet away from Toby, who was now casually walking toward them.

"Kate, he's got a gun. He's got a damn gun. Get us out of here," Megan screamed.

Kate threw the car into drive and sped around the side of the house, racing toward the entrance. A black pickup truck had pulled in front of the entrance and was blocking it. Two large, bearded men were climbing out of the pickup. Both were in shirtsleeves and jeans. They did not look friendly. A silver SUV was just pulling to a stop behind the pickup truck.

Kate leaned on the horn and waved her hands.

"Let us out. Let us out," Megan screamed.

One of the bearded guys picked up a piece of lumber from the ground and used it like a baseball bat, swinging it into the windshield on Megan's side. The board made a loud sound as it struck the windshield, which immediately cracked into a spiderweb pattern.

Megan screamed.

Kate shouted, "Shit. Oh my God. Oh my God." She threw the car into reverse again and floored it. The guy with the piece of lumber swung again, hitting the hood of their car and leaving a dent running across the top of the hood.

Kate raced past Toby, who had to jump out of the way. He spun around as one of the bearded guys shouted something. Toby aimed his pistol and fired three or four times.

"Kate. Kate. Oh my God, he's shooting at us," Megan screamed.

The car suddenly leaned decidedly to the left. Kate fought to control the steering wheel as Toby casually walked around to Kate's side of the car and fired three more times. As Kate stepped on the accelerator, the car rumbled and jerked as it struggled to go in reverse.

"He shot the tires. We can't go. We can't go," Kate screamed. She slammed on the brakes, put the car into drive, and stomped on the accelerator. The car shook and rumbled forward slowly. Smoke and the scent of burning rubber began to fill the interior. The bearded guy with the piece of lumber slammed it into the driver's window. The window cracked, and he hopped for a step or two before he hit the window again. The window curved to the inside of the vehicle.

"No. No. Get away from us. Leave us alone," Kate screamed. The smoke was so thick inside the car they couldn't see out.

The third time he hit the window, it exploded, sending small chunks of glass across the front seat.

The board caught Kate on the right side of her face, near her cheekbone. Her eyes rolled up into her head as her skull bounced off Megan's shoulder. As Megan screamed, another guy reached through the shattered passenger window and turned off the ignition before he tore open the door.

Megan, still screaming, attempted to wrap her arms around Kate just as the passenger door was ripped open. A massive arm wrapped around her neck. A hand yanked her by the hair and dragged her from the smoke-filled car.

A voice half-laughed and said, "Take it easy, Nessan."

EIGHT

Dillon reached for his coffee mug and drained the remnants. The coffee was cold. There were grounds lining the bottom of the mug, but he swallowed it without flinching or even making a face. He set the mug back on his desk, rubbed both hands over his face, and looked at the clock on the far wall. It was after seven. He was the last person in the office. He decided he'd read for another twenty-five minutes, knock off at 7:30, and head home.

For the last four hours, he'd been reading background information on Dublin cocaine rings, five at last count and growing. The American connection with the Sands brothers appeared to be unique. Almost everyone else involved was homegrown, meaning Irish. One thing was clear. There was a new generation taking over, thugs in their mid-twenties. They'd committed six murders around the country in just the past nineteen days. Friends killing supposed friends. Shootings were occurring while people picked up kids at school, attended a funeral, went grocery shopping or simply drove down the road. A number of individuals were going to ground, hiding in hotels and AirB&B's. But with one exception, they were all Irish criminals.

The exception was an Iranian who'd lived in Ireland for the past ten years. He was thought to have committed at least a dozen murders but was never charged. He'd been shot in the head while attending a wake at a home in Coolock just the week before. At no surprise, with twenty people in attendance, no one saw anything.

The thing that caught Dillon's eye was the fact that the Iranian was an asylum seeker. Having fled Iran, he ended up in Ireland and was granted asylum. Amazingly, his asylum was never revoked, despite numerous run-ins with the law. So much for one hand knowing what the other was doing.

At 7:30 Dillon returned the files to the file room. He locked his desk and headed out to his car. He stopped at the Eurospar on the way home, purchased a rotisserie chicken, and drove the final two blocks to his attached house. He pulled into the parking area in front of his home, closed the gates behind his car, and unlocked his front door. He input the four-digit code on his alarm system just inside the door then called for his dog, Lucifer.

After he called a second time, he heard a noise from upstairs in the bedroom as Lucifer jumped off the bed, stretched, and made his way to the top of the stairs. A moment later, a black face peeked around the newel post.

"Lucifer, come on outside." The dog didn't move. "Lucifer, come on. Time for a treat. Outside."

The offer of a treat seemed to attract Lucifer's attention. He bounded down the stairs and headed for the front door. Dillon stepped into the kitchen, grabbed a dog biscuit from the cookie jar on the counter, and returned to the front door. As he opened the door, he tossed the biscuit. It bounced off the front of his car. Lucifer bounded off the front stoop and caught the biscuit before it hit the ground.

When Dillon closed the door, he noticed an envelope on the floor. The handwriting read, 'To Whom it may Concern.' He recognized the handwriting. Deitora, his permanently unhappy, humorless next-door neighbor. He was pretty sure he knew what the note would say before he read it. He opened the envelope and pulled out the note, sure enough, he was right.

'It has come to the attention of a number of your neighbors that your front garden is in desperate need of attention. Specifically, droppings for your untrained, ill-mannered, properly named dog. Please be a little more respectful of those of us who make an effort to maintain a modest amount of respectability in our neighborhood and clean up your property.'

The note was unsigned. But it was her. He recognized the distinctive penmanship that hadn't been taught in the schools for sixty years. He looked out the door. Lucifer was in the process of finishing his business on the concrete parking area. Dillon was tempted to pick up the piles, he counted five, and toss them over the wall into Deitora's rose garden. Fortunately, cooler heads prevailed, and with a plastic bag wrapped around his hand, he picked up the offending debris and deposited them in the trash bin. He wheeled the bin out onto the front sidewalk for the morning pick up. He called Lucifer, and together they hurried into the house and locked the door behind them. He didn't detect any movement from next door, but he was sure Deitora had been watching.

NINE

Megan called, not for the first time. "Kate. Kate, are you all right?" She could see her, Kate. They were on the ground in the stone building. Megan was chained to the side of an old tractor, and Kate was tied to the end of a farm implement. Both items were rusty and looked like they hadn't been used in years. "Kate? Kate, can you hear me?"

Kate's head moved, and she groaned. Her left eye seemed to flutter open for a brief moment before it closed again, and her head dropped, resting her chin against her chest. Her right eye was now black and had swollen shut from the guy hitting her with the board when he broke the driver's window. After being dragged from the car, they'd both been punched and kicked. Kate ended up face down in the dirt, unconscious. That had given the two bearded creeps the opportunity to direct their undivided attention toward Megan. They kicked and pawed her as she tried to crawl away. All the while laughing, like it was one big joke.

They dragged them both into this building that looked like an old barn, except it was stone. The bearded pair pulled the girls' jeans down around their ankles before they chained Megan to the tractor and tied Kate to the rusty farm implement.

Megan's lips were swollen and split. She couldn't breathe through her nose, but at least it had stopped bleeding. It still throbbed and hurt. Blood had dripped and splattered down the front of her torn top.

"Ugh. What happ . . . Megan?" Kate suddenly called in a raspy voice and coughed a few times.

"Kate. Kate, are you okay?"

Kate raised her head and attempted to focus her one good eye on Megan. "Where are we? What happened?" She tried to move then screamed once she became aware of the rope tying her up against the rusty implement. She strained against the rope, attempting to pull herself free, but to no avail.

"Kate. Kate, don't. Don't, Kate. They've got us chained to these things."

"Ahh. Ahh," Kate started to scream. Almost immediately, her voice cracked, and she broke into a coughing jag. After a minute or two, she said, "What happened? Who the hell did this? Where—?"

"I don't know. We followed that Toby person. Remember? He was going to take us to the McGovern's Guest House. Only he—"

"Toby?"

"The guy we met at the Swordsman. He bought us the Guinness and paid for our lunch. Remember?"

Kate nodded her head slightly. "Yeah, I think so. Toby?"

"We followed him out here, and he said something about no one would hear us scream. We tried to get away, but two guys parked their pickup truck across the entrance, blocking our way out. Toby shot the tires on our car. They pulled us out of the car, beat us up, and dragged us in here."

Kate gave a slight nod, coughed, and looked at her jeans pulled down around her ankles. "Did they—"

"No. No, they didn't, Kate. We're okay. Now we just have to get out of here. It's getting dark outside, so I think it must be around nine at night. We've been in here for almost five or six hours. I heard them drive away, but then they came back sometime later, and I think they took our car."

"What do they want?"

Megan shook her head. "I don't know. They said something about us liking to party or something. It didn't make any sense to me, but I was having trouble focusing. They were pretty rough. How's your head?"

"My head?"

"Yeah. That guy was battering your car window with a board. Once the window broke, he hit you in the head with that board. I think you were knocked out. He grabbed you around the neck, choking you, and pulled you out of the car. Anyway, hitting you with the board, that's how you got the black eye."

"Black eye?"

"Yeah, it's swollen and black. Does it hurt?"

"I, I can't tell. I mean, I hurt all over. My knees, my elbows, my back is killing me, and I've got a really bad headache. I need some water. Do you have anything to drink?" Kate said.

"No. honey, I don't. Maybe close your eyes and see if you can get some sleep. You'll feel better after you get some sleep."

"I need some water first. I'm so thirsty."

"See if you can sleep, Kate, and I'll try to get you some water."

"Okay. Thanks, Megan."

Kate closed her eye, and a moment later, her head dropped onto her chest. Megan watched her in the fading light, desperately looking for any movement suggesting she was breathing. Just as she was about to call her name, Kate's head rose, and she coughed a few times. Her head sank to her chest again, but at least Megan could hear the occasional cough. Megan leaned her head back against the rusty tractor frame. Closed her eyes and, after a while, drifted off.

TEN

Dillon was back in the office a little after 7:00 the following morning. Suel was already at his desk, going over a stack of files. "Reading up on our drug friends?" Dillon asked once he crept behind Suel.

Suel half-jumped in his desk chair and shouted, "For the love of God. You sneak up on a hard-working lad first thing in the morning and almost give him a heart attack? That's the way you start your day?"

Dillon laughed. "Sorry, didn't know you were so into the read." He glanced at the file open on Suel's desk. "Christy Byrne, nasty guy for somcone in his late twenties."

"Mercifully, we won't have to worry about him. He was killed last March, ripe old age of twenty-six, actually."

"Was he the one tied to the steering wheel and someone set the car on fire?"

"No, that was his brother, Casey. Christy apparently committed suicide, shot himself in the head twice."

"Shot himself twice?"

"It was a setup, Dillon. Bit of a message sent to some other idiots who are probably waiting for their personal interviews with the devil. Six murders in the past nineteen days. Twelve the month before. All related to the drug gangs."

"Well, don't get hung up on those numbers. It's still early in the day."

"One can only hope. Be nice to put them all in a cage, let them kill one another. Whoever ends up the last one standing, we just lock him in some dark hole and throw away the key. There you go, problem solved," Suel said and followed up with a laugh.

"Until the next batch comes along, which would probably be in about twenty-four hours."

"Aw, Dillon. Now I don't think it would take that long."

"I'm going to make some coffee. You interested?" Dillon said.

"Not on your life. But I'll have a tea while you force down that rotgut you try to pass off as coffee."

"Give me five minutes to brew some coffee and join me in the break room. The Sands brothers just finished their first night in Mountjoy. I've got my fingers crossed the rumors McCabe mentioned preceded them."

"I'll make a call to someone I know over there, see if anything happened."

Dillon headed to the break room. He dumped the remaining half cup of his coffee down the sink. He rinsed the grounds out of the pot, filled the pot with water up to the ten-cup mark, and poured the water into the coffee maker. He added ten scoops of fresh coffee grounds and turned the pot on. He filled the water kettle halfway full and turned it on. When the kettle came to a boil, he poured it over a breakfast tea bag.

"Paddy, tea's ready," he called to Suel. He poured himself a mug of coffee and settled into a chair next to the window with a birds-eye view of the parking lot.

Suel entered the break room a moment later. He lifted the tea bag up and down a half-dozen times before tossing the bag into the trash. He topped the tea up with a teaspoon of milk and joined Dillon.

"I'll never understand how you're able to drink that coffee shite straight like that without so much as a drop of milk to cut the edge," Suel said and nodded towards Dillon's half-empty mug.

"I learned to drink it in the army. I was all of eighteen, and some guy in the mess hall handed me a mug. We'd just run five miles. The sun wasn't even up and—"

"Please," Suel said, holding his hand up to stop Dillon mid-sentence. "You've told me that tale more times than I care to remember. Can we dwell on something a little more pleasant, like the murders of these drug dealers?"

"So far, we've been lucky. No one innocent has been killed," Dillon said. He swallowed some coffee and grimaced.

Suel shook his head. "I'm afraid it's only a matter of time. These knackers are shooting one another in pubs, outside of schools, or when they answer the door in their home. How long will it take before someone's child is killed? Or their wife? Or God forbid, an innocent family that simply ends up in the wrong place at the wrong time? These bastards are nuts, and they're playing for keeps. God help the poor soul who mistakenly gets in the way."

ELEVEN

Megan slept fitfully for a few hours. She eventually woke up around four in the morning, moved her head from side to side, and heard her neck crack. She rolled her shoulders as best she could, which brought about more cracking. Kate was still, but thankfully, she occasionally coughed, so Megan knew she was at least alive. She heard something scurry off to the right, maybe a mouse or worse, a rat. Her stomach growled, and her throat felt dry.

Dawn began to gradually approach, and the little bit of sky she could see through the cracks in the wooden doors began to lighten and turn grey. At some point, she must have dozed off because she jerked herself awake when she heard a car. A moment later, she heard two car doors slam.

She thought about calling for help but almost immediately decided against it. No telling what would happen if it turned out to be the horrible people who'd beat them up yesterday. She heard footsteps approaching and then a sound at the doors.

She hadn't noticed it before, but then it had been dark for most of the time she'd been chained to the tractor. The two wooden doors rattled as a chain was pulled through a hole in the doors, a moment later, one of the doors opened. The sunlight coming in was blinding, and Megan had to close her eyes. After a few seconds, she squinted and was able to make out two figures approaching. Fortunately, they didn't appear to be either one of the bearded thugs who'd hit the car windows with the board and pulled them out of the car to beat them up.

The bad news was the one she recognized was Toby, the creep who had set them up in the first place. He was followed by a man Megan didn't recognize. She closed her eyes as they approached.

"Let's try her first. The other bitch got hit pretty hard when Nessan broke the car window," Toby said to Brennan. Although he'd been there yesterday, neither Megan nor Kate had actually seen him.

Megan immediately recognized Toby's voice. There was no doubt. She kept her head down and her eyes closed, pretending to be asleep. A moment later, something jerked the bottom of her foot. She half-jumped and let out a little cry. Not that it hurt, it merely surprised her. She opened her eyes and squinted just as Toby kicked her again on the sole of her foot. Only this time much harder.

"Wake up, honey. We've got some questions for you."

Megan squinted and tried to ask what they wanted, but her throat was so dry she had trouble speaking. She attempted to clear her throat a couple of times and groaned out the word, "Water." She had trouble recognizing her own voice. She tried to speak again, but between the dry throat and her swollen lips, she was unable to even sound out the words.

"Get that bottle of water from the car," Brennan directed, and Toby hurried back out the door. Brennan squatted down next to Megan and appeared to be studying her. Toby rushed back in the door with a plastic water bottle. "Give her a couple of swallows, or we'll never be able to understand what she's going to tell us."

Toby unscrewed the plastic cap off the top of the bottle. He placed the bottle against Megan's lips, tilted the bottle up, and Megan gulped down the cold liquid. She was taking audible swallows, but after just three, he pulled the bottle away.

"No, no. More, more please," Megan groaned leaning as far forward as possible in an effort to get just one more swallow.

As Toby stepped back, Brennan stood and pulled something out of his pocket. "What's your name?"

"Please help us. We didn't do—"

"You want more water," Toby said.

"Please. Please."

"Then answer the damn question. What the hell is your name?"

"Meg—" She swallowed and took a deep breath. "Megan," she said.

"You're right," Brennan said and closed a small blue-covered booklet. It took a moment before Megan realized it was an American passport, obviously hers. "And your friend over there. What's her name?"

"Kate. Her name is Kate, and she should see a doctor."

"Give her a little more water," Brennan said.

Toby looked like he was about to say something but thought better of it. He bent down and placed the bottle against Megan's lips. She took three or four more gulps before he pulled it away.

"Let's check out the other one," Brennan said, and they walked over to Kate.

Toby kicked her on the foot a couple of times. Kate's head slowly began to move.

"Give her some water so we can understand what she says," Brennan said and stepped back so Toby could kneel next to Kate.

Toby knelt down and placed the bottle against Kate's lips. Megan heard her gulping four or five times before a sudden burst of coughing and gagging began.

Toby jumped back and half-shouted, "The stupid slapper, she puked me ring."

"What are you worried about? She didn't get any on you."

"Fine mess if you ask me," Toby said.

"More," Kate said in almost a scratchy whisper.

"All right, Mrs. You'll get some more. I need you to tell me your name first."

"Kate. I'm Kate. What are you—"

"Who's your friend over there?"

Kate raised her head and attempted to focus with her one good eye. "Megan. That's Megan. Why are you—"

"Give her a little more," Brennan said. As Toby bent over and shoved the water bottle into Kate's mouth, Brennan walked back outside. Kate took four more gulps, this time much slower. Toby finally pulled the bottle away and followed Brennan outside.

Brennan pushed a button on his key fob, and the doors on the Range Rover unlocked. "Dump them in the back. They stay here much longer, they're' liable to be found."

"Brennan, the place has been abandoned for fifteen or twenty years. They can scream all they want, and no one will hear them. No one ever comes out here. We can leave them here and—"

"We've got too much riding on this. We have to find out where those fecking Sands brothers hid the rest of that shipment before the Guards do."

"You think they'll talk?"

"Kevin and Sean? They were sent to Mountjoy last night. Who knows what will happen? I wouldn't put it past the Guards to try and pull something. We can't take the chance. These two slappers had a rough go of it yesterday. Now, we're going to be nice and polite, get them cleaned up, fed, and hopefully, they'll start talking."

"And if they don't?"

"Then we dump their bodies in the Dublin mountains, someplace where they'll never be found."

"And if they talk?"

Brennan smiled and gave a little laugh. "You kidding? We'll still dump their bodies up in the Dublin mountains."

TWELVE

Dillon had been going through files covering the various drug wars over the past thirty-six months. Even after taking notes, and he had pages of notes, he had difficulty keeping things straight. What gang the various individuals were with, who had been killed, who was still alive, who had a price on their head. Amazingly, and to Suel's earlier point, it was a new generation of youngsters taking over the trade. The body count for the past three years was over sixty, and of those killed, only three individuals had been older than thirty years of age.

He was in the process of making a note on a recent victim, Terry McArdle age twenty-two. McArdle was, among other things, an amateur boxer. He was murdered in a hotel at the weigh-in twenty-four hours before his scheduled St. Patrick's Day bout. He'd been shot six times by two individuals posing as security.

The incident had been caught on someone's cell phone, thirty-seven seconds of pandemonium. The video was mostly images of chairs being knocked aside and the floor as the holder of the cellphone ran for cover. The audio was what you'd expect, automatic weapons fire, and all sorts of people screaming. It never did focus on anyone pulling a trigger. There was maybe a two or three-second clip of McArdle in red silk boxing trunks jumping off a temporary stage. Dillon had watched the video a half-dozen times and learned absolutely nothing.

He had just finished making a quick note on McArdle and the date of his murder, March sixteenth, when he felt his cellphone vibrate in his pocket signaling a text message coming through.

He was about to pull the phone out when DCI McCabe's voice boomed through the office. "Suel, Dillon. My office, now, if you please."

Dillon looked up just in time to see McCabe turn in the doorway and head back to his desk. He glanced across the room at Suel on the phone. Suel nodded and held up his index finger, signaling he'd be off shortly. Dillon drained his coffee mug, grabbed his notebook, and headed towards McCabe's office.

"Yes, Dillon, take a seat. Where's DI Suel?"

"Just finishing up a phone call. He'll be here any moment."

"Anything on the Sands brothers?"

"I think that's why Suel was on the phone. He's got some contacts at Mountjoy. The Sands brothers were headed there after their court appearance yesterday. No doubt they were celebrating the first of many nights they'll be spending there, compliments of the court system."

McCabe smiled and chuckled. "Yes, well one can only hope . . . Ah, DI Suel, thank you for joining us. Any word on the Sands brothers after their initial night at Mountjoy?"

Suel got an evil grin on his face and laughed. "Seems they made it to the Joy in time for dinner. Someone cracked a food tray over Sean Sands' head. His brother Kevin stepped in to play the hero and promptly had his nose broken. Not sure who did the dirty work. Neither one spent time in the infirmary. They were both sent back to their cells. Still, a bit of a wakeup call to the pair that their stay at the Joy may not be all that relaxing. Nothing like a memorable welcome to send a message."

"Not nearly memorable enough for the likes of those two. Keep me posted," McCabe said and handed a sheet of paper across the desk to Dillon. "A bit of a problem out in West Meath. I'd like the two of you to look into it."

"West Meath?" Suel said.

"Yes." McCabe paused for a moment and gave them both a look that suggested they'd be best served if they simply listened. "I just got off the line with Eric Bergman over at the US Embassy. Seems a car, rented by an American woman, was found along the Royal Canal outside Mullingar. The car had been torched. No word of a robbery or anything out of the ordinary. No sign of the American woman."

It was a fairly common practice to steal a vehicle and use it in a crime. Usually, it would be used in a bank or Post Office robbery, maybe once in a great while in an assassination. After the crime was committed, the vehicle would be set on fire in an effort to destroy all evidence.

"The woman have any links to someone? Maybe the car was stolen and she's still unaware of that fact," Suel said and glanced at his watch. "It's not quite ten. This hour she could be having breakfast, out for a walk, or even still in bed."

"You'll note the local Fire Brigade extinguished what remained of the vehicle at six-thirty-five yesterday evening." McCabe nodded at the sheet of paper in Dillon's hand. "The vehicle was rented by a Kathleen Murray, age twenty-four, traveling on an American passport. She only arrived in Dublin yesterday aboard a Delta airlines flight stemming from the middle of the US, someplace in Minnesota. According to records, it appears to be her first time in Ireland. I don't think I have to mention the potential for some very bad publicity. I'd like the two of you over there this morning, looking into this. Hopefully, there's some logical explanation, although that particular option seems to be getting thinner by the minute. The case falls under the Mullingar department's jurisdiction. Offer assistance, but they're in charge. Because she's an American, I'd like you to take the lead, Dillon."

Dillon nodded.

"Mullingar. You want us out there? This morning?" Suel said.

"Yes, I do. If you hurry, you can make it before the noon hour," McCabe said in a tone that ended all questions.

Ten minutes later, with Suel complaining as he drove, they headed towards the M50. "Like we don't have enough to do with those two bleeding eejets, Kevin and Sean Sands. Now, an American slapper who probably left her keys in the car down in Temple Bar. I'm thinking some group of malcontents drove it out to Mullingar just to set the damn thing on fire."

"Strange she's only just arrived and the thing is torched the same day, a few hours later. I hope it was stolen and she's okay," Dillon said.

THIRTEEN

Shauna Hanlon tossed the morning's Irish Times on the kitchen table and swore. "For the love of God. I knew it was a bad idea from the get-go. Two American knackers, fake passports. The two of 'em lit out of their minds for the better part of a week. Of course, it makes perfect sense that they'd end up with a couple of American slappers and now they're off to the Joy, and we're out six million euros."

Shauna was in her late forties and currently blonde. She didn't look a day over thirty-five, the benefits of Botox, enhancements, and a fat checkbook. She'd eventually taken over the family business after her Uncle Myles had been murdered last fall. He'd been shot a half-dozen times as he stepped out of a Finglas pub for a cigarette. His murder set off a family battle for control, where essentially, the family formed in a circle and simply began firing at one another. Smart Shauna had remained out of the circle and fired from behind.

Not for the first time, Mickey O'Hara closed his eyes and prayed for patience. "What would you have us do, Shauna? You jumped on board at the first mention of it. Two Americans. Untraceable. They were supposed to know what they were doing. As a matter of fact, it was you what sold the likes of the rest of us on the deal. You're the one who said there was no way in hell they'd ever be tracked. From the looks of it, I'd say the Garda had the number on those bastards before they ever arrived in Dublin. Now they're off to the Joy for an extended vacation. We've no trace of them two slappers. They literally seemed to have disappeared into thin air. For all we know, they're down on the Costa del Sol tanning themselves and laughing at the likes of us. And just in case you didn't hear me the first time, let me remind you. You're the one what got the rest of us to buy into this. What I want to know is, just how in the bloody hell are we going to be paying everyone off? Wee Timmy Bixby in particular."

"You don't need to remind me. I get it. All right? So stop your complaining and help me figure out how we're going to come up with that much money in the next few days."

"If I knew the answer to that, I'd be out there putting it together. I'm thinking we just might be better off joining those two slappers on the beach in Spain for a bit until things cool down."

"Until things cool down? Are ye daft? Six million euros, Mickey. It ain't never going to cool down. And there ain't no place I can think of that's far enough away to hide. Certainly ain't the Costa del Sol. Feck's safe, Wee Timmy's lot would have us spotted before sunset."

"I know. I know. So what's the plan?"

"First, we have to make an example of the Sands brothers."

"Kill 'em?"

"Not at first. I'm thinking we maybe give the two of them a small taste of what they're in for. We back off for a day or two before we take 'em permanently. Bleed 'em out in their cells, very private. Send a nice message to anyone thinking we're on the back foot."

"That all sounds like one hell of a tall order, Shauna."

"Which is exactly why I'm in charge, Mickey. Your job is to figure out how in the hell we're going to find six million euros, and fast."

"I'm maybe back to the Costa del Sol."

"I told you that's not going to work. Were you even listening? We'd be dead before sunset."

"I get that part. But the two Americans, those women, the blonde and the redhead. I'm thinking, if they led the Garda to thirty kilos, there's maybe a better than even chance they know where the other thirty kilos are hidden, and just maybe they're waiting until things quiet down and they can make a move."

"That seems like you're pinning our future on a pretty thin hope. We're talking days here, Mickey, not years."

"I know, damn it. I know."

"So think of something else and make me another tea while you're at it." Shauna's cell suddenly signaled an incoming call. She glanced at the screen and gritted her teeth. "Oh for feck's sake. Speak of the devil, Wee Timmy." She waited two more rings before she answered. "Mr. Bixby, I was just about to call you."

FOURTEEN

Brennan backed his Range Rover up to the double doors on the stone storage shed. He turned the car off, walked to the back, and lifted the rear door. A large sheet of heavy plastic lay folded in the corner. He proceeded to unfold it and spread it over the carpet.

In the meantime, Toby was busy untying Kate from the rusted farm implement. Her head swayed up and down, and she groaned as he undid the rope around her arms. Once he had both arms untied, her head sank onto her chest, and she slowly leaned over to her left side, coming to rest in the dirt.

"She needs a doctor. She has a serious head injury," Megan called and then strained against the chains holding her in place.

Toby ignored her and untied the rope around Kate's ankles. He dragged her a few feet away from the rusted implement, rolled her over, shoved his hands into her armpits, and lifted her. Walking backward, he dragged her towards the Range Rover. As he dragged her, one of Kate's shoes came off.

"I said she needs to see a doctor. She needs medical attention," Megan shouted.

"Let me pull her jeans up before you dump her in the back," Brennan said as he reached down to pull up Kate's jeans.

"When you get 'em up, grab her ankles and guide her into the back," Toby said.

"Watch her head. I want it to look like we're trying to be careful. Get the one doing all the yelling to think we're trying to help."

"Think she needs a doctor?" Toby asked.

"What difference does it make? It's not like we can take her to the hospital or get someone to check her out."

Brennan took hold of Kate's ankles and carefully guided her legs into the back of the car. Toby groaned and lifted her upper body in, trying to make sure her head didn't hit anything. He let go of her before she was completely settled, and her head bounced off the floor of the SUV. She gave a slight groan but not loud enough for Megan to hear.

"Get the other one and walk her over here. Don't say anything to her. Let me do the talking. You have the key?"

"I gave it to you," Toby said.

Brennan got a questioning look on his face and quickly shoved his hands in his pockets. He pulled out a small brass key. "Sorry, guess I forgot. Did it look something like this?" Brennan joked.

"I think that should work," Toby said and hurried over to Megan.

"Is Kate going to be okay?" Megan said as Toby knelt down and reached behind her.

He ignored her and slid the key into the padlock.

"I asked you if Kate is going to be okay. Is she even breathing?"

He unlocked the padlock holding the chain in place and began to unwrap the chain from around Megan's right arm.

"Oh, God, finally. That feels so good," Megan said. She began to move her arm back and forth while wiggling her fingers, trying to get the blood flowing again. Toby leaned across her and loosened the chain around her left arm.

Megan pulled her left arm free and began to roll her shoulders and move her head from side to side.

"Let's get you on your feet," he said, taking hold of an arm and raising her up onto her feet. "Pull up those jeans, buckle your belt, and I'll help you to the car."

"Where are you taking us? What's this all about?"

"Pull up your damn jeans."

She pulled up her jeans, buckled her belt, and zipped the fly. "There. Happy? Now, where are you taking us?"

Toby took hold of her arm and led her out to the Range Rover.

As they approached the car, Brennan flashed a broad, welcoming smile.

"We want you to climb in here, careful not to disturb your friend. We'll be taking you on a short, little ride."

"I'm not getting in until you tell me where you're taking us and what in the hell this is all about. We didn't do anything to you. Why don't you just let us go, and we won't tell anyone. Just let us go. Please."

"That's what we're going to do. Thought it might be a good idea to let you get cleaned up and fed first. Then we'll let you go. Terrible mistake. Now if you'll just climb in here, we can—"

"Why can't we ride in the backseat? Kate? Kate, are you okay? Kate?"

"Get in the damn car," Brennan said.

"I'm not getting in until you tell me where you're taking us."

Brennan looked at Toby and said, "Get her ass in there and let's go."

"I'm not getting in there until you—"

Toby slapped Megan hard, half spinning her around. He threw a couple of right-handed jabs into the back of her head.

"No. No. Stop it. Stop hitting me. Stop—"

"Get your ass in the damn car. Come on. Get in there. Now." He grabbed a handful of Megan's hair and yanked it, pulling her head toward the back of the Range Rover. He kept pulling her hair as she attempted to climb in.

"Ouch. Stop it. Stop it. Damn it. I'm trying to get in, if you'd let go of my hair, I could get in. Just stop it. Please, Ouch. Stop it, damn it. You're hurting me."

Toby released his grip on her hair, and she hurriedly climbed into the back. She wasn't quite settled in when he tossed a sheet over both Megan and Kate. Megan's head made a thumping sound as he forced her to lie down. Suddenly, all was quiet except for little sobs coming from underneath the sheet.

FIFTEEN

S uel was in the process of driving through a round-about on the N52, a two-lane highway. They were just outside of Mullingar. Dillon was on the phone with Eric Bergman at the US Embassy, in the process of getting an update. As he listened to Eric, he wrote down information in a small pocket notebook.

Eric continued, "Here's what we know so far. Kate Murray left the Minneapolis airport with her girlfriend, Megan Gaffney. They flew Delta to Atlanta and then Atlanta to Dublin. They arrived yesterday morning. They were seated next to one another on both flights. Passports were issued approximately forty-five days earlier. Records indicate it was the first time out of the US for both women. In the past twenty-four hours, there have been two charges to Kate Murray's credit card. It's a VISA credit card through Capital One. The first charge was for a rental car, a red Nissan Micra, automatic transmission specified. The car was rented from Enterprise Car Rental at the Dublin Airport site. I'll be heading there as soon as we're off the phone. The second charge was from an AirB&B on the edge of Mullingar called McGovern's

Guest House. Now, that charge came through this morning, and it was for two guests. Maybe the girls made their way there, and someone stole the car. We can only hope. But check out that place. I'll text you the address and phone number in just a moment."

"McGovern's? I think we might have passed a sign for it a little ways back. I appreciate the update, Eric. Did McCabe give you any other information?"

"No, nothing. Well, other than you were on your way out to Mullingar."

"We're here now, in fact, the canal should be just a mile or two ahead. I'm going to ring off. Anything else comes through, please let me know. I'll keep you posted on what we find out here."

"Ditto. Hopefully, you'll find the girls at that B&B."

"Appreciate the update, Eric."

"Later," Eric said and disconnected.

"Any good news?" Suel said.

"Maybe. Two charges on Kate Murray's credit card. One from the car rental agency yesterday at the airport. More importantly, a second one this morning from a B&B here in Mullingar."

"This morning? So she checked into some place. Maybe dealing with the time change, they were in the B&B, and the car was stolen. Some local knackers decide after riding around, the safest thing to do is torch the damn car, get rid of their fingerprints. Meanwhile, the girl is safe and sound at the B&B."

"Make that girls. Apparently, they flew over to-gether, this Kate Murray and another girl named Megan Gaffney. Keep your fingers crossed they're at that B&B."

They suddenly drove over a small bridge with a sign marking the Royal Canal running beneath the bridge. Suel slowed and pulled to the side of the road as Dillon looked out the window.

"You see anything that looks like a burned-out ve-hicle?" Dillon said.

"I'm not seeing shit," Suel said.

"Maybe they've already towed it away."

"You have a more positive impression of the Irish work effort than I seem to have. Let's stretch our legs for a minute and maybe we can see something." Suel put the emergency flashers on and waited for a truck to pass be-fore he climbed out of the car. They walked back along the bridge and looked down. Sure enough, there was the Royal Canal and running along the far side of the canal an asphalt path. In the distance, they could see a couple riding their bikes along the pathway. Nothing remotely resembling a burnt car or a scorched area where a vehicle had recently been burned was visible. On the opposite side of the canal from the bike path, a gravel road seemed to run parallel to the N52.

"Let's see if we can find an entrance to that road," Suel said and started back to the car.

Dillon took a final look around, running his eyes up and down the canal a few times, but saw nothing. Suel had the car started and the blinker on by the time Dillon climbed into the passenger seat. He took off before Dillon had the door closed. "You in a hurry?" Dillon asked.

"This is beginning to look more and more like a wild goose chase. I've got a fiver that says we'll find these two asleep in the B&B nursing hangovers. Then I'd like to get back to Dublin and deal with a real problem."

"I hope you're right," Dillon said.

SIXTEEN

There was just a sliver of light coming from under the sheet, but it was enough to allow Megan to make out Kate's face. She brushed Kate's hair back and whispered, "Kate, it's Megan. Are you all right? Kate? Kate, it's Megan."

Kate's left eye fluttered open and, after a moment, seemed to focus on Megan. "Where? Where are we?" She asked in a raspy voice.

"Don't worry. You're going to be all right. I'm going to get you to a doctor just as soon as we can. You just close your eyes and rest. You're going to be okay. I promise, Kate. Don't worry. Just close your eyes and rest."

Kate gradually closed her eye, and her breathing seemed to sound a little more regular. A few minutes later, Megan felt the car slowing and then turning. It began to pick up speed, but she sensed they weren't traveling nearly as fast as before. After a few minutes, they slowed and drove over two large bumps. The car turned again and came to a stop. She heard voices, Toby and the other man who'd put them in the car, although she couldn't make out what was being said. Two car doors opened and then closed. Megan waited for the rear door to be opened. Then she waited some more.

After what seemed like an hour or two, she heard voices again. The voices grew louder as they approached. A voice she recognized as the man who appeared to be in charge said, "Get them out and bring them inside. Separate rooms. Put the redhead in the back room. Careful with the blonde, she seems in pretty rough shape."

A moment later, Megan heard a beep, and the rear door opened. Suddenly, someone tore off the sheet covering them, and bright sunlight flashed in, momentarily blinding her. A large pair of hands seemed to lift her effortlessly out of the back of the vehicle and set her on her feet. Megan blinked a few times and focused on one of the bearded men who'd beaten her and Kate yesterday.

"You and me, we're gonna have one hell of a good time, bitch," he whispered into her ear.

Without thinking she formed a fist and aimed a reverse Karate punch at the man's neck, striking him directly on his Adam's apple. His eyes grew wide, his tongue stuck out, and he gasped. He automatically placed both hands around his neck. Megan took a half-step back and kicked him squarely between his legs. His groan was cut short the moment his head bounced off the rear bumper of the Range Rover, and he collapsed onto the ground.

A hand grabbed Megan by the hair, swung her around, and threw her on the ground. Her head bounced off the concrete just as a massive weight seemed to crush her chest. She opened her eyes, and there was the man in charge, sitting on top of her. She tried to struggle, attempting to roll first left and then right, all in an effort to slide from beneath him. Her movement only seemed to pin her down tighter.

All the while, the bearded man, now in a fetal position, gasped and groaned off to the side.

As she continued to struggle, the man on top of her suddenly reached behind his back and pulled out a gun. He placed the barrel against the tip of her nose and pushed hard. "Here's the thing, honey. You try something like that again, I'm going to shoot your friend first. Then, I'm going to make you watch her die. Once she's dead, I'm going to shoot her again just to be sure. After that, I'm going to shoot you. Do you understand?"

Megan just blinked and hoped he didn't pull the trigger.

"Answer me. Do you understand what I just said? And make no mistake. Your girlfriend's life depends on what you say. Now, do you understand what I just said?"

Megan swallowed, nodded, and said, "Yes." The voice she heard didn't sound like hers. It sounded more like it came from a little girl. She fought to stop the tears from welling up in her eyes, but that didn't work either.

SEVENTEEN

Suel drove down the N52 for another half-mile. An asphalt walkway began to run alongside the highway, and they passed an older couple who looked like they were just out for a casual stroll in the beautiful weather. They drove past a sign indicating another roundabout and the road to Dundalk and Delvin. Suel took the first left off the roundabout. Thirty feet later, he made another left onto a gravel road barely wide enough for the car. They were now heading in the opposite direction, back towards the canal. They passed a large industrial building on the left, rounded a bend, and there, just ahead, sat three cars, two of which were Garda vehicles with lights mounted on top and blue and florescent green paint along the sides and across the back. Suel pulled behind the vehicles and parked.

As they climbed out of the car, a uniformed Garda officer approached. She was a dark-haired woman with hair about even with her jawline. She wore a dark blue protective vest with high-visibility green stripes. In the heat, her face looked flushed, and the beads of sweat on her forehead made her look like she'd just run a couple of miles.

"Can I help you, gentlemen?" She said, sounding like help was the last thing she wanted to offer. Looking at her, 'happy' would not be a word that sprang immediately to mind.

Suel and Dillon automatically flashed their badges and warrant cards.

"DI Suel, Dublin, special branch."

"US Marshal, Jack Dillon, Dublin, special branch."

She seemed to look at Dillon for a long moment before she said, "What are you two doing here?"

"There was a torched car last night?" Suel said.

"Yeah, it's a rental. A Nissan Micra. That's about all we know."

Dillon pulled out his pocket notebook with the notes he'd taken while talking to Eric Bergman. "Car is, or rather was, a red Nissan Micra. It was rented to an American woman yesterday at Dublin Airport. She and a friend had just flown in from the US."

"The car's just up ahead," the officer said. "The blaze was extinguished early yesterday evening. No sign of a body. Follow me, and you's can see for yourself," she said. "What's this got to do with Dublin?"

"We got a call from the American Embassy. The woman who rented the car was traveling with a friend, another woman. Both twenty-something Americans."

As they passed the parked vehicles, they could see the burnt-out wreckage up ahead, or what was left of it. Of the wheels, only the metal tire rims remained, the tires themselves were gone, as were the seats. All that remained of the interior were the two metal frames from the driver and passenger seats. The car was, or rather had been, a two-door model. The body was so charred, it was impossible to determine visually what the color had originally been. The dashboard, steering wheel, upholstery, and floor mats had all disappeared. The windows were gone. The grass and weeds around the wreckage were scorched for about ten feet in all directions.

Two men stood talking to one another. Once they were close enough to hear, from what Dillon could pick up, it sounded like they were discussing a football match. As they approached, one of the men looked up and said, "What do you need?" It sounded more like a trespassing accusation than an offer of assistance.

He was stocky but certainly not what you'd call fat. He had close-cropped salt and pepper hair. He wore jeans and a long sleeve, light-blue shirt. The sleeves on the shirt were rolled halfway up thick muscular forearms. The man he was talking to was taller, leaner, and older. Dillon guessed he might be around fifty. He was bald, with strands of long, dark hair poorly styled in a combover that only seemed to focus more attention on his bald head.

Suel didn't bother to take out his badge or warrant card. Instead, he just said, "We're with Special Branch in Dublin. We got a call from the American Embassy this morning. This vehicle was rented yesterday, at Dublin Airport, by an American woman. We think she and a girlfriend drove it out here. Are any of you familiar with a place called McGovern's Guest House?"

"You drive out here on the N4 and turn onto the N52?"

Suel nodded but didn't say anything.

"Then you damn near passed the place. It's just a couple miles back on the N52."

"That'll be our next stop. Any idea what happened here?"

The stocky guy frowned and said, "Yeah, someone torched a car. My guess, it was a couple of feckin' muppets out for a joyride." He waved his hand, indicating the other man and the female officer. "The three of us have wasted the better part of a day standing around, waiting for the flatbed to show up. Odds are we'll never find the stupid bastards what done this. Hell, for all we know, they're watching us right now and having a good chuckle about their little adventure. Now you two show up, and that brings the number of coppers doing absolutely nothing to a total of five. That seems to be our damn tax dollars hard at work."

Suel laughed out loud. "Well, sounds like you and I think a lot alike."

EIGHTEEN

Once Brennan climbed off Megan, he shoved the gun into his belt. Toby hurried over, took her by the arm, and quickly led her through the back door and into the rear hallway of a large brick house. The structure looked old, and once inside, it smelled of mothballs and mold. The hall entrance was dim, and the ceiling was low. He kept hold of her arm at the elbow.

They walked along the hallway, past a kitchen on one side and what looked like a dining room on the other. Both rooms had large fireplaces with dingy framed landscape paintings hanging over the mantel. The kitchen fireplace had a large iron pot hanging in the center of the fireplace. The walls of the dining room were covered with wood paneling in need of a good cleaning. The hall split into two narrower halls due to a staircase in the middle.

Things grew a little brighter in the entryway at the base of the staircase. There were windows on either side of a heavy-looking wooden front door. Megan quickly glanced at the front door as Toby turned, gave a tug on her arm, and headed up a creaking staircase with worn wooden treads. The echo from their footsteps seemed to grow louder the further up the staircase they climbed.

Megan gave a quick glance into the front rooms situated on either side of the staircase. They were sparsely furnished with old, worn pieces of furniture. Threadbare upholstered chairs sat on either side of the large fireplaces beneath two more dingy framed landscape paintings. The floors were covered with shabby, threadbare Oriental rugs. An end table next to a rickety wooden chair was layered with dust. Lots of dust. Megan quickly had the sense that, though somewhat furnished, no one had lived in the house for quite some time, maybe generations.

At the top of the staircase, a narrow hallway ran toward the front of the house on either side of the staircase. The hallway looked like it had been wallpapered eighty years ago. The wallpaper had a faded, gloomy cream background with images of cheerless, washed-out blue flowers. The wallpaper appeared to have been unattractive since the day it was installed, and eight decades had done nothing to improve the situation. Toby turned right at the top of the stairs. There were three doors, and he stopped at the third one. He produced a black skeleton key from his pocket and unlocked the door.

"Home sweet home," he said just under his breath as he pulled Megan into the room. The room was small and windowless. The only semblance of furniture was a thin, stained mattress lying on the floor in a far corner.

The grimy walls were an unattractive off-white and appeared to have last been painted about the same time the wallpaper had been hung.

Toby closed the door behind them and quietly said, "Let me give you some advice. Brennan may look like a nice gentleman, but he's tough as nails. He wasn't fooling. He could have just as easily shot you. A word to the wise. Be careful. Now, I'm going to bring your friend into another room then I'm going to take you to the bathroom. You can shower and get cleaned up."

"What do you want from us?"

"We need to ask you some questions. Hopefully, you'll be able to help. Once you cooperate, we're going to see about getting Sean and Kevin out."

"Who are Sean and Kevin?"

"Not to worry, you can stop pretending. You'll be safe here with us," he said and closed the door. A moment later, Megan heard the lock click into place. She racked her brain, trying to figure out who Sean and Kevin were, but she couldn't come up with anyone.

Toby headed downstairs and back outside. Brennan was standing next to the open rear door on the Range Rover. Liam, the bearded man Megan had punched, was seated on one of the steps leading into the house. He was leaning forward and appeared to be taking deep breaths. He did not look up at Toby.

"How'd it go? She give you any problems," Brennan asked.

Toby shook his head. "I did like you said. Told her we needed some help getting Kevin and Sean out. Told her I'd be back and lead her to the bathroom soon as I escort this one to her suite."

Brennan glanced in the back of the Range Rover. Kate seemed to be sleeping peacefully. "I suppose I'll have to help you with this one since shit for brains, Liam, over there, had to try and play it tough. Might as well get it over with." He reached in the back of the car, took hold of Kate's arm, and pulled her halfway out. Toby took hold of her other arm, and together they roughly dragged her out of the back.

"No, no, no. Wait. Just wait a little second. No," Kate groaned and kept her left eye closed.

They began to walk towards the door, but after just three steps, Kate's legs shuddered and stopped working altogether. She sagged halfway to the ground. Her feet, only one had a shoe, dragged along the ground and up over the threshold past Liam as they stepped into the back hallway.

"Jesus, hang on a minute," Brennan said. He stopped, reached down, and grabbed Kate's ankles. At the same time, Toby got behind her and wrapped his arms around her chest. Brennan lifted her ankles, and they carried her halfway down the hall and into a small pantry. Brennan lowered her legs, and Toby set her down on the floor in front of a large built-in cabinet.

"Grab a cushion from one of the chairs in the sitting room, place it under her head, and lock her in. I'll get a water bottle and put it in here. Probably leave the light on for her."

Brennan retrieved a water bottle from the recycling bin, filled it with tap water, brought it back to the pantry, and set it on the floor.

Toby came back with an almost flat cushion from one of the chairs next to the fireplace.

"Is there even any stuffing in that?" Brennan asked.

"Enough to do the job. We give her one that's too full she's liable to have some real neck problems. You think she's going to make it?"

Brennan shrugged. "What difference does it make? We just have to get the other one . . ."

"Megan."

". . . Yeah. To tell us where the rest of the shipment is hidden. We have to get to it before the Garda do, or we're all dead. You better take her to the bathroom, let her shower and get cleaned up. Give her some space. It's time we get her to start thinking, as long as she cooperates, the two of them will be free to go."

"Yeah, free to go to the Dublin Mountains," Toby chuckled.

NINETEEN

Suel backed the car up to a space where he could turn around. He smiled, gave a final wave to the three cops, and mumbled, "Worthless bastards. Let's find this McGovern's Guest House place, tell those two women their car's been stolen, and get the hell back to Dublin. Honest to God, by the time we get back, the entire day will have been wasted. God save me." He glanced over at Dillon, pressing keys on his cellphone. "Now who in the hell are you calling?"

"I'm not calling anyone. I'm setting the GPS to give us directions to McGovern's Guest House."

"Were you listening back there? They just said it's a couple of miles. We'll probably be there before you get it set up on your phone. I don't know why in the hell you waste your time—"

"Take a right onto the N52 in fifty meters," the voice from Dillon's cellphone suddenly said.

"You were saying?" Dillon laughed.

Suel followed the directions through the roundabout, heading back the way they'd come on the N52. They drove over the Royal Canal bridge, and maybe a mile and a half later, the directions instructed Suel to take the third left on the upcoming roundabout. They turned onto the L1703 road, and a minute later, the voice said, "Your destination is on the right." Suel turned onto a lane with several shade trees along either side. Up ahead, they could see a two-story pink stucco structure with a circular drive in front of it. It looked like just about every square inch of space was covered by a pot of hanging flowers. Trimmed hedges and more flowers lined the gardens on either side of the steps leading up to the front entrance. A white and gold sign over the front door read, 'Welcome to McGovern's.' On the other side of the circular drive was a spotless lawn and a brick patio with four tables, each with four chairs neatly arranged around each table.

"Will you look at the state of this place. They must have a crew of gardeners," Suel said.

"Or a bunch of their own kids they put to work. It definitely looks like the sort of place a couple of women would find enjoyable," Dillon said.

"Yeah, the likes of you and me, we'd be happy with a room on the second floor of a pub." Suel pulled into the circular drive and parked the car just beyond the entrance. "Let's meet the ladies and tell them they'll have to find another means of transportation," Suel said, and half-laughed.

"You're actually looking forward to this, aren't you?"

"Like I told you on the way out, I really want to get back to Dublin and attend to the full plates we both have.

Ladies first," he said as he held the front door for Dillon to enter.

They stepped into what had probably originally been a sitting room but now looked more like a hotel lobby. The room had an oval rug with a couch and two matching chairs positioned in front of the fireplace. A coffee table stood in front of the couch with three different 'Things to See & Do in Ireland' magazines. Behind the couch and against the far wall was a wooden counter. A silver bell, the kind you'd ring for service, rested on the counter. Suel walked over and hit the bell three times. A moment later, a woman pushed open a swinging door. She wore jeans and a white t-shirt that had 'McGovern's' written across the front of it in pink letters. She wore a white apron around her waist, which at the moment she was using to wipe her hands.

"Gentlemen, good afternoon. How may I help you?"

"We'd like to see one of your guests, Kate Murray," Suel said.

A questioning look came over the woman's face, and she said, "May I ask what this is about?"

"We're with An Garda Síochána," Suel said. "Afraid it's a personal matter regarding her rental car. We understand she was a guest here last night."

The woman shook her head. "Oh, dear. Unfortunately, no, she wasn't here. She had a reservation, a reservation for two, actually. But they never checked in."

"But her credit card was charged," Dillon said. "The charge came through this morning."

"Yes, that's our policy. We take reservations. As a matter of fact, we've been fully booked for most of the month. It's high tourist season. Let me look," she said and opened a drawer behind the counter. She pulled out a book and tugged on a silky blue ribbon which opened to yesterday's page. Yes, here it is." She turned the book so Dillon and Suel could read it.

"You didn't hear from her? She didn't cancel?"

"She had a reservation for one night, which was last night. She made the reservation way back in March. Check-in time begins at three in the afternoon, and our policy is you can cancel anytime up until check-in time. We held the room for them through yesterday evening. I know we turned away at least three other couples. That's why we charged them for the room this morning."

"Do you have a contact phone number for Kate Murray?" Dillon asked.

"Yes, I'm sure we do, just a moment." She opened a small wooden file drawer and pulled out a 4 x 5 card. "Yes, here's the information. A note says we placed three calls to this number last night. No answer on any of the calls."

As Suel looked at the number, he punched it into his phone. He placed the phone against his ear and said, "It's ringing." A moment later, he shook his head and said, "Dropped me into voice mail."

"Is there a problem?" The woman said.

"There is now," Dillon replied.

TWENTY

The mattress on the floor was barely two inches thick. It was a striped material, stained in a number of places, and Megan didn't want to consider the various possibilities as to what had created the stains. She lifted the mattress to check the bottom side. It looked even worse. At least nothing scurried out from underneath it when she raised it off the floor. She took her shoe off and slapped the mattress several times, but that only seemed to raise dust, and in short order, she stopped.

She walked around the edge of the small room, checking the floor for mouse droppings. Thankfully, she didn't find any. She placed her ear up against all four walls and held that position for many minutes but never heard a sound from anywhere else in the house. At one point, she thought she might have heard a car drive away, but without any windows, there was no way to be sure, and she figured it could have just as easily been a car passing on the road.

Maybe an hour or two later, there was a knock on the door as it opened. Megan was sitting on the floor opposite the door with her back against the wall. Her stomach had been growling for almost as long as she'd been locked in the room.

"How are you doing?" Toby asked.

Rather than give a sharp answer, she just stared at him.

"Well, um, I figured if you wanted to grab a shower, I could show you where the bathroom is."

"Oh, wow, there's a bathroom here. Who knew?"

"You want to get cleaned up? Or do you want to sit there and complain? Your choice."

"Will it be private?"

"Yes. No one will be in there with you. If you want, you can give me your clothes. I can run them through the washer and dry 'em. You can shower and clean up in the bathroom while I wash them."

"Our suitcases are in the trunk of our car. If you could get those, I could maybe change into something clean, and you wouldn't have to—"

"Yeah. Well, see, that's not really going to be much of an option. I'm not sure where your car is right now."

"So what your telling me is I can take a shower and then climb right back into the same stuff I've had on for the last two days. Or, I can sit around naked and have all you guys stare at me and make comments."

"No one's going to be staring at you. The bathroom is nice and private. Besides, after the way you kicked Liam's ass, everyone is going to keep their distance. Where'd you learn to fight like that, anyway?"

"Self-defense course, it's big in the States. Is there a lock on the bathroom door?"

"There is, and it works, but I gotta warn you. If you try anything, like lock the door and jump out the window, Brennan is going to take it out on your friend. I told you before he wasn't kidding, and I meant it. So please remember that, 'cause if you try something he will go crazy, and there's nothing I can do that'll stop him. So, you want that shower?"

"You said there's a lock?"

"Yeah, on the inside of the door."

"Do you have anything like a towel or do I have to drip dry?"

"I think I can find you a towel and a washcloth."

"And some soap?"

"Yeah, that too."

"Okay, but you better not be lying to me."

Toby held up both hands in mock surrender. "I'll be right back."

He closed the door. Megan heard him insert the key and lock the door. Amazingly, he was back in about five minutes and knocked on the door again as he opened it.

"Yes," Megan said, as Toby stood in the open doorway.

He held a dingy bath towel and washcloth. At one time, they had probably been white, but now they looked like a more mottled grey. "Here, found these for you and this bar of soap." The bar of soap was cracked in places and covered with dirt from whoever had used it last.

When he handed it to her, the soap felt dried out, and Megan guessed it had probably sat on some sink in a barn for the last few years.

"Gee, thanks," she said, not meaning a word.

"Okay, follow me." He stepped out into the hallway. Megan was tempted to push him over the stair railing, but then what would she do? And as stupid as he might be, she believed every word when he said that Brennan guy would take it out on Kate. So, she followed him down the hall and into the bathroom.

It could have been worse. The sink was reasonably clean, and there was a medicine cabinet with a mirror above the sink. The toilet was next to the sink, and two large rolls of toilet paper rested on the floor next to the toilet. The shower was a small, glass-encased thing with an antique shower nozzle. Actually, it was just a copper pipe that was attached to the wall and then curved. A shower head had been attached at the end with what looked like duct tape. The whole affair appeared to be homemade, like something you might find in an old lake cabin back in the States. The floor was a greenish-grey linoleum with a buckled seam running down the center. The color on the floor had worn away around the entrance, apparently from all sorts of people coming in and out of the room.

"Here's how you lock the door from the inside," Toby said. He turned towards the door and slid a deadbolt lock into place. The lock was rusted where the brass finish had worn off, and the barrel receptor attached to the door frame was held in place with a single bent nail.

Megan didn't think it would keep anyone out who really wanted to get in. In fact, if someone pounded too hard, they were liable to knock the lock off and open the door.

"If you want to toss me your clothes, I can wait outside. You can hand them out the door, and I'll run them through the washer. I promise I won't peek."

"Okay. Um, thanks for doing this."

"We'll get you fed after your shower."

"Thanks, I'm starving. You'll give Kate some food, too?"

"Yeah, of course, as long as she's up for eating."

Megan locked the door, such as it was, as soon as Toby stepped outside. She looked at the keyhole beneath the doorknob, actually bent down and peered out. She could see Toby standing about two feet from the door. She draped the towel over the doorknob, made sure it was covering the keyhole, and quickly undressed. She stuffed her thong in her jeans pocket and folded her bra inside her t-shirt before she unlocked the door. She tossed her clothes out the door onto the hall floor and quickly locked the door again. She left the towel hanging on the doorknob, grabbed the washcloth and soap, and headed for the shower.

Amazingly, the water came on, and she could adjust the temperature. She stepped in under the water and let it run over her head and down her shoulders. She held the bar of soap under the stream of warm water and rubbed it with her hands until all the dirt disappeared, then she rubbed it some more just to be sure. She soaped up twice and rinsed off, taking her time. When she turned the water off and stepped out of the shower, she landed in a large puddle stretching across the linoleum floor. Apparently, the drain on the shower wasn't working all that well. She dried off as best she could and wrapped the towel around her.

There was a small window in the room, and she used the washcloth to wipe away the steam and look out. All she could see were trees. No cars, no other homes, nothing. She sat down on the floor, as far away from the puddle as she could possibly get, and leaned back against the wall. Eventually, she drifted off to sleep.

TWENTY-ONE

Dillon was sitting on the couch in the lobby of McGovern's Guest House. Suel sat in a chair next to him. He was focused on eating a chicken sandwich and sipping a cup of tea. Dillon was on the phone to Ina Nolan, a cousin of Suel's who worked in the Garda's computer forensics department.

"The phone number I just gave you is for a woman named Kathleen Murray. She's the missing American we had hoped to find over here in Mullingar. Unfortunately, she never showed up at the B&B where she had a reservation."

"You ever think she might have met someone in a pub last night?"

"We're past that point. I'm hoping you could pass on that number to someone who can trace it. Hopefully, it will turn up at some luxury hotel back in Dublin, but I have my doubts."

"Why aren't you calling DCI McCabe? He can have someone run this and—"

"Because he's not answering his phone. He's probably in a meeting somewhere. Look, Ina, if you can't help, no problem, but I'm beginning to get the sense we're on a short leash that's getting shorter with every minute we waste."

"Calm down, Dillon. I didn't say I wouldn't help. I just wondered if maybe she was out partying and now can't remember where she parked her car. Not that it's there, because some knacker stole it, and it wouldn't be there anyway."

Dillon rolled his eyes at Suel and shook his head. "Ina, can you put me in touch with someone who can track this? Yes or no?"

"Hold on, Captain Crabby. I'm transferring your call now."

"Thank you, Ina," Dillon said, but she was already off the line. After a couple of clicks on the phone, it began to ring. Halfway through the second ring, the call was answered, and a male voice said. "Hi Ina, change your mind?"

"Sorry to disappoint you," Dillon said. "Is this Tommy Walsh?"

"It is. Who's this?"

"US Marshal Jack Dillon, assigned to Dublin Special Branch. Tommy, I'm out in Mullingar, working a missing person case. Ina was kind enough to transfer my call. I'm hoping you can get a triangulation on a cell phone number. We're trying to locate this individual and—"

"I've heard of you. Weren't you involved in that incident out at Dublin airport a few years back?"

"That was maybe three or four years ago, but who's counting? Can you help us?"

"No and yes."

"What the hell does that mean?"

"First, why don't you give me that number and I'll get on it. Once I start the program, I'll get back on the line. Should only take a minute or two."

"Now, this is an American number. I don't know if any calls have been made on it. As far as we know, the phone is with the individual. She flew into Dublin yesterday morning, rented a vehicle at Dublin airport. She was supposed to stay at a B&B in Mullingar but never showed up."

"So give me the number, Dillon. I can't begin tracking it until I get that from you."

"Oh, yeah, sorry about that." Dillon gave him the number.

"Okay, thanks. Now, stay on the line. I'm going to put you on hold. I'll be back in a minute." Dillon heard a click and pulled the phone away from his mouth. "I think he's running the program now."

Suel chewed two or three more times and swallowed. "You think or you know?"

"Why do I even bother? Go back to eating."

"You going to finish your sandwich?" Suel said and looked at Dillon's half-eaten chicken sandwich sitting on the plate in front of him.

"Don't even think about it. For your information, I—"

"Marshal Dillon. You still there?" Walsh said, coming back on the line.

"I'm here, Tommy."

"Give me your number, and I'll send this map to you."

"Map?"

"Yeah with the location of that cell phone. You're calling from out Mullingar way?"

"I am. We're right on the edge of town not far from where the N4 and the N52 meet."

"N4? Oh yeah, I see it on the map. You can't be more than maybe fifteen minutes from the location. Looks to be rural."

"And you're sending me a map?"

"Yes, the phone is listed as belonging to a Kathleen Murray. She's a younger-looking, blonde woman."

"That sounds like it. And you have a picture of her?"

"Yeah, with her name and a red marker indicating the specific location."

"That location marker is good to what, about 350 feet?"

Walsh laughed. "No offense, sir, but time to get into the next century. It's accurate down to just a couple of feet."

"A couple of feet? You can get that nowadays from cell tower triangulation?"

"You're talking about obsolete technology. That's the way it used to work. Now, they track based on about a dozen low flying satellites."

"No kidding? That's a hell of a program you've got."

"Truth be told, sir, it's a free program available from most cell phone providers. Who's your provider?"

"My provider? Um, Vodafone."

"Yeah, they've got a free program you can download. It'll be exactly like the one I just used. You should download it. It'll save you the time spent harassing me." Fortunately, Walsh followed up with a laugh.

"Thanks, Tommy, I'll keep that in mind."

"You should get that map link in just a few seconds. Anything else I can do for you?"

"No, that should do it. Thank you."

"All right just sending that information off now, so you should see it shortly. One more thing. It looks like a text message was sent yesterday afternoon around one-fifteen from the Swordsman pub on the outskirts of Mullingar. Just off the junction of the N4 and the N52. It's indicated on the map as well. Anything else?"

"No, Tommy. We ever meet in person, I'll buy the first round. Thank you so much for your help."

"My pleasure, glad I could be of assistance. You run into any problems, just let me know. Oh, and next time you talk to Ina, put a good word in for me and tell her I'm still waiting for her call."

"I'll be happy to do that, Tommy. Thanks for the help," Dillon said and disconnected.

No sooner had he hung up than his phone signaled a text message coming in. When he clicked on the message, it was identified as coming from An Garda Síochána. He opened it, and the message read, "This file is unable to be downloaded. We'll keep trying." It displayed a small revolving wheel suggesting it was attempting to accomplish the download.

"Wouldn't you know? The guy sends me the link, and my phone can't download the file. Honest to God. I just want to scream."

"Call him back. Have him send it to the Mullingar station. We can head over there."

"Yeah, I suppose. Damn it."

Dillon clicked on the phone number for Tommy Walsh. The phone began to ring a few seconds later. After several rings, Dillon was thinking he was about to be dumped into voice mail when Walsh finally answered.

"Hi Tommy, Dillon again. Sorry to bother you, but that file you sent is apparently too large for my phone to open."

"Too large? That doesn't sound right. What does it say?"

"The message?"

"Yeah, what does it say?"

"It said the file was too large to download, but they'd keep trying, and there was this little wheel turning, but nothing happened."

Walsh laughed for a moment. "When was the last time you shut off your phone?"

"Shut it off? You mean like actually turned it off?"

"Yeah, when was the last time?"

"I don't know, a couple of months back, maybe around Christmas or New Year."

"So, six or seven months?"

"Yeah, probably."

"That's most likely the problem. You need to update your program."

"How in the hell do I do that?"

Walsh chuckled for a moment. "All you have to do is turn the thing off, let it sit for a minute, and turn it back on. That will cause it to update automatically, then try to open that message. You shouldn't have any problem."

"Really?"

"Yeah really. It would be a good idea to do that at least once a week. It gets rid of all sorts of cookies and bullshit, cleans up your system. Give it a try. If it doesn't work, call me back."

"Yeah, okay. Thanks, Tommy. Who knew?"

"Most people your age and above don't," Wash said, laughed, and hung up.

"Well?" Suel said and drained his tea mug.

"I'm going to have to shut the phone off, let it sit for a minute or two, and turn it back on. He thinks that will work."

Suel shook his head but didn't say anything. Dillon turned off his phone. He waited three minutes before he turned it back on, just to be sure. The phone made it's chiming sound as it came back to life and spelled out the name SAMSUNG while a little bell tone sounded.

"Oh, man. If this works, I'm telling you," Dillon said.

Suel shook his head.

Dillon waited a moment before he clicked on the 'Messages' icon. The text message for Tommy Walsh appeared. He clicked on it, and a moment later, the map appeared with the small image of Kathleen Murray and a red dot indicating the location of the cellphone. A second icon indicated the Swordsman Pub. "Paddy, call the woman's number. See if she picks up."

Suel dialed the number and a moment later shook his head. "Immediately dropped me into voice mail. She hasn't been on the thing. Where does that map locate her?"

"Not all that far from where that burned-out car was. I'm guessing ten minutes, tops."

"Let's see if we can get those Mullingar Guards involved. They'll know their way around. Chances are they're still cooling their heels waiting for the car to be picked up."

Dillon nodded. "Good idea. If this continues to shape up the way I fear it's going, we'll have to get them involved in the very near future anyway. Might as well do it now, so they don't get a burr up their ass thinking we were trying to make them look bad."

"I'll drive," Suel said.

Dillon picked up what was left of his chicken sandwich and headed out the door. Suel drove back to where they viewed the burnt-out car and met the Mullingar cops. He hadn't driven ten yards on the gravel road when a tow truck appeared from around the distant bend followed by the three cars, two of which were Garda vehicles. Suel slowly pulled off the gravel path. He and Dillon stepped out of their car and waved the tow truck past.

The stocky guy with the crewcut was behind the wheel of the first vehicle. He pulled to a stop and lowered his window. "What's wrong? Couldn't find your way out? There's only one road."

TWENTY-TWO

Megan was aware of a distant noise, but she couldn't tell if it was real or if she was still dreaming. The sound of someone clearing their voice woke her, and she slowly opened her eyes. She was seated on the floor of the bathroom, supposedly with the towel wrapped around her. Unfortunately, when she dozed off, the towel had come undone and left her exposed.

Toby stood a few feet away, leering. He cleared his voice again and said, "Um, I've got your clothes here. They're mostly dry, I think." He held her jeans and t-shirt in one hand, her bra and thong in the other, and continued to stare.

Megan quickly reached down and pulled the towel around her. "If you can just hand them to me, that'll be fine."

He smiled, splashed through the puddle on the floor, and handed her the t-shirt and jeans. He tossed her thong on top of the t-shirt. He made a show of reading the tag with her bra size and smiled before he handed the bra to her. "Nice," he said.

"Let me just put these on, and I'll be out," she said, ignoring his comment.

"How'd all this water get on the floor? Did you forget to close the shower door?"

"No, I didn't forget to close the shower door. Your drain must be leaking somewhere. All I know is, when I stepped out of the shower, that puddle of water was all over the floor. It kind of looks a little smaller than it was, so it must be slowly going somewhere."

She absently ran a hand over her jeans. "These still feel damp. How long did you set the timer for?"

"Set the timer?"

"On the dryer, you know, you set the timer."

"Um, no, I don't know. I hung them out on the line. They were out there for a good hour or so, and there's a nice breeze today."

Megan thought, Oh my God, but didn't say anything. "Well, thanks. If you can maybe give me a minute, I'll put them on."

"Oh, yeah. Good. Then I'll take you back to your room, and we can see about getting you something to eat."

"Thanks, because I'm starving. Is Kate going to shower?"

"She said she wanted to sleep a little longer and she'd let me know," Toby lied. He waited for a long moment, hoping she'd get dressed while he stood there, or maybe the towel would fall off again. Neither happened, and eventually, he slowly made his way to the door. He pulled the door open and glanced back, trying to get lucky, but that didn't work either, so he stepped out of the bathroom and closed the door behind him.

Megan waited a minute or two, just to make sure he wasn't going to come back in. She quickly rose to her feet and hurried to the door. She pushed the deadbolt in place and draped her towel over the doorknob, covering the keyhole in the process. Her thong and bra were damp and cold, but that was nothing compared to when she put on the t-shirt and worked it down to her waist. She stepped into her wet jeans and pulled them up her legs an inch at a time. She was very uncomfortable standing there in her damp clothes but not about to say anything.

She undid the deadbolt lock and opened the door. Toby stood about three inches from the door, smiling, and she had the very unpleasant feeling he'd been trying, unsuccessfully, to peer through the keyhole.

"All set?" He said.

"Yeah, thanks for doing the wash. It's great to be in clean clothes again. You mentioned something to eat?"

"Yeah, let's get you back in your room, and I'll bring it up to you."

"I could just follow you downstairs."

He shook his head and said, "I don't think so."

They walked down the hall. Ever the gentleman, Toby opened the door to the little room with the stained mattress and stepped aside. Megan walked in the room, took about five steps, and turned around just as the door closed. She heard him insert the key in the lock, and a moment later, the lock snapped.

It wasn't even ten minutes, and Toby was back with food, such as it was. Megan had been thinking pancakes or maybe scrambled eggs and buttered toast. He held a bowl of cold cereal, cornflakes or something, with milk. He handed her the bowl along with a spoon. Next, he reached into the front pocket of his jeans, pulled out a banana, and handed it to her. He set a plastic bottle of water on the floor. He took out a small piece of bright red plastic from his back pocket, and at first, Megan thought it might be a placemat.

It looked like a small sheet, maybe just eight by ten inches. He put his mouth on the corner and proceeded to blow it up. When he was finished, he tossed it onto the mattress, smiled, and said, "Thought you might like a pillow. Make your sleeping just a little more comfortable."

"Gee, thanks," Megan said, meaning anything but.

TWENTY-THREE

Dillon focused on the stocky guy with the crew cut. "We did a trace, and we've located the woman's phone. Kate Murray. Wonder if you might help us find it?"

"You traced it?"

Dillon nodded, clicked on his cellphone, and handed it to him. Crewcut studied the map briefly and said, "I think I know where this is. Hold on just a moment. Let me check with the boss. He walked back to the other two cars. The female officer drove the second car. He said something to her, she nodded and drove off, following the tow truck carrying what remained of the burnt-out Nissan Micra. He spoke to the tall, thin man with the combover. They seemed to discuss things back and forth for a moment. Eventually, the thin man nodded, put his car in gear, and followed the other two vehicles down the road.

"Sorry about that. That's DCI Jamie Roach. Poor bastard has been fighting a cancer for the better part of the year, and he's not winning. We end up doing any search, and try as he might, it's not going to go well for him." He shook his head and watched Roach's car turn off the gravel road and onto the highway. "Name's Eamon Turley," he said and held out his hand to Suel.

"Paddy Suel," Suel replied, nodding and shaking hands.

"Jack Dillon," Dillon said, extending his hand. Turley shook hands. Dillon squeezed his hand, not hard, just an average grip, but it was like squeezing a brick.

"Dillon? Yeah, I thought I picked up the accent. You're that American Marshal, right?"

Dillon nodded and said, "Yeah, we say US Marshal, but yeah."

"I've been trying to teach him the ways of a proper investigation. It's been an uphill battle all the way," Suel said.

"Well, look, Dillon, why don't you and your cellphone ride with me? Suel, you can follow us. Let's see what we can find out there. If your map is to be believed, we're not that far away."

Dillon climbed into the passenger side of the Mullingar squad car. Suel ran over to his car, made a quick U-turn, and pulled in behind Turley as he headed out on the gravel road. Turley took a right then slowed at the roundabout for a truck and a couple of cars. He took a left onto the roundabout and almost immediately another left onto the N52.

"Let me take a look at that map, Dillon."

Dillon clicked on his phone and brought up the image. Turley took the phone, glanced at it for a quick moment, and said, "Hmm, out past Wallace's bar and

Dalystown National School. I'm not aware of anything else out that way, but let's see what we find."

"Your jurisdiction extend out this far?" Dillon said maybe five minutes later.

"Pretty much, at least from the standpoint that there's no one else and we're the closest. Police, fire, and emergency. Not much out this way, the odd farm or a corner with a home or two. With the way things have changed, probably half the estates have been abandoned and fallen to ruin over the last thirty to forty years. It would be rare that somewhere out this way a place would be housing a young family today. Small farms can't survive nowadays."

"Here we go," Turley said and put on his right blinker. There was no oncoming traffic, and he turned onto a road marked L1127. If you didn't know where the small sign was, you'd never see it, and not for the first time Dillon was amazed at how easy it was to get completely lost in rural Ireland. The road was maybe wide enough for a car and a half. There was no shoulder. Once they turned, an official brown highway sign indicated a campsite four kilometers down the road in the opposite direction.

Turley veered to the left, past Wallace's bar. A nice enough looking building with two wooden picnic tables out front and no vehicles in sight. They drove on for another mile or two. Turley put his blinker on, made a right-hand turn, and pulled over.

"This is it?" Dillon asked, looking out at farm fields and the occasional tree.

"No, but we're close. I'm guessing one, maybe one and a half kilometers. Just want to double-check. Of course, it's not like there's a lot of places to turn off from here on."

They headed down the road. No homes or structures of any kind were visible. The road suddenly turned to gravel, and Turley slowed his pace. He glanced from time to time at Dillon's phone screen. As they rounded some sparse looking trees, a structure appeared up on the right. "Here we go," Turley said and accelerated ever so slightly.

He pulled to a stop in front of the entrance to the lot. The small, single-story house that looked like it couldn't hold more than two rooms appeared abandoned. The house sat back behind a small wall, no higher than two feet, and no more than maybe twenty feet from the gravel road. A dead tree, not much larger than Dillon's forearm, stood at the far corner of the house. A couple of pieces of lumber lay scattered in front of the house. Turley and Dillon climbed out of the car as Suel pulled up behind them.

"The phone is in this shithole?" Suel said.

"Looks more like it's behind the place," Dillon replied, looking at his phone screen.

"I think we'll just walk back," Turley said and headed through the entrance in the wall. Definite vehicle tracks appeared in the loose gravel surrounding the place, but it would be next to impossible to determine how long they'd been there.

"Any idea when this place was abandoned or who lived here?" Dillon said.

Turley shook his head. "Hard to say, but my guess, it's been empty for at least twenty years."

They rounded the structure and stopped. The rear door was open, and the small window next to it was broken. Large chunks of what appeared to be burnt rubber were scattered across the open gravel yard. Dillon picked up on bits of glass scattered amongst the gravel. The gravel was mounded in two distinct areas, suggesting a vehicle may have skidded to a stop. In the distance was a stone structure, maybe a storage shed or a small barn with two weathered wooden doors. The doors were open, and a length of chain hung from one of the doors.

"If this thing is accurate, the phone should be right around—" Dillon had walked maybe ten feet in the direction of the stone structure and stopped. "I'll be damned, there it is." He pointed to a sparkly pink item on the ground.

"Leave it there," Turley said. "I'm calling our Technical Section now. Let's get them out here and do things by the book. Look around at all this shite," he said, indicating the chunks of rubber and the sparkly pink cellphone case on the ground. "Something sure as hell went down out here."

Dillon took a deep breath and pulled his pistol from his belt. "While you're on the phone, we'll do a quick check of the house. Say a prayer it's empty. Then the three of us can check that thing." He nodded toward the stone building with the open doors.

Suel followed Dillon to the open backdoor of the house. As they entered, Dillon noticed dried leaves in the open doorway. More leaves had blown across the small room. Most likely, an indication the door had been open for an extended period of time. They stepped into what had been the kitchen. There were no appliances, although there was an empty area between two wooden cabinets where a small stove would have been. The worn wooden planks on the floor creaked as they slowly crossed the room. It looked as though a finish had never been applied to the floor. Two electrical outlets were installed in the wall above a linoleum countertop. There was a small white porcelain sink with a drainboard beneath the broken window. The faucet was missing from the sink. They stepped from the kitchen into a small sitting room with a fireplace. The fireplace was small and shallow, built for coal burning. Whatever tiles were once there had long since been pulled off.

There were two small front windows. Resting on the windowsill of one of the windows were the remains of a small bird, really nothing more than a pile of feathers and a beak.

A wooden door was on one side of the sitting room. Suel pushed open the door using his foot. The door creaked as it swung open into what had, at one time, probably been the bedroom. The only bedroom. The room was empty except for a mildewed wool blanket in the far corner that looked like it had been there for years. A window with four panes of glass looked out onto the gravel yard. One of the panes was missing. Dillon could see their cars parked out just beyond the small wall.

"I'd guess this dump has been empty for a pretty long time," Suel said.

"Let's check that rear building," Dillon said and headed for the back door.

Turley held a stack of crime scene evidence markers in his hand, yellow plastic A-frames, maybe four inches high. Each one had a black number on it. A dozen of the A-frames were already scattered around the rear area.

"I've put one by the phone. Found what looks like blood over there. Marked some of the tire remnants. I also found a number of brass shells, look to be nine-millimeter. Technical section should be out here in the next thirty minutes. What did you find inside?"

"A dead bird," Suel said.

"Looked like it had been there for a year or two. Really nothing more than just a pile of feathers," Dillon said.

"If it's all right with you, I'd like to wait until the tech team arrives before we check that outbuilding. We've walked through the site. I don't want to disturb things any more than we already have."

Dillon thought about that for a long moment, and as much as he didn't like it, he had to agree. It made sense. "We'll wait outside next to the car."

"I'll be along in a moment," Turley said. "Just want to secure the area with a few more of these." He indicated the stack of yellow plastic A-frames in his hand.

Dillon and Suel headed out front to their car.

"This is turning into a right bollocks," Suel said. "Your woman's phone, blood, shell casings, the car torched. What in God's name did they get themselves into?"

TWENTY-FOUR

Megan wasn't all that impressed with the bowl of cornflakes, but since she hadn't eaten in over twenty-four hours, she dug in. It only took a minute or two to spoon in every last cornflake. She lifted the bowl to her mouth, swallowed the remainder of the milk, and licked the sides of the bowl. She set the bowl next to her on the floor and carefully peeled the banana. Bits of the peel still appeared a little green, suggesting the banana wasn't quite fully ripe. Not that it mattered. She stuffed a third of it into her mouth, closed her eyes, and savored the taste. She'd never, ever, had such a delicious banana.

She was in the process of licking her fingers for the second time, savoring the final bit of banana from her fingertips, when she heard voices from outside the room. It sounded like whoever was talking was coming up the stairs and she wondered if Toby was maybe bringing Kate up for her shower. The voices grew louder and then suddenly stopped. A moment later, she heard a key being inserted in the lock and the door opened. No knock this time.

Toby stepped into the room, carrying a wooden stool. He set the stool on the floor in front of Megan. He didn't look at her. He seemed to focus on the floor and stepped back just as the man he had referred to as Brennan suddenly appeared in the doorway. Brennan smiled and pulled the stool a little closer to Megan as he sat down.

She automatically tried to slide back on the floor but immediately ran into the wall. She drew her knees up and wrapped her arms around her legs, not realizing she'd just assumed a protective posture.

"Did you enjoy your breakfast, Megan?" Brennan said, looking at the bowl with nothing but the banana peel in it.

"How is Kate?"

"She's just fine, not to worry."

"I want to see her."

"You'll see her in plenty of time. She's eating her breakfast, right now. She had some cereal," he said, nodding at the bowl on the floor next to Megan. "She said she didn't want a banana, so we gave her an orange instead. Oh, and she had a cup of tea earlier. She was a little worried breakfast might not stay down, but I think the tea seemed to settle her stomach."

"I need to see her."

"I'm sure you do, and I want you to see her, just as soon as possible. But what we need to do first is get some information from you."

"Information?"

"We just need the answer to a couple of simple questions, and you can see her. In fact, what I'd like to do is put you both up in a hotel suite. Have you pampered after all of this, you know, as a way of saying thanks for helping us out and—"

"What are you talking about? What kind of information do you need? I'll tell you anything I can."

He smiled. "Good, I knew we'd get along once you had some time to think it over. Now then, Kevin and Sean."

"Kev—"

"Your information apparently helped the Guards. They would never have thought to look in the paint cans. And I don't blame you. You certainly didn't have much of a choice. Now, all we need to know is where they hid the rest of it."

Megan had a confused look on her face and slowly shook her head.

Brennan flashed a quick smile. "Oh, come on now. No pressure. After all, the trial is over. It's okay, you can tell me. I really need to recover the rest of that shipment. I'm thinking there could be a nice little payment in there for you, too. The both of you's."

"I'd love to help you, but I have absolutely no idea what you're talking about. If I could maybe see Kate. You know, to check on her—"

Brennan's face turned red. "You think I'm fucking around with the likes of you? I warned you. You spoiled little bitch. Didn't I warn you? I told you, if you didn't cooperate, there would be trouble. Apparently, you seem to think I was kidding. Okay, have it your way. Why don't we see what your friend Kate has to say about it when she gets my undivided attention?" he said and half-jumped off the stool, knocking it over in the process. His face was red. His eyes flared, and his hands were clenched in fists at his side.

"I really have absolutely no idea what it is you're talking about. Who did you say? Kevin and who? I don't know what you mean. If I did, I would tell you. Really I would. Please, you have to believe me. We only just arrived and—"

"And partied your pretty little asses off. I know all about it. We all do. And we don't give a damn. Good for you, for both of you. I hope you were able to ride as many guys as you wanted. It's fine with me. Hell, I couldn't care less. But now, we just need your help to find the rest of the shipment before the Guards do. Because if they find it first, you and your little friend are going to be in some very serious trouble. You think I'm kidding? All right. Maybe it's time for a little lesson. Toby, take her to the back window."

"Do you think that's a good idea? I mean, maybe if we just gave her some time to think about it, she—"

"Shut the feck up, ya bollocks, and do as I say. Take her to the damn back window. We'll be out there shortly. You can watch what happens, sweetheart. We'll give you an hour to think about it, and then it's going to be your turn. You'll be next."

"I don't know what you're—"

"This is on you, bitch," Brennan shouted and stormed out of the room.

"Damn it, Megan, I told you," Toby said. "He's not kiddin' here. We're getting desperate, and he's feckin' serious. You're not protecting anyone, and you sure as hell aren't helping yourself."

TWENTY-FIVE

Dillon, Suel, and Turley were on Suel's cellphone with DCI McCabe. The cellphone was on speaker, and they were seated in Turley's squad car. Turley had moved the car about twenty feet further down the road, so the Mullingar Technical Bureau vehicle could park just beyond the entrance into the yard.

"Last update we got, they were going to be at least another hour or two," Suel said.

"And they haven't even entered the outbuilding, yet," Dillon added.

"We're short-handed as it is out here, sir. If you could spare the lads for an additional day or two, it would really help. You know how it is, the longer it takes to find the women, the less our chances of finding them alive."

"Yes, I'm aware of that. Dillon, Suel, work it out and keep me posted. Tell me, how's DCI Roach doing? I haven't heard an update lately," McCabe said.

"He's doing his best, sir," Turley said. "But to be honest, we all fear he's on borrowed time. He's been fighting the cancer for the better part of a year. He's frail, and he's lost a good deal of weight. Poor soul is exhausted by the middle of any day. All that said, he's in there fighting every day and not about to give up."

"God Bless, one hell of a man in his day."

"And still is, sir," Turley said.

"All right. Look, keep me posted. Dillon, Suel, stay on this for the next seventy-two hours, and we'll touch base at that time. Hopefully, this comes to a positive conclusion before that. You're going to head back to Dublin tonight?"

Dillon looked at Suel, who nodded.

"Just to pack a change of clothes and some incidentals in a bag," Suel said. "If we leave shortly, we can be back out here a little after midnight."

"We can manage without them for a bit, sir," Turley said. "But starting early tomorrow morning, we'll be knocking on doors and asking questions."

"Supposedly, the Murray woman sent a text message from a location here yesterday around the noon hour," Suel said. "We can check that out on our way back to Dublin. It's right on the way."

"Damnedest thing," McCabe said. "No sooner do we whisk two Americans named Kate and Megan back to the States than two more arrive on the same day, only to disappear twelve hours later. Christ on a bike, I don't get it. All right, keep me posted. Anything else?"

Suel gave a quick glance around and said, "I think that about covers everything at the moment, sir."

"Very well. Good luck, lads. DI Turley, nice to make your acquaintance. Please pass on my best to DCI Roach."

"I'll be sure to do that, sir."

McCabe disconnected, and Turley said, "He seems like a nice enough sort."

Suel nodded and said, "Yeah, until he decides to nail your ass to the wall. And believe me, he's more than capable of doing that."

"You said your woman sent a text message. Do you know to who?"

Dillon shook his head. "Don't know who, but we can check. She sent it from a place called the Swordsman. Is that a store, or a restaurant, or something?"

"A pub, just off the N4. You would have had to pass it on the way here. You can follow me there. I want to check with the tech lads and see how much longer they'll be."

"If it's like Dublin, however long they tell you, add at least an hour," Suel said.

"Give me a minute, and I'll be back." Turley climbed out of the car and hurried over to the Technical Bureau vehicle. The Tech van was a white panel vehicle with a florescent yellow stripe edged in blue running all around the vehicle. Flashing lights were mounted on top of the van, and the words 'Technical Bureau', in both Irish and English, were painted in blue on either side of the van.

Just then, three individuals in white hazmat suits, boot covers, and blue latex gloves were in the process of bagging the various items DI Turley had marked, along with a number of additional items the technical crew had identified. One of the guys in the hazmat suits was placing an armful of evidence bags in the van as Turley went over to talk to him.

"You pick up on McCabe's comment?" Dillon asked.

"McCabe's comment? You mean we got seventy-two hours to sort this mess out?"

"No, the bit about two Americans named Kate and Megan going back to the States and two more arrive with the same names, on the same day, only to disappear twelve hours later."

"I'm not following."

"What if this is a mistake, and these two missing women were thought to be those two we sent back to the States? They were held in secret, assisted in the conviction of the Sands brothers, and then we snuck them out of the country and back to the US. It could be a major screw up."

"Sounds to me like you're grabbing at the proverbial straw, Dillon."

"I don't know. So far, the only image we have is of this Kate Murray. I mean, she's young. She's an American."

"Yeah, and she's blonde. Kate Betto, now in the custody of the DEA, was a redhead if you'll remember."

"But Paddy, think about it. Kate Murray and Megan Gaffney, a blonde and a redhead. Kate Betto and Megan Ganino, a redhead and a blonde. Murray and Gaffney are Americans. They suddenly show up in Mullingar, just at the end of the Sands brothers' trial. Maybe someone makes a mistake and grabs them."

"Two things, first you have to find someone that stupid. Then, why grab them? It's not like they're going to be able to get the Sands brothers out of prison. The other thing is, I think it was a pretty well-kept secret the girls showed us the paint cans with the drug stash."

"Maybe," Dillon said.

Turley climbed back in his car. "They'll be here for a few more hours. They haven't entered the storage shed yet, but they can see a woman's shoe. Pink and looks new, lying on its side in there. By the way, they've recovered eight brass shell casings so far. All nine-millimeter. They're guessing all fired from the same gun, but that has yet to be confirmed."

"You're going to lead us to the Swordsman?" Suel said.

"I will. I'm going to turn around here, and you can follow me," Turley said.

Dillon and Suel hopped out of Turley's car and headed to their own.

TWENTY-SIX

Toby took hold of Megan's arm, squeezed it, and yanked her toward the door. As they stepped into the hallway, she could hear Brennan shouting down on the first floor, but she couldn't make out what he was saying.

"Don't let him hurt Kate. She's not well. I told you she needs to see a doctor. When that asshole hit her, he did some real damage."

Toby seemed to ignore what she said and pulled her down the hall.

"Hey, did you hear what I just—"

"I warned you, Megan. Brennan warned you, but apparently being nice doesn't seem to work. You either don't think we have the balls, or I don't know, maybe you've got a death wish for your friend Kate. Is that it? You want to take her out of the picture, and then you can have everything for yourself. You that cold-hearted?" He said and yanked her arm again, dragging her down the hallway.

"No, no, it's nothing like that. I told you before. I don't know what you guys are talking about. Neither of us do. We just got here yesterday."

They passed the door to the bathroom. There was still a puddle on the bathroom floor but nowhere near as large as it had been just an hour ago. Megan didn't notice. She was too busy trying to keep up with Toby as he pulled her down the hall. It felt like he was going to yank her arm out of the shoulder socket, and she stumbled to keep up.

There was a window at the end of the hall with a shade drawn. Toby yanked the shade two or three times. It suddenly snapped up to the top and rolled around a couple of times. He let go of Megan's arm and raised the window.

Megan rubbed her arm and rotated her shoulder. It hurt.

"Get down here, and you can look out. Wouldn't want you to miss anything," he said. He suddenly grabbed a fistful of her hair and yanked her down towards the open window. He tried to force her head out the window, banging her forehead against the lower rail of the window.

"Ouch, damn it," she shouted.

"Shut the feck up, bitch, and get your damn head out there or you'll miss the show," he shouted. He raised the window another few inches and shoved her head out.

Her forehead was throbbing, and she could feel a burning sensation running across it.

Brennan suddenly appeared below. Kate was with him, or rather, he was dragging her. His right hand held a clump of her hair, and his left arm was wrapped beneath her arms. Her feet, only one had a shoe, were two or three inches off the ground. Her right eye was still black and swollen. Blood had crusted around her nose and mouth and splattered across her torn top. Her left eye was closed, and she appeared limp and unconscious.

"Kate. Kate, are you all right? Kate," Megan screamed.

"Forget it, she can't hear you," Toby said and laughed.

"You ready for this?" Brennan shouted as he looked up at Megan. "This is all your fault. Because you let your friend down. Because you won't answer a few simple questions, this is what happens when bitches don't play nice." He let go of Kate's hair, and her head immediately dropped and hung limply. Her chin rested against her chest. Brennan suddenly reached behind him and pulled out a large carving knife.

Megan screamed, "Don't, don't, don't! Please don't hurt her."

"This is all your doing, Mrs. Because you can't be bothered to answer a few simple questions, this is what happens." He raised the knife above his head. The blade seemed to glisten in the late afternoon sun. "This is all on you, Megan."

"No. No, wait. I'll tell you. I'll tell you whatever you want. Please don't hurt her," she screamed. "Please don't. Please don't." She suddenly broke down into deep sobs. Toby released the handful of her hair, and she sank onto the floor of the hall. She curled up in a fetal position and began to sob.

Toby waved out the window, smiled, and gave the thumbs-up to Brennan.

Brennan nodded, slipped the knife back into his belt, and using both hands, dragged Kate back into the house.

TWENTY-SEVEN

They were back driving on the N4. Mullingar was maybe ten miles behind them, and they were headed toward Dublin. DI Turley was in front of them, leading the way to the Swordsman pub. Another mile out of Mullingar and Turley put on his blinker. He pulled into a parking area next to a two-story white stucco building with a double front door painted red. The sign above the door read, 'The Swordsman Pub.'

"I could do with a pint," Suel said, putting on the blinker and turning into the parking area.

"We're on duty, aren't we?" Dillon said.

They pulled in next to Turley and climbed out. Turley was standing just a few feet from his car, looking at the parking area. It was only half-full, but then again, it was still early.

"Fancy a pint?" Turley said.

"Dillon tells me we're still on duty," Suel laughed.

"Exactly, and we're going to be asking some questions of your barman inside. What better way to win him over to our side than buying a round? It's bound to make him more likely to answer questions if we present ourselves as good paying customers."

"I can't really argue with your logic there, Eamon. What do you say, Dillon? We need to get some answers."

"Okay, okay. A pint, but only the one. Besides, DI Turley, Suel said he'd buy."

That brought a round of laughs, and they stepped in the door. There was a nice hum of conversation, but Dillon noticed it dropped ever so slightly as they made their way to the bar. After all, this was a country place, a local. And everyone knew everyone else. Their families had probably known one another for the last four or five generations. Now, all of a sudden, in walked three strangers.

"Eamon," someone yelled from the far end of the bar, and Turley gave a wave. Apparently, not everyone considered them strangers. They stood at the bar for no more than half a minute before a heavyset man in a blue shirt said, "What can I get you, lads?" He wore a white apron around his waist, and his shirt sleeves were rolled up to his elbows.

Turley said, "Three pints of Guinness." Then looked from Suel to Dillon and back at the barman, just to make sure everyone was in agreement.

"He's paying." Dillon nodded at Suel.

"Because I'm the only responsible one in the group," Suel said.

The barman poured three glasses of Guinness, filling them three-quarters of the way full. He set them next to the tap to let them settle.

"While you're waiting on those, Dillon, show him your picture of the girl," Turley said.

Dillon pulled out his cellphone as the barman said to Turley, "Been a while, Eamon. How you been keeping?"

"Not a bother, Gerry. You know the bit, kids driving us crazy. The wife is cracking the whip. Take a look at the picture there. The woman he's gonna show you apparently was in here yesterday."

"About twelve-thirty," Dillon said.

"Just before lunch," Turley added. "She sent a text message to someone. We're wondering if you might recognize her."

"What's she done?" The barman asked.

"Nothing, just looking for her. She rented a car over at Dublin airport. We found it, just want to check and make sure she's all right."

The barman raised an eyebrow and gave a look suggesting he didn't quite believe Turley's version of the story. He leaned forward to look at Dillon's phone.

"No, no, can't say that it rings a bell. Twelve-thirty, you say?"

Turley nodded and added, "In the afternoon."

"Good chance, if she was here, I might have been in the kitchen, getting things ready for the lunch crowd. What you should do is talk to Megan. She's in the backroom waiting tables. You know her?"

"Not hard to look at, dark hair? She have a little heart tattoo on her wrist?"

"That's her. Nice enough girl, but she's more than capable of dealing with the three of you's. She was tending bar while I was in the kitchen." He grabbed one of their pint glasses and topped it up, leaving a creamy head on the top. He slid the glass toward Turley and topped up the next glass.

"Thanks, Gerry. We'll check with her. Megan, you say?"

Gerry nodded, and slid the pint to Dillon. He topped up the last glass, and as he slid it to Suel, he said, "That'll be eighteen euros."

Suel took out a twenty and handed it to him. "Keep the change, Gerry, and thanks for the help."

"And the pints," Dillon added.

Turley gulped down almost a third of his pint before he headed for the backroom. Along the way, he stopped and exchanged one-liners with two different guys sitting at the bar. The backroom had a stage in the far corner that was empty at the moment. Two little boys, maybe six years old, were sitting on the stage, each held a Mac tablet, and they were busily running their fingers across the screens. An attractive, dark-haired girl, maybe twenty-two or three, was just bringing a tray full of empty glasses to the back bar. The barman looked all of sixteen, and he quickly placed the glasses in a green dishwasher rack. He mixed two drinks, tossed a cherry in each, and pushed them back across the bar.

Turley wandered past a half-dozen tables and settled onto a stool at the bar. Dillon and Suel followed suit. A few minutes later, the girl returned with another tray of empty glasses.

Turley set his glass on the bar and said, "Megan, how's the night going?"

She smiled and said, "So far, so good, Eamon, but it's still early." She ran her eyes over Dillon and Suel, appraising them in a way that suggested they wouldn't be in the Swordsman unless it happened to be work-related. "You working?"

"Unfortunately," Turley said. "Say, Gerry thought you might be able to help us."

"Oh?"

"These lads are with An Garda Síochána, over here in Mullingar from Dublin. We need some help trying to find a woman. Wonder if you might have seen her yesterday."

Dillon handed her his cell phone with the image of Kate Murray on the screen.

Megan took the cellphone, glanced at it, and said, "Yeah sure. That's Kate. She was here with another girl, Megan. Americans. They were here and had lunch. They wanted directions to, let's see, um, McGovern's Guest House. You know it? It's a B&B just off the N52. I told them it was about ten minutes from here." She began removing the empty glasses from her tray and lining them up on the bar. When the tray was empty, she picked it up and looked at Turley. "Is there a problem?"

"Did they leave here for McGovern's?" Turley asked.

"That was kind of the deal. See, they got here before the lunch crowd. We've had people stop in here before looking for the place. They're pretty strict on not letting anyone check in before three. I told the girls, Kate actually, I told them that, and they decided to stay and have lunch. I think she said they'd just flown into Dublin. They were sitting in the booth, maybe beginning to nod off. Then Toby bought them a pint." She seemed to think for a moment. "A pint and a glass, actually. They were talking about things. I don't know what, exactly. Nothing kinky or anything if that's what you were worried about."

"Who's this Toby?"

"He's in here from time to time. Don't know his last name."

"He local?" Suel asked.

Megan shook her head. "No, started coming in, I don't know, maybe a couple of months ago. No idea where he's from, but there's a bit of the west in his accent. Don't know where he lives for that matter. Nice enough lad, never any problem. Pretty much keeps to himself. Something happen to the American girls?"

Turley shook his head. "You haven't seen them since?"

"No. In fact, Toby was going somewhere, and he said he had to drive past McGovern's. They were going to follow him there. I think they left a little before three. You know it's only about ten minutes from here."

"Toby pay with a credit card?" Dillon asked.

Megan shook her head. "No, God bless the lad. Always cash and always leaves a nice tip."

"What's he look like?"

"Toby? I don't know, nice enough looking. Curly hair, a shade of brown. Maybe your height," she said to Dillon.

"You remember what he was wearing yesterday?" Turley asked.

"The usual, um, jeans, blue jeans, and a U-2 t-shirt."

"The girls make any phone calls while they were here?" Suel asked.

Megan shook her head. "No, least not that I know, but I wasn't checking. The lunch hour gets pretty busy here. Gee, they were really nice. I hope they're okay," Megan said.

"You think of anything else, give me a call," Turley said and handed a business card to Megan.

She looked at the card and nodded. Someone maybe three tables away raised an empty glass and called, "Megan."

"We'll let you get back to it," Turley said.

"Shit," Suel said and drained his pint. "What do you think?"

"I think we need to find out more on this Toby knacker. Let's check with Gerry."

They headed back out to the main bar. Gerry waved them over as they stepped into the room then said something to the younger man working the bar with him. As they came alongside the bar, Gerry stepped out from behind and said, "Let's talk in my office. We're getting into the busy time, and we won't have any interruptions in the office. You's need another pint?"

"Thanks but we better not. Looks like we might be working late," Turley said.

They followed Gerry down a hallway marked 'Toilets.' They walked past the ladies room and the men's room. Gerry pulled a ring of keys from his pocket and unlocked a door, flipped on a light switch, and said, "Make yourselves comfortable, lads. Wherever you can find a spot."

They had to step around three stacks of liquor boxes. Each stack was three boxes high. A picture of Gerry and a woman, Dillon guessed his wife, hung on the wall next to his desk. The desk itself was stacked with files and what looked like about ten feet of adding machine tape. Behind the desk were two computer screens with live images of the parking lot from different angles. As Gerry settled in behind the desk, Turley hurried into the good chair opposite the desk. Suel snuggled into a space on a worn couch, the rest of which was littered with files.

"Toss that shite onto the floor. What'd you say your name was, Dolan?"

"Dillon."

"Yeah, well toss them files onto the floor, Dillon. So, Megan able to help?"

"Maybe," Turley said. "She mentioned a lad, curly hair, maybe from the west. Name is Toby. Usually pays cash."

Gerry nodded. "Nice enough, lad. Never any trouble. Not sure where he's from, exactly, but yeah, a bit of the west in his speech. What's he into? Guns? Drugs?"

"No, nothing like that. We're thinking he might be able to help us. The woman we're looking to talk to, he had a chat with her. Nothing out of line. Just wanted to check with him."

"He's here off and on. Don't know that I'd call him a regular, but he stops in from time to time. Has a pint or two and leaves. Always tips the girls."

"You have a surname on him?"

Gerry shook his head. "Just know him as Toby. Nice enough lad."

"How old would you guess?" Turley said.

"On Toby, old enough to be legal, Eamon, if that's what you're getting at."

Turley shook his head.

"I'm not sure. I'd say he's not thirty, but he could be twenty-six, maybe twenty-eight. Young enough. Always on his own, keeps to himself, but nothing that would make you wonder about him."

"You've no cameras in the pub?" Dillon said.

Gerry chuckled, "What's the point? Everyone's been coming in here since before they were born. It's the odd one who's not a local. I've cameras out in the parking lot." He moved his head to indicate the computer screens behind him. "God forbid, but we get the occasional fender bender."

"Can we look at yesterday afternoon's film?" Turley said.

"I suppose. If you must," Gerry said, not sounding all that pleased.

"Just from maybe one to three in the afternoon," Turley said.

Dillon and Suel nodded in unison.

"It'll take me a minute to get it set up for you."

"Let me call Tommy Walsh and see if he can find out where her email was sent," Dillon said. He stepped out of the office and into the hall.

TWENTY-EIGHT

Megan was sitting on the floor of the little room, silently crying. They were going to kill Kate. She had no doubt. They were going to kill her. She had no idea what they wanted, but she felt determined to play along as best she could until she could find a way to get the two of them out of this mess. She took a deep breath and vowed she was done crying. There was too much riding on how she acted from here on in.

It was another hour before she heard the footsteps coming up the staircase. A moment later, she heard the key being inserted in the lock. No knock this time. The lock clicked, the door opened, and Toby stepped in. He smiled, walked over to Megan, and handed her a bottle of water.

The plastic bottle was cold and wet with condensation.

"Sorry about that bump on your head, but that's the kind of shit that happens when you don't cooperate."

"Is Kate even alive?"

"She's fine. She's just resting now."

"First of all, you're lying to me. She's not fine. She looked to be unconscious. I'm guessing she's been like that ever since you brought us here. I told you she needed help. You didn't listen, and now it's a pretty safe bet she's in even worse condition. She needs a doctor."

"Well, you should have cooperated and things would have worked out better. We told you. We warned you. And you decided not to listen."

"Let me tell you what I've decided, Toby. I've decided that you're full of shit. I've decided I'm not going to deal with you anymore. I'm just wasting my time. I don't want to make a deal with you. In fact, let me rephrase that. I'm not going to make a deal with you. I'm only going to deal with your pal, Brennan. So, why don't you go back downstairs and tell your boss I've determined you are a worthless piece of shit. If he wants me to answer his questions, to tell him what I know, then he better talk to me directly."

"You don't have to get all bitchy, Megan. I just—"

"I'm not talking to you, Toby."

"You better watch what in the hell—"

"No, Toby, you better watch out what in the hell you say or do. You cross me again or do anything to hurt Kate, I'm going to tell Brennan, and I'm going to tell him to kick the ever-living shit out of you. Now get the hell out of my sight and send Brennan up here. I have some things to tell him."

Toby looked like he was about to say something but apparently thought better than to open his mouth. He walked out of the room, slowly shaking his head. He slammed the door closed and locked it. Megan heard his footsteps hurrying down the stairs.

A moment later, Toby yelled, "Brennan. Brennan."

Megan exhaled and placed the cold plastic bottle of water against her forehead. The cold felt good against the bruise, and she gently ran an index finger along her forehead. The lump had to be at least four inches long, and she vowed Toby would pay for what he'd done. Both he and Brennan would pay. She didn't know how. But if it was the last thing she did, she was going to get her revenge on both of them. Revenge for her and Kate. She didn't care what it took.

She quickly tried to gather what little information she had. The names Kevin and Sean Sands. They were brothers, and they had something Brennan wanted. They were either dead or in jail. Paint cans were involved. Apparently, there was another Megan and Kate. They were with the Sands brothers. They were Americans. Brennan, Toby, and the two bearded bastards that beat them up didn't know those two women, or they never would have taken her and Kate.

She heard footsteps coming up the stairs. Slow, steady footsteps. They sounded heavier than Toby's. She heard the key get inserted in the lock. The locked clicked, and there stood Brennan, smiling. He carried a bowl of something steaming. The scent of the food gradually drifted into the room, and Megan's stomach immediately began to growl.

"You know, Megan, I'm afraid we got off on the wrong foot. Sometimes, I just let my emotions get the better of me, and that's not a good thing. Toby tells me you've come to your senses," he said and handed her the bowl.

It looked to be a meat stew of some sort. A spoon was resting in the bowl. Megan slowly pulled out the spoon, thinking if it had been a fork she could have used it to stab Brennan in the eye or the throat. It would only take one to the eye to incapacitate him. Then she could stab him in the other eye and go find Toby. Unfortunately, it was a spoon.

"One simple question, Megan. Where did the lads hide the rest of the stash?"

Megan took a spoonful of stew and placed it in her mouth. It was hot, delicious, and her stomach growled, causing Brennan to smile.

"Sounds like you're going to enjoy that."

"Yes, it's delicious. Did you make this?"

"Tell me where the rest of the stash is hidden," he said. The smile had suddenly vanished from his face. He looked deadly serious.

"That's just it. I mean that's the problem. I can't tell you."

"What the hell?" He raised his voice.

"Relax, Brennan. I can't tell you, because I don't know the names of places and streets. But I can show you. If you can get me back to where the paint cans were, I can show you where they hid the rest of it."

TWENTY-NINE

illon stepped back into Gerry's office. Gerry, Turley, and Suel were gathered around one of the screens. Gerry had his hand on a mouse and was scrolling through images. The images were all black and white and seemed to jump as he scrolled through them. A twenty-four-hour digital readout in white appeared in the upper right hand corner of the screen, it currently read 14:19, nineteen minutes after two.

"You learn anything?" Suel asked without taking his eyes off the screen.

"Yeah, I'm still a Neanderthal," Dillon said.

"We could have told you that," Turley said.

"The text message was sent to the States. I called the number but got dumped into voice messaging. Apparently, the number belongs to some woman named Mary Ann. I'll try it again in another hour. You finding anything here?"

The digital readout now read 14:23.

"Nothing so far," Suel said.

They continued scanning through the images, and then at the 14:43 digital readout Dillon half-shouted, "Stop."

Gerry went through a half-dozen more images before he stopped. "You sure?"

"Yeah, go back to that image," Dillon said.

Gerry slowly backed them up, one image at a time. "Stop," Dillon said.

Gerry went one image too far. He moved forward and froze the image.

"That's definitely them opening the car doors. How long between images?" Dillon asked.

"Five-second delay," Gerry said.

Suddenly, there they were, Kate and Megan. Blonde-haired Kate looked like she was saying something to Megan across the roof of their rental car. It was the first time Dillon or Suel had seen what Megan looked like.

"They've got the car doors open. Go to the next image and see if we can see them."

Gerry clicked the mouse. The next image came up, but neither woman could be seen. The car doors were still partially open, but the girls were apparently sitting in the car. A reflection from the sun bounced off the windshield, obscuring any chance of viewing inside the car.

"Back up a couple of images and see if we can see them walking to the car."

As Gerry reversed through the images, there were three shots where the women could be seen walking to their car. But they were filmed from the back, and only because they'd seen the image at 14:43 were they aware the three images were of Kate Murray and Megan Gaffney."

"What's this other screen show?" Turley said, looking at the blank computer next to him.

"Same area, different angle," Gerry said.

"Bring it up to those time frames and let's see what we get," Dillon said.

Gerry gave a groan and shot an unhappy face at Turley, but he turned on the second screen.

"Relax, you right plonker," Turley said. "We're going to be mentioning you in all the newspapers. You'll have folks coming in by the busload just to buy a drink from the man what solved the crime."

That seemed to put a smile on Gerry's face, and he raced through the images to the 14:20 point then slowed down. There was a frontal shot of the women approaching their Nissan Micra, and then, just behind them, a man. He had curly hair and wore a dark t-shirt emblazoned with 'U-2'.

"Is that your man Toby behind them?" Turley asked.

"Oh yeah, that's him. Nice-looking lad, isn't he?" Gerry said.

THIRTY

Brennan said, "I'll bring the both of you's there, and as soon as you show me where they hid the rest of the delivery, I'm going to put you up in an expensive hotel. In fact, make it a hotel of your choice. Give you girls more coke than you ever thought possible. You and Kate can snort and party to your heart's content, Megan."

Megan smiled and gave a little shrug. "Brennan, that sounds like just what the doctor ordered. You do that, and I'll make it worth your while. Very worth your while. Just you and me. What do you say?"

Brennan chuckled. "A side of you I didn't see. I think we could work out a little something."

"Sounds perfect. I can't wait. What I want to do is, on the way we can drop Kate off at a hospital. Let her get—"

"Are you fecking nuts? Drop her off at a hospital? How in the hell is that going to work? What? I'm supposed to check her in and give them my name. That's the craziest thing I ever—"

"Brennan, I meant what I said. You just drop her off. No identification. No passport. You don't even go in. No one goes in. We simply leave her at the door. It makes everything so much easier. You don't think there's going to be a problem leaving her in the car in Dublin? Even if she's asleep, someone might knock on the window. Someone might remember the car with the sleeping woman in it."

"We could put her in the back, cover her up."

"Yeah sure, that works fine until she throws up or does something worse and the car begins to smell. This way, you leave her at the hospital in Mullingar, no one knows who she is or where she's from. If things go wrong for us, the police can't pin anything on you. Even if they did link her to you, what's the worst that would happen? The only thing you did was take her to a hospital. What's more, if you put her in the car, she's liable to take up space you're going to need to store your product. She's bound to get in the way of some of the things I might have planned for us."

He seemed to think about that.

"Please," Megan said. "I think you might find it worth the few minutes it would take to drop her off. We can do it tonight, once it's dark. It'll only take a minute or two. Save you a problem later on. It's not like she can ID you, she's been out the last two days. Think about it, baby."

"Brennan. Hey, Brennan," Toby called from downstairs.

"Feck sake," Brennan growled. "Hold that thought," he said and stepped out into the hallway.

"What the hell is it, Toby?"

"We need to talk."

"What the—"

"Down here. I got some information. Saw something."

"Ahh, for the love of God," he said and hurried down the steps. "What the feck is it, and it better be good."

"I don't know that it's good, but the Garda have sealed off the farmhouse where we kept the two Americans."

"What? Who told you that?" He grabbed Toby by the shirt collar, half-lifted him and pushed him back against the wall. "Who in the hell have you been talking to?"

"Will you calm down and get ahold of yourself? I haven't been talking to anyone. I went out there."

"You, you went out there? Why on earth did . . . Someone might have seen you. You're a right plonker. Why the hell did you go and do that—"

"Brennan, will you shut up and listen? No one saw me. Jesus, no one ever goes out that way. Well, except for the Guards, apparently."

"The Guards?"

"Yeah. No, they weren't there when I went past. And no, before you ask, I didn't stop. I drove past. But they'd been there. They had strips of blue and white tape stretched across the entrance. Right on the tape, it says 'An Garda Síochána DO NOT CROSS' in bold letters.

There wasn't a vehicle there, but they sure as hell had been there."

"How did they know?"

"All I can think of is maybe someone heard the shots I fired and—"

Brennan slapped Toby across the back of the head. "You worthless plonker. Shooting up the place and some bastard heard you. Called the Guards."

"You got a better way of stopping your woman from driving away? I suppose you being the gentleman, you probably would have asked her to stop, nice and polite-like. Maybe winked at the same time and you could of landed in bed with the two of em."

"Enough, we're leaving tonight. We'll get rid of your one," he nodded towards the little room where Kate lay on the floor. "And I've got the other ready to show us where the Sands brothers hid the rest of the stash. We go tonight, there's a good chance we can grab it before the Guards find it. I've no doubt they're turning every-thing upside down looking for it."

"Tonight? Your woman knows where it is?"

"She says she can show me, but she can't tell me where because she doesn't know the names of the streets. She said, if I can get her back to where the paint cans were, she can lead me to it."

"You believe her?"

"What choice do I have? Besides, I turned on the charm. She's got other plans," he said and smiled.

THIRTY-ONE

Dillon grabbed the coffee mug from Turley, took a sip, and grimaced. "Oh, God."

"Yeah. I could never understand why you lot went for coffee when there's tea to be had," Turley said.

"Don't tempt him, Eamon. Better for all of us if he doesn't know what he's missing."

They were seated around Turley's desk in the Mullingar station. A room with cinder block walls, a dozen desks, and ringing phones. The investigative section, the same the world over.

They had been going over the initial reports from the Technical Section. There was nothing really new in the reports. At this stage, about all they had to look at was more of a laundry list of items recovered. Everything from brass casings to hair samples and a pink shoe. One thing was interesting. The hairs recovered belonged to a blonde and a redhead. The blonde hairs had been found on a farm implement in the storage shed, and the red hairs had been found on a rusted, antique tractor in the same shed. Both pieces of equipment appeared to have been unmoved in the storage shed for a number of years. The shed was the same place where the pink shoe had been found. Indications were, whoever the hairs belonged to had been bound to the equipment for an extended period of time. A rope was next to the farm implement, and a fairly substantial length of chain was wrapped around a portion of the antique tractor.

The odds had increased to about ninety-eight percent that the two American women, Kate Murray and Megan Gaffney, were the victims. Dillon and Suel were now convinced the women had been mistaken for the two American women with the same first names who had corroborated with the Garda, led them to the drugs stored in the paint cans, and were now in the custody of the DEA after being quietly flown back to the US.

Dillon had placed a call to Eric Bergman at the American Embassy in Dublin but was still waiting for a reply.

"So just for the sake of discussion," Turley said, "let's say your hunch is correct. The two women are mistaken for the pair that was with the Sands brothers. Why? I mean, does someone want to kill them for providing evidence? For cooperating with the Garda?"

"That would be my guess," Suel said.

Dillon shook his head. "Maybe. But maybe that's only half-right."

"This is why you should drink tea instead of coffee," Suel said.

"Remember what McCabe mentioned the other morning? That it was a good-sized recovery. What was it, thirty kilos of coke?"

Suel nodded.

"But what if that represents just a portion of the shipment? There were another fifteen empty paint cans. Does that mean there were fifteen more kilos hidden somewhere or fifteen more kilos to be delivered?"

"So what are you getting at?" Turley said.

What about this angle? Let's say the cocaine in the possession of the Sands brothers was only a portion of a shipment. What if they hid the rest somewhere else? What if it was en route to them? What if whoever grabbed these two women expects them to know where the rest of the shipment is, and they're willing to kill them to find out?"

"A hell of a lot of ifs," Turley said.

Dillon looked disgusted and shook his head. "Yeah, it is. What'd we find out about this Toby character?"

Turley shrugged. "Not much. We know he was driving a grey vehicle, a Datsun or possibly a Nissan. No license number available. We don't have a surname, a license, or registration. We don't have anything like an address or a phone number. About all we have is a grainy black and white image of some knacker with curly hair."

"And we know that he has a pint at the Swordsman from time to time," Dillon said.

"Who are your main dealers out here?"

"Dealers, in the drug business? Nothing like the heavy hitters in Dublin, leastwise not yet. The players out here are mid-range," Turley said. "There was Myles Hanlon he was the biggest player, well, until he was taken out maybe October or early November of last year. The family got into it with one another, started shooting, and in short order pretty much eliminated themselves. There's talk of someone else coming on board, but the kind of numbers your talking, three to six million euros, I don't see it. It would have to be someone big, someone already established."

The Sands brothers did have a connection out there," Suel said. "It never came out exactly who, that I'm aware of. Might be in the investigative research from their trial if we can get access to that. At least some suspicions."

"Then I think we need to get back to Dublin. See if we can get access to the investigative research on the Sands case," Dillon said.

"And see what the status of the Sands brothers is at the Joy. Get a line on who might be trying to apply some pressure in there. And then get our asses back here as fast as possible," Suel said.

"In the meantime, we'll ratchet up the pressure trying to locate your man, Toby," Turley said. "I've a sense he can't be too far, and he's probably been right under our nose all along."

"Maybe something will turn up with the evidence your tech team collected."

"Or maybe your man, Toby, will just call the station and turn himself in," Turley said, shaking his head.

THIRTY-TWO

Megan sat on the floor of her room. Brennan had run out of the room and down the stairs, leaving the door open. She stuck her head out the door. Brennan and Toby had moved away from the base of the stairs and into a room on the first floor. Megan could hear the murmur of their conversation but couldn't make out what exactly was being said.

She took a deep breath and tiptoed down the hall. She stopped at the first door and tried the doorknob. It was locked, as was the case with the next two doors. She tiptoed back to her room, listened to the muffled voices for a few seconds, and hurried past the staircase to the doors on the other side. The first one she tried was locked. She hadn't taken two steps to the next door when she heard a door open downstairs on the first floor, and the voices immediately grew louder.

She hurried back to her room, praying they wouldn't see her as she went past the staircase. She stepped into her room and closed the door just as she heard footsteps on the staircase. She sat down on the floor next to the empty bowl of stew. She looked at the spoon, licked it clean, and then slipped it into the pocket of her jeans. A moment later, the door opened, and Toby stepped in.

"Have we calmed down, yet?"

"I told you before I'm not talking to you. Here," she said, pushing the empty bowl toward him. "I'm finished so you can get this out of here."

Toby reached down and picked up the bowl. He flashed a quick smile and said, "You know, if you weren't such a bitch, I'd give you an update on your friend, Kate. But seeing's how you know everything, anyway, what's the point?" He turned and started to head for the door.

"No, wait. Wait. Please. I'm sorry, Toby. It's just that I'm so frustrated. I feel like you've kept me in here for a month. I'm worried to death about Kate, so don't tell me she's just resting, because I saw how she looked when Brennan was going to stab her. She's not resting. She looks like shit, she's unconscious, and she needs a doctor. Please tell me what the update is. Please."

"What's in it for me?"

"What's in it for . . . What do you want me to do? I can't give you any money. You took my purse. You've got our luggage. Go ahead and keep the rental car, except it needs all new tires and windows. What do you want from me? I told Brennan I can take him to the rest of the stash if that's what you want. All you have to do is get Kate to a doctor. It's not like she can tell anyone where she was or what you guys even look like. She's been out the whole time, and it's getting dangerous, Toby. You have to—" She started sobbing, which led to uncontrollable crying, and she didn't care.

"Hey, all right. Calm down. Calm down. Soon as it gets dark, we're going to put you two in the car, drive your friend Kate, to the hospital, and drop her off. Then me, you, and Brennan are going to Dublin."

Megan coughed a couple of times, sniffled, and wiped the tears from her face using the back of her hand. "Really, you're going to take her to the hospital? Promise?"

"Yeah, but look, under the circumstances, we're just going to drop her off at Midlands Regional. It's right here in Mullingar. They'll take care of her. But it's going to be up to you to make sure we get her there. You try something stupid, yelling at someone, God forbid signaling the Garda, or trying to run out of the car, and I'm warning you. Brennan will kill her without giving it a second thought. And then that'll be all on you. You get what I'm saying?"

Megan nodded. "I promise I'll be good. Honest. I won't cause any trouble. Just get her to a doctor, the sooner, the better, please. I'll do anything you want. Anything. But she needs help."

It was just after nine-thirty when Brennan pulled out from behind the house. Megan was lying on the floor of the backseat. Her ankles and wrists were taped together. Kate sat in the corner of the backseat, still unconscious, with the seatbelt holding her in place, as they drove, her head moved from side to side. Toby sat in the front passenger seat, keeping an eye on both of them.

It was a short drive, no more than ten minutes. The area outside the car suddenly became illuminated and, from her position on the floor, Megan saw the white sign with blue letters, Midlands Regional Hospital. The car slowed as Brennan made a turn, and suddenly a four-story, red-brick building with white windows came into view.

"Soon as I stop, you drag her out and just set her in one of those wheelchairs by the entrance. They'll take it from there. Make it fast. I don't like staying here any longer than we have to."

"You're gonna be okay, Kate. You're gonna be okay," Megan said from the floor of the backseat.

"She'll be in good hands. The HSE will take good care of her," Brennan said.

That brought a chuckle from Toby.

Megan felt the car slow and heard the passenger door open before the car had even stopped.

"Hurry up, Toby. Oh shit, there's a car coming in behind us."

Toby tore open the passenger door and fumbled with Kate's seatbelt.

"Come on, come on. What the hell is taking you so long?"

"It's the damn seatbelt. It won't unbuckle."

"Hurry up, that fecking car is pulling in, closer. Come on, damn it."

"There, got it," Toby said. He wrapped his arms around Kate's chest and pulled her out of the backseat.

"I love you, Kate," Megan called.

"Shut the hell up," Brennan said as Toby slammed the rear door closed with his hip. Brennan looked in the rearview mirror and said, "Bloody hell, it's the Garda. Hurry up, Toby. Hurry the hell up."

Megan tried to sit up, but with her ankles and hands wedged between the front and backseat, she couldn't. As Toby pulled Kate out of the car, Megan noticed that now both her shoes were missing, and only one foot was covered with a white athletic sock.

"Oh, shit, we're out of here," Brennan said and suddenly drove off, leaving Toby to fend for himself.

"You need a hand, sir?" The officer said from the patrol car as Toby settled Kate into the wheelchair.

"No, we're okay. She's having another reaction to her medication. They're expecting us," Toby said and wheeled Kate in through the automatic door. He pushed her in, stopped about fifteen feet inside the door, and left her there, unconscious, in the wheelchair. He headed down a hallway, walking quickly but not running, hoping the officer wasn't following.

THIRTY-THREE

ickey O'Hara disconnected his cellphone and leaned toward the driver. "Petey, turn around and head for the Swordsman. You know it? It's out on the N4?"

Shauna Hanlon suddenly came awake, opened her eyes, and half-shouted, "For feck's sake, Mickey. I'd just as soon head home. It's already been a long, frustrating day, and neither one of us is any closer to finding our way out of this shit storm."

Without saying a word, Petey, the driver, pulled to the curb and decided to wait it out. The two of them, Mickey and Shauna, had been at each other for the better part of the day, and for his part, Petey had just about had enough of it.

Mickey turned towards the backseat and Shauna. "Well, while you were resting your eyes, I got a phone call. Seems Garda detective Eamon Turley was at the Swordsman today."

"So your man is fond of the occasional pint. What's that got to do with the likes of you and me?"

"Might be all three of us are apparently interested in a pair of missing girls."

"Missing girls? What you do in your spare time is no concern of mine. I'm just thinking you'd better be coming up with an idea pretty damn fast, or we're going to have to—"

"What if I told you the missing girls were American?"

"American?"

"Yes, two of them. A blonde and a redhead. Fancy a guess as to what their names are?"

"Don't tell me."

"Sure as we're sitting here. All right, Petey. The Swordsman. Let's get a move on."

"You heard him, Petey. Let's go," Shauna said.

Petey quickly checked the rearview mirror before making a U-turn and heading back the way they'd come.

"Two American women, blonde and a redhead, named Kate and Megan," Mickey said. "The Garda found their car torched not far from the Royal Canal. No sign of either one of the Americans."

"So what's the Swordsman got to do with it?"

"They were on the CCTV tape along with some plonker by the name of Toby."

"At the Swordsman? I wonder if that wasn't young Toby McDade," Petey said.

"Who the hell is Toby McDade?" Mickey said.

"A young knacker from out in the west, Kerry or someplace. You know who his cousin is? That right bollocks, Brennan McDade."

"McDade? Crazy Brennan McDade? Your lunatic man with the temper?" Shauna said.

"Yeah, that's him. I'd say he uses a little too much of his product, a bit what you might call unstable," Petey said and laughed. He looked in the rearview mirror. "Ma'am, remember when your Uncle Myles got into it with a knacker over the horse racing scheme, maybe two years back? He was ready to have him taken out. In fact, someone had been dispatched to do just that when your man came groveling on his knees to Myles, begging forgiveness. That muppet, the one on his knees, was Brennan McDade. Myles always figured your man Brennan was missing a couple of screws. There was a rumor floating around he had something to do with the Sands brothers, but to my knowledge, it's never been confirmed, least as far as I know."

"But then it would make perfect sense he has a handle on the two women. He knows where they are. He talks them into joining him for a party, and they lead him to the rest of that stash," Mickey said. "For feck's sake, he probably torched their car to throw everyone off the trail. Meanwhile, that bollocks is fixing to get his hands on the rest of the shipment."

"Ain't that just the way it works? We've been beating ourselves up looking for the answer, and all along, there it was right in front of us. Crazy Brennan McDade. Saints preserve us," Petey said.

"Step on it, Petey. I don't believe it. Maybe our luck is finally about to change. It's about damn time, honest to God. Wee Timmy gave us forty-eight hours to come up with the payment. If we can follow the likes of Brennan and get hold of the rest of that shipment, it'll be a lifesaver. Literally," Shauna said. "Mickey, we need to let our friends in the Joy know it's time to take the Sands brothers out. We find these two American slappers, give them the added incentive there's no place safe, even in the Joy. We can have this wrapped up in twenty-four hours and be back on top. Make the call and get the word to the Joy."

Twenty minutes later, Shauna was seated at the bar sipping a glass of white wine with Petey. Since their faces were well-known in Mullingar, the men on either side of them had fled from their stools about sixty seconds after they sat down. The conversational hum in the bar had dropped by about fifty percent, and people were choosing to leave rather than become collateral damage after sitting near Shauna Hanlon.

Gerry stepped over and topped up Shauna's wine glass. "Don't want to scare you off, Ms. Hanlon," he leaned forward and almost whispered. "I just got a call. Three Garda detectives are headed this way. They've been in and out all day reviewing our CCTV footage from the parking lot, asking a lot of questions of my customers. You're certainly welcome to stay," he lied. "Just thought you might appreciate it if I gave you a heads-up."

"Thank you. I appreciate the information. We heard a little about that. Who were they looking for?"

"They never told me. Young lad, curly hair, driving a grey car is all I know. As a matter of fact, they locked me out of my own office then proceeded to go through the tapes. Lord only knows what or who they were looking for. I'm sure, in the next day or two, the CCTV system will go on the blink. They'll swear it's not their fault, and it'll cost me an arm and a leg to get it fixed. No one knows better than you how they can be."

She nodded and took a long sip as Gerry stepped away. A moment later, Mickey stepped into the bar. He looked around, spotted Shauna and Petey at the bar, and headed toward the empty stool next to Shauna.

"You're not to order anything," Shauna said.

"What?"

"Your man just warned me. The Garda are on the way. They've been going through his CCTV tapes for the better part of the day. We don't need to meet up with them tonight. You two can take me home. Then I want you to find crazy Brennan McDade. He knows something, and I want that information. I don't care what you have to do to get it. Now let's be off before those knackers from the Guards show up. Come on, the both of you," she said and drained what was left in her glass.

"But my pint, I've barely finished it," Petey said.

"Not a problem. Give Mickey the keys. He'll drive me home, and you can walk."

"Walk? It's over twelve miles."

"Then maybe you should come with us," she said and headed out the door.

"Don't say a thing, Petey. You'd be preaching to the choir," Mickey said and followed her out the door. Petey took some heavy gulps, set his glass on the bar, gave a longing look at what remained, and hurried to catch up.

THIRTY-FOUR

Toby made his way out the front door of the hospital. He had walked to the opposite end of the building from the Emergency Room. He moved as fast as possible without drawing attention to himself. Fortunately, it was dark, and once he stepped outside, there was no sign of the patrol car. He headed in the direction of Brennan's house. It was only a couple of miles. He pulled out his cell phone, called Brennan again, and got dumped one more time into voice mail.

"Brennan, me again. Walking back to get my car. Let me know what you want me to do," Toby said and hung up. An hour later, he looked behind him for any headlights. When he didn't see any, he walked up the drive to where his car was parked in the back. He slid in behind the wheel and checked his phone one more time to see if he might have somehow missed Brennan's phone call. Nothing showed up on his phone.

He debated what to do, felt his stomach growl, and decided if he hurried he might be able to grab a plate of chicken wings or a burger before the kitchen closed out at the Swordsman. Under the circumstances, it seemed like the better idea rather than spend another minute in town tonight. No doubt, by now, someone on hospital staff had found the American woman. He shook his head. If only he'd had the chance to strangle her. He wouldn't feel like he'd left a loose end just hanging out there. Fifteen minutes later, he pulled into the Swordsman parking lot. The lot was nearly full, but he managed to find a space in the back corner of the lot, next to the dumpster. He headed into the pub and took an empty stool at the bar.

"What can I get you?" The barman asked as Toby settled in.

"I'll take a pint of Guinness, and is the kitchen still open?"

Gerry studied the handsome face, the curly hair, and picked up on the bit of the West in the man's accent. "Not to worry," he said and reached for a menu. He tossed it in front of Toby and said, "You want something, just let me know, and I'll have them make it up. Let me get that pint for you."

He filled the pint glass three-quarters of the way full, set the glass next to the tap, then stepped around the corner and placed a call while the Guinness settled for three minutes.

Turley had just stepped out of his car and was about to head in the house when his phone rang. The number came through as unknown, but he answered it anyway. "Turley," he said then listened to pub noise in the background.

"D.I. Turley, glad I caught you. It's Gerry from the Swordsman. Sorry to bother you."

"Yeah, Gerry. Not a bother. What's up?"

"You're not going to believe it. Guess who's here?"

Turley closed his eyes and took a deep breath. It had already been a very long day and he sure as hell wasn't about to guess. "Go ahead, Gerry. Surprise me. Who is it?"

"It's him."

"Him?" Turley said.

"The nice-looking lad with the curly hair. From the parking lot CCTV tapes. Remember? He was the one with the two American girls," Gerry said.

Turley was already climbing back into his car. "Keep him there, buy him an extra pint. Hell, buy him two. I'll even pay," Turley said as he backed his car onto the street.

Gerry topped up the pint of Guinness with a rich, creamy head and delivered it to Toby. "Here you go, lad. It's been a long day. This one's on the house."

Toby got a surprised look on his face and said, "Really?"

"You look like you could use it, son."

"You'll never hear me say no to a free pint."

"You decide what you wanted?" Gerry said and nodded at the menu.

"I'll take the chicken wings."

"Coming right up. Now, enjoy that pint, and I'll get things moving on those wings."

THIRTY-FIVE

When Turley's call came through Dillon answered his cell phone, "US Marshal Dillon at your service." He and Suel were on their way back to Dublin for a change of clothes and a night's sleep before heading back to Mullingar in the morning.

"Dillon, Turley here. Just got off the line with your man Gerry from the Swordsman."

"Everything okay?"

"Yeah. Toby, the lad with the curly hair from the CCTV tape, just settled in for a pint."

"He's there now?"

"I told your man to buy him a pint, so he stays put. I'm on my way over there now." Turley heard Dillon relay the information to Suel.

"Do you want us there?" Dillon said as Suel indicated the sign announcing the next exit in two and a half kilometers. "We could probably be back there in forty-five minutes or so. We're already on the M4."

Turley thought for a moment and said, "No, keep going, get a night's sleep. I'm not going to bring him in. Right now, we don't have enough to question him. If he's in any way involved, he'll deny it. As far as we can prove, all he did was park his car near them. I'll follow him and see where he goes once he leaves the Swordsman. Be nice to at least have an address and a license number."

"You sure? We can turn around if you want."

"Yeah, I'm sure. Don't. I'll see you in the morning. Give me a call once you're on the road tomorrow morning. Anything out of the ordinary happens tonight, I'll send you a text message."

"All right. Thanks for the heads-up. Watch yourself, and good luck." They disconnected, and Turley increased his speed, heading for the Swordsman.

"He's not going to bring him in?" Suel said.

"No. He's right. At this point, he's got nothing to stand on. The guy will deny everything and probably lawyer up if he does know something. Turley's going to try to get an address and a license number, which is about all we can hope for."

"What happens if he's got the girls locked up in a closet somewhere? He's not going to put some pressure on this knacker?"

"Turley's of the opinion that would do more harm than good. It would only warn this Toby character that he's a person of interest. If he's brought in, probably the first thing he'll say, in fact, the only thing he'll say if he's got any brains is, I want a lawyer."

"We say solicitor here."

"Okay, so he's going to solicitor up then. But it's not going to help us get any closer to where those two girls are. You know, I'm just wondering if we might not pay a visit to those idiot Sands brothers in the Joy tomorrow before we head back over to Mullingar. They'll be sentenced sometime next week. We could gently remind them that their sentence will be handed down next week. This would seem to me to be the perfect time to let them know this is the last opportunity they'll have to cooperate and maybe get that sentence reduced."

"Cooperate? Those two bastards. If they were thinking of doing that, they would have copped a plea weeks ago."

"Still be a shame to miss the opportunity. I know they've done time before. But you have to admit, the Joy is a little different experience. I think it's at least worth a try," Dillon said.

"Okay, go ahead if you want, and then when they refuse to cooperate, you'll once again have the experience that I was right."

THIRTY-SIX

Turley had just ordered a pint when Toby's chicken wings arrived. The lad took his time eating them, licking all four fingers and his thumb before starting in on the next wing. Turley had been thinking on the drive out to the Swordsman that he might get a little something to snack on but watching Toby attack his chicken wings seemed to eliminate any semblance of an appetite.

Turley took a sip from his pint and set it aside. He stared at the whiskey bottles lined up in front of the mirror behind the bar. He could watch Toby's reflection in the mirror without having to turn his head. Ninety minutes and three pints later, Toby finished up and paid his bill. Turley placed a ten euro note on the bar, gave a nod to Gerry, and casually made his way out the door. He saw Toby heading towards the back of the parking lot.

Turley hurried to his car. He climbed in behind the wheel before Toby had even opened his car door. He waited until Toby turned on his lights, drove past and out of the parking lot before he turned the key in the ignition and backed out of his parking place. He'd been right on his guess when they were running through the tapes earlier that afternoon. Toby was driving a grey Nissan, a Nissan Juke to be exact. It looked like a 2018 model. Based on the license plate, it was purchased in County Kerry in the first six months of 2018. The two hundred and sixty-fifth car sold in Kerry in 2018.

Toby headed back to Mullingar, driving just slightly over the speed limit. Turley debated calling a squad car. Three pints over the course of the last two hours would definitely put him over the limit. But then what? Better to see where he went and take things from there.

He followed Toby at a distance. For the most part, he was able to keep another vehicle between the two of them. Eventually, Toby headed into an older section of Mullingar. More stately, older homes ran along both sides of the tree-lined street. Toby turned at the far end of the street and headed out of town. Turley followed, letting the distance grow between them. After a kilometer or two, Toby turned into the drive leading up to a stately, older, two-story brick home. The home appeared dark, without a light on anywhere inside. As Turley drove past, he saw the car park at the rear of the house. The headlights had just been turned off, and Toby was in the process of climbing out of the vehicle.

Turley rounded a bend and drove further down the lane. He made a U-turn in a distant neighbor's drive and headed back toward the brick structure. He pulled to the side of the road just before the bend, got out, locked his car, and trotted towards the brick house.

There was a light on in a back window of the place now. Turley studied the house and the area around it while standing out on the road before he moved closer. He walked along the side of the house and noticed that the mortar between the bricks was in bad shape. He passed two darkened windows and attempted to peek inside only to be prevented by drawn window shades. The wood frames around the windows appeared to be devoid of paint and were soft to the touch, the wood slowly rotting. The shades covering the windows were old, yellowed, and curled along the sides. Still, they prevented him from glimpsing anything inside the house.

He peeked into the room with the light on. Fortunately, there wasn't a drawn shade. The room appeared to be an old kitchen. There was a single lightbulb hanging from the middle of the ceiling and an ancient gas stove against a far wall. Heavy looking wooden cabinets hung on the wall. The cabinet doors had glass panels, and Turley could see stacks of plates, bowls, cups, and saucers stacked in the cabinets. Even peering in from outside, he had the impression the items were probably a hundred years old. A cereal box and a whiskey bottle, Paddy Irish Whiskey, rested on the wooden counter beneath the cabinet. The bottle was maybe half-empty, and the cap to the bottle rested on the counter next to the bottle. There was an old-style kitchen sink with a stack of cups and plates waiting to be washed. Turley couldn't see Toby anywhere.

He scurried around the back corner of the house to Toby's car. He pulled a pen from his pocket and wrote down the license number on his hand. He took out his car keys. Next to his house key was a small steel bottle opener with a sharp end. He glanced at the back door leading into the house. It was solid wood with no window and looked to be a hundred years old. He crouched down next to the rear wheels on the car. He stabbed the side of the rear tire with the bottle opener and pulled it out. A soft hiss could be heard as the air slowly ran out of the tire. He moved to the opposite corner of the car and repeated the process creating two flat tires. Now, even if Toby changed one of the tires, he still wasn't going anywhere.

Turley hurried around to the far side of the house, hoping to see inside and possibly catch a glimpse of Toby, but all the rooms appeared to be dark and more curled, more yellowed, antique shades were drawn over the windows. He quickly walked back onto the road and headed to his car.

He drove back to the Mullingar Garda station and did a search on the license number and the address of the property. Two names came up. The car was licensed to a Tobias McDade, age twenty-eight, listed as residing in Tralee, County Kerry. Turley smiled at the mention of Tralee. The best thing about the town was said to be the road leading out of it. The house and the surrounding 20 hectares were the property of a gentleman named Xavier Brennan McDade. Brothers? From his quick look at the structure, he guessed it might have been inherited. There didn't seem to have been any active farming, and Turley had the sense the place was slowly but surely falling to ruin.

He glanced at the clock on the wall, 11:30. He began to search the Garda records for Tobias and Xavier Brennan McDade.

THIRTY-SEVEN

Megan had listened to two male voices from downstairs. It sounded like they were arguing. One of them was clearly Brennan, and she presumed the other would be the friend he referred to as the strange one, named Cormac. The voices were loud at times. Then they'd fade, sometimes laughter followed. Another argument would occur, and the same routine would begin all over again. After several hours, things seemed to settle down, and she prayed she wouldn't hear the lock in the door snap open.

It had been quiet for quite some time, and she wondered if they'd left or gone to sleep or maybe passed out. She certainly had no desire to see either one. Not for the first time, she tiptoed to the door and slowly turned the doorknob. It stopped halfway through the turn, locked, just like the previous half-dozen times she'd tried to open the door.

She went back to study the window again. There was a side panel, maybe eight inches wide and two feet tall. The panel opened a half-dozen inches or so, and she wondered if maybe, just maybe, she could slip out. She stood on the bed and tried a half-dozen different ways to wiggle her way out, head first, one leg at a time, both legs, shoulder first. Eventually, she concluded that nothing would work.

She examined the larger window that didn't open. It was double pane glass, and about the only way she could figure out how to break it would be to kick it. But then what? She was on the second story. It was a long drop down to the ground. She'd be going out a broken window with all sorts of shards of glass still in the frame, not to mention all the glass that would be down on the ground where she would land.

Maybe she could tie the sheets together, break the window, crawl out and halfway down the side of the house. But then, by the time she did all that, no doubt idiot Brennan would be waiting for her when she eventually dropped to the ground.

She searched the bed frame for a loose piece of wood she might be able to use to club him over the head. Thinking if she could maybe knock him out next time he came in the room, she'd be able just to walk out the front door. But no such luck. The bed frame was old and, unfortunately, solid. Her stomach growled again, and she looked out the window. The sun was beginning to set. It was still light out, but the sun was behind the houses on the next street over. If only she saw someone, maybe she could signal them.

She studied the windowsill. It appeared to be granite but more than likely concrete. Still, it looked rough. She pulled the spoon she'd taken when Toby fed her the other day and held it in her hand. She reached out through the side panel, and holding the spoon upside down by the head, she slowly began to drag the handle of the spoon back and forth across the rough windowsill. After a few minutes, she examined the end of the handle, one side was slightly filed back.

There was a noise downstairs, someone coughing. Definitely a man. A moment later, footsteps plodded up the staircase. Oh no, please don't come in here, she prayed. Whoever it was groaned outside her door, but she couldn't determine whether or not it was Brennan. There was another groan and then the unmistakable sound of someone using the bathroom, definitely male.

Whoever it was, they didn't bother to close the bathroom door and certainly didn't flush. A moment later, she heard footsteps heading slowly back down the staircase. She took a deep breath, exhaled, and hoped they'd just stay away. The house remained quiet, and Megan eventually drifted off to sleep.

THIRTY-EIGHT

O nce Suel dropped him off at the station, Dillon climbed in his car and headed home. He waited for a car to pass then made a left-hand turn off St. Pappin's Road and onto Dean Swift. It was just a little after midnight. As he pulled into his parking area next to the front door, he felt a wave of exhaustion wash over him. He was tired, and he was scheduled to meet Suel at the Special Branch tomorrow morning at 7:00. He turned off the car and sat for a moment. He rolled his shoulders and moved his head from left to right. The timer on his sitting room light was still on but set to turn off at 12:15. He glanced next door. Fortunately, the lights were off, and he could only hope Deitora was fast asleep. She was the last thing he needed tonight.

He climbed out of his car and quietly closed the door. He slipped his key in the front door lock, opened the door, input his alarm code, and then pressed the button on his key fob to lock the car door. The headlights blinked, and the horn chirped. He glanced across the street and one house over. Tara lived there. A friendly single woman who always gave him the impression she could be interested. It looked like she was entertaining tonight. There was a strange car parked in front of her house, and the light from the master bedroom suggested candlelight. He closed the front door.

He walked into the kitchen and spent the next few minutes picking up the trash Lucifer had scattered around the room. He filled the coffee maker with enough water and grounds for four cups, set the timer, and slowly made his way upstairs. Lucifer was asleep on one of the pillows on the bed.

Dillon thought about waking him up, hustling him outside, and quickly decided against it. He undressed, draping his clothes over the chair in the room. He brushed his teeth, looked at his tired self in the mirror, and climbed into bed.

It seemed like only a minute or two before his alarm went off. Lucifer buried his head under the pillow as Dillon groaned and slowly climbed out of bed. It was barely sunrise and raining, a soft rain, steady but without the thunder and lightning that would usually accompany a rain back in the States. He made his way across the hall into the bathroom and stepped in the shower. He let the water rush over his shoulders for a number of minutes, gradually coming awake. He took a long shower and felt better as he stepped out and dried off. He pulled on a pair of casual trousers and a long sleeve shirt, promptly rolling the sleeves up to his forearms.

Lucifer was still asleep, and he decided to let him stay that way for another fifteen minutes. As he stepped out of the bedroom, he could smell fresh coffee brewing in the kitchen. He poured himself a cup, took a sip, and turned on the tv. He caught the tail end of the morning's Brexit report. He tuned out the news while he tossed two pieces of bread in the toaster and cracked two eggs into the frypan.

The eggs were almost ready to be flipped when the newscaster announced, "Breaking News from Mountjoy Prison." Dillon glanced over his shoulder at the familiar reporter's face telling him two prisoners in Mountjoy prison had been found dead. No concrete information at this time other than unconfirmed sources mentioned two Americans, possibly brothers, as the victims. Names were unavailable. There was a press briefing scheduled for ten o'clock that morning.

The forecast came on next. Dillon just stared at the screen, still focused on the tv. The smell of burning fried egg brought him back to reality. He scraped the eggs off the pan and onto a plate, tossed the toast on top and placed the plate on the kitchen counter.

His phone suddenly vibrated in his pocket, and he knew it had to be Suel before he even pulled it out.

"Don't tell me it was the Sands brothers killed at the Joy," was how he answered the phone.

"Bloody hell," Suel half-shouted, confirming Dillon's worst fears.

"How in God's name is this even possible? Both of them? Kevin and Sean?"

"Apparently hung in their cells. They're looking at it as a suicide pact."

"A suicide pact?" It was Dillon's turn to shout.

THIRTY-NINE

M ickey chuckled and said, "I told you before, Petey saw a young lad with curly hair pulling in there last night. The car fit the description. It was grey." He took another sip of tea.

"I know the car fit the description, for lord's sake. My question was, why, in God's name, do we have to go there at this dreadful hour?" Shauna said.

"Just a wild guess," Mickey said. "But could it be because Wee Timmy Bixby gave us forty-eight hours to come up with the payment?"

Shauna was sitting in the backseat of the car and not at all happy. She took another sip of tea and wrinkled her nose. It tasted desperate, but then at this hour of the morning, with the sun barely up, and the reminder of Wee Timmy Bixby, she couldn't think of anything that would taste good.

They were headed to Brennan McDade's home, just a kilometer or two outside of Mullingar. Shauna had been there for Deidre's wake, six or maybe eight years ago. Deidre had been a distant acquaintance and was Brennan's eternally disappointed mother. Always inserting herself after her less than worthless son seemed to turn every situation into a major disaster. If memory served, the home had reminded Shauna of a dusty antique store. In need of an industrial cleaning and some serious updating, she recalled faded couches and chairs all sitting on worn, moth-eaten rugs. The floors creaked. A fair amount of the lights either didn't seem to work, or the light bulbs had simply burned out. Deidre's wake was one of those events where one stayed only long enough so that the host, in this case, Deidre's idiot son Brennan, made note of your presence. Shauna had made some flimsy excuse about an evening meeting she couldn't get out of and quickly fled the scene. She hurried home and vowed she'd never, ever become old and senile. For the next few years, every time poor Deidre's name was mentioned, the conversation would immediately return to her wake in the dilapidated mansion, one story topping the next.

After they left the Swordsman last night, Petey and Mickey had a dram of whiskey down in the kitchen. Petey had swung by the McDade estate on his way home. He was just in time to see a young man with curly hair pulling a grey car into the entrance and parking at the rear of the house. He'd phoned Mickey a little over an hour ago, at the ungodly hour of 5:00 am, and now here they were. She took another sip of her tea and made a face. It hadn't improved. She set the paper cup in the holder on the back of the driver's seat and closed her eyes.

"What do you want to do with the two of them?" Mickey said. "Shauna? You awake? Shauna?"

"Hold your horses. I'm trying to think," she growled.

Mickey guessed, if it weren't for the sunglasses, he'd know for sure if she had drifted back to sleep. Never a pleasant individual first thing in the morning, today was no exception.

Petey pulled over to the side of the road. Just ahead, on the opposite side of the road, sat the McDade home. Even from this distance, it appeared abandoned and un-attended. The overgrown hedges across the front hadn't been trimmed in years. Newspapers and trash seemed to have found a permanent residence along the base of the hedge. What remained of the front lawn had been over-taken by weeds at least a foot high. There appeared to be a half-dozen newspaper circulars scattered around the front stoop.

"How do you want to handle this?" Mickey said.

Shauna thought for a moment and said, "Go ahead and pull in but leave the car blocking the entrance. Mickey, the two of us will go up to the front door. Petey, you go around to the back just in case they try to run out that way. Guns out, gentlemen, and be alert. Your man Brennan McDade isn't called crazy for no reason."

Mickey lifted his shirt and pulled the pistol out of his belt as Petey drove down the lane and pulled into the entrance. The three-foot wall across the front of the lot was covered with graffiti. They came to a stop just inside the wall, completely blocking the entrance. They climbed out of the car. Petey hurried along the side of the house as Shauna and Mickey made their way through the field of weeds where the lawn used to be and headed toward the front door.

Once they finally arrived at the door, Mickey reached to push the doorbell only to find a hole in the doorframe with a bare copper wire hanging out.

"You hear anything from inside?" Shauna said as she kicked some newspaper circulars off to the side and swore under her breath. Mud, leaves, and the remnants of weeds covered her Christian Louboutin heels.

Mickey shook his head. The door was weathered oak and appeared to have been devoid of any finish for the last fifty years.

"It's been at least six years since I was here. It was a disaster then, and nothing appears to have changed in that time. Look around. I'd say crazy Brennan McDade has once again proven he is one worthless bollocks. The place has gone to ruin. Amazingly, he's managed to find a way to disappoint his mother, even after her passing. Pound on the damn door and wake up crazy Brennan. I need a decent tea."

Mickey switched his pistol to his left hand and pounded on the wooden door with his right. The pounding sounded like an echo in a hollow cavern. He pounded again and again then waited for a moment.

Upstairs, Toby groaned but kept his eyes closed. He took a couple of breaths and was just beginning to drop back to sleep when the racket started up again. He rolled over on his side and pulled the pillow over his head. The noise continued, and his first thought was thunder and an approaching storm. He pulled the pillow off his head and fluttered his eyes open. Sunshine drifted in around the curled edge of the window shade.

Outside at the front door, Mickey took the pistol in his right hand and pounded the butt of the weapon against the center panel of the oak door. Each time he struck the oak panel, the pistol left a gash in the wood.

There was the noise again, only this time even louder. Toby ran his tongue over his lips and grimaced at the hint of whiskey. The pounding didn't stop, his head throbbed, his eyes felt raw, and whoever in the hell was making that racket was going to pay the price. He groaned out of bed and stumbled down the stairs, leaning against the railing for support as he headed for the front door.

"Maybe you should just kick it in," Shauna said.

"You sure?"

"I'll lose what's left of my mind if I have to listen to that pounding much longer. Go ahead. We've given the bastards a chance. Crazy Brennan is probably off somewhere in la-la land after using his product. Kick the damn thing in."

"You're the boss," Mickey said as he took a half-step back, raised his leg, and aimed just to the left of the brass doorknob.

"I swear to God, I'm going to kill whoever is out there," Toby said out loud as he turned the doorknob and pulled the door open.

"Ahh," Mickey screamed as the door opened and his right leg shot out into the open air. His left leg automatically flew out from underneath him, and he almost seemed to levitate for a brief moment before landing on his back on top of the doorjamb. He groaned for just a nanosecond before the wind was knocked out of him, and the pain shot up his spine. His pistol bounced off the hundred-year-old tile on the entryway floor, cracking two of the tiles.

Toby was suddenly wide awake, taking in Mickey lying on his back with wide eyes and speechless. Behind him stood the wicked witch of Mullingar, Shauna Hanlon, with both hands covering her open mouth and eyes focused on Toby.

It took him no more than half a second to process the scene and race toward the backdoor, followed by shrieks from the wicked witch. He tore open the backdoor, jumped across the landing, and stopped.

A smiling Petey sat on the hood of Toby's grey Nissan Juke. He held a pistol that he casually raised, clicking the hammer back with his thumb as he did so. "Perfect timing, young man. I'd like a tea with sugar and no milk."

FORTY

Megan slowly opened her eyes and took in the room. It was small, with just a single bed pushed into the corner. Thankfully, Brennan had untied her wrists and ankles. She didn't know how long she'd been asleep. It had been dark when they arrived, and now the sun was shining outside. She sat up in the bed, moving her wrists and ankles, and thought of Kate. At least she would be safe in the hospital and hopefully on the road to recovery.

For the first time, she could look at the sheets and the pillowcase. They were filthy. The yellow sweat stains on both suggested they hadn't been changed in a year or possibly two. The bed was the only item in the room, no chair, no wardrobe, no mirror, nothing.

The bed reeked like some awful locker room or a laundry basket full of sweaty clothes after someone had worked in a garden all day in the heat. She raised the window shade and peeked outside. There was a very small backyard with a patch of grass in desperate need of cutting and lots of dandelions. A tall wooden fence surrounded the yard.

Her hair felt greasy to the touch, and she could smell it. She needed a shower, clean clothes, and to get away from these maniacs. She also needed a toilet, now.

She rose off the bed and quietly took three steps to the door. She slowly turned the doorknob, but it stopped after half a turn. Locked. She knocked softly on the door.

"Hello. Hello, is anyone out there? Hello, I have to use the bathroom. Can you let me out? Can you let me out please? I need to go to the bathroom."

She stopped to listen, but all was quiet.

"Hello, hey, damn it. I need to pee. Let me out of here," she shouted and then pounded on the door hard.

A moment later, a male voice called out, "All right, just relax. I'm coming at a dead run." She could hear footsteps slowly climbing up a staircase. The footsteps approached, and then all was quiet. She was about to say something when she heard the lock snap, and the door opened, forcing her to take a step back.

Brennan stood there with a smile on his face and bloodshot eyes. He was holding the key to the door. "How did you sleep?"

"I need to use the bathroom."

He made a theatrical sweeping gesture with his arm, directing her to the end of the short hallway where a door was half-open. There were white tiles on the floor and what looked like a glass wall to a shower. "Your carriage awaits, madam," he said and giggled at his own joke.

She hurried down the hall and into the bathroom. "Is it all right if I take a shower? I really need to. I'm just filthy. Can I, please?"

"You look pretty good to me."

"Please, I need to get cleaned up."

He seemed to think about that for a long moment.

"Please? I promise I won't take long. And I need to use the bathroom, the toilet, like right now."

"Yeah, but don't lock the door. And don't take too long. I'll be standing out here, and we gotta get going pretty soon."

"Yeah, I know, but if I can take a shower, it will help me concentrate on where we need to go. Otherwise, I'll be worrying that I'm all sweaty and greasy and that I need a shower. Okay? So let me get cleaned up. Please."

"Okay, go ahead. But don't lock the door."

"Fine," she said, pushing the door closed and hurrying toward the toilet. Along with the toilet, the bathroom had a sink with a mirror and a small shower stall. The lower area of the shower stall and the ceiling above the shower appeared to have a dark green mold.

She grabbed a plastic shampoo bottle and a bottle of shower gel off the sink and set them on a small shelf in the shower. She pressed the button on the electric shower, and the water began to flow from the shower head. She adjusted the temperature, moving the dial from four to six, then quickly pulled off her top, her jeans, and her undergarments and stepped into the shower.

The water felt wonderful, and she squirted shampoo into her hand and soaped up her hair. She scrubbed for a long minute then rinsed her hair under the shower head and scrubbed herself clean. She scrubbed herself a second time, shampooed again, and began to relax ever so slightly as the water ran over her shoulders and down her back.

After a few minutes of just letting the water run over her, she quickly scrubbed her thong and her bra. She turned off the shower and opened the door. Two towels were hanging from hooks on the wall. She avoided the soiled white cloth and reached for the navy blue one, only because it hid the grime that no doubt was on it.

She dried off and quickly dressed, wringing out her thong and bra. She picked up a comb from the bathroom sink, ran it under hot water for a couple of minutes, and quickly ran it through her hair.

The bathroom window was made up of two windows. The lower two-thirds of the window was a frosted piece of glass in a stationary steel frame. The upper third was in a steel frame that swung open maybe four inches. She opened the upper portion and peeked out.

The window looked out onto the street with an industrial area just across the way. Brennan's car was parked on the sidewalk in front of the house. The street curved, and she could see that this side had identical houses all along it. Four white stucco units attached to one another. At the end of the four, there was maybe a ten-foot plot of grass or a concrete pad and then another four units. Every unit had the exact same windows on the first and second floors, which suggested they all had an identical floor plan.

One thing was clear. There was no way she was going to escape out the bathroom window, and at the moment, there was no one walking past that she could call for help.

There was a sudden knock on the door, and Brennan said, "You about finished in there?"

"Be out in just a moment," Megan said.

The door immediately opened, and Brennan stood there grinning foolishly. He held a lowball glass. The glass may have been crystal. It held two ice cubes and a brown liquid. Megan doubted it was iced tea he was drinking. The smile vanished from his face when he saw the small open window. "Thinking of going somewhere?"

"Are you kidding? I doubt I'd fit," she laughed. "No, I wasn't planning on going anywhere. But the bathroom got all steamy, and I thought it would air out better if I opened the window."

He seemed to think about that for a moment and took a sip of his drink. He indicated with a nod of his head that she should follow him. He headed down the stairs and into a small kitchen area.

There was a two-burner stove, a small refrigerator, and a table with chrome legs, a red top, and two chairs. The table had a dirty plate with remnants of a fried egg and a crust of toast. A carton of milk sat in the middle of the table.

"Have a seat, and I'll get you some breakfast."

When she sat down, Megan noticed the open whiskey bottle on the counter next to the stove. He poured some cornflakes into a bowl, ignored the ones he spilled across the counter and onto the floor, and handed her the bowl and a spoon.

As she poured the milk into the bowl, Brennan topped up his glass with more whiskey and another ice cube. He slurped some whiskey before he sat down across from her.

"We'll leave as soon as my pal gets back," Brennan said and took another sip. This time, he didn't slurp.

Megan nodded and stared at her cereal bowl.

"You're looking pretty good," he said. "You like your shower? You sure seemed to enjoy it."

She shot a quick look at him for a half-second and then refocused on the bowl of cornflakes. She began to shovel the cereal in as fast as she could, and in no time, the bowl was empty. She pushed the empty bowl toward him without looking up.

"Yeah, you're one shy thing, ain't you?"

He took another sip and waited for an answer that she privately vowed would never come.

After a painfully long couple of minutes, he stood, topped his glass up with more whiskey and another ice cube. "Come on. Best you're in your room when Cormac gets back. He's a strange one."

How much stranger could *he* be? She wondered. She followed him out of the kitchen and up the stairs. He held the door for her, and she stepped into the room. A moment later, she heard the lock click and breathed a sigh of relief.

FORTY-ONE

Toby groaned and cried some more. "Aww, aww, my God."

Shauna reached over and slapped him on the back of the head, not for the first time, and said, "For the love of God. Would you ever stop your damn whining? I can't think for lord's sake, you miserable little bollocks."

"But my hands, my hands. You cut off two of me fingers."

"I hear any more from you, and I'll have them cut out your tongue. Now shut the feck up."

Mickey slowly made a half-turn in the passenger seat. "Oh my god," he said and groaned with the back pain. "She's right, quit your whining, you stupid knacker. Besides, we was being nice. It was your little fingers what we took. You don't never use them anyway. You're damn lucky I didn't take that thick head of yours off. God, my back is killing me after what the likes of you did, opening that damn door."

"Next time maybe we just cut his thumbs off. Course we'd have to pull them out of his ass first," Petey said and started to laugh.

Toby swallowed his groan and tried to ignore the pain. He was seated in the backseat, in the opposite corner from Shauna. His left eye had swollen almost closed, compliments of Petey. Slicing the fingers off had been Mickey's idea, although he seemed to be permanently bent over after landing on his back and had handed the carving knife to Petey.

Shauna had scrounged two dishtowels from a kitchen drawer, tossed them at Toby, and told him to wrap his hands. Threatening him along the way, that if so much as a drop of blood landed on the upholstery of her car, she'd cut off more than a finger.

They wanted to know about the two American girls. Most importantly, where the hell they were. Toby decided the wise move would be to not mention dropping the one off at Midlands Regional Hospital, and he quickly informed them that both women had gone to Dublin with Brennan.

"Dublin?" groaned Mickey. "Why in the hell would your man bring them back there?"

"They're going to show him where the rest of the Sands brothers' stash is hidden. It's about thirty or forty kilos."

"Thirty or forty kilos," Mickey said, and Toby watched as all three of his assailants did some quick math in their heads.

"And you know where this is?" Shauna said.

Toby shook his head no. "I've no idea. I only know Brennan was going to take her, I mean them, the two of 'em, to Dublin. They said they didn't know the street names, but once he took them to where the Sands brothers had been staying, they could show him where the stash was hidden."

"They're liable to be running straight into the Garda," Mickey said.

"Where are they staying in Dublin? Some hotel?" Shauna said.

"No, not a hotel. They'll spend the night with Brennan's friend, Cormac. Bit of a strange one, he is."

"You know where this Cormac lives?"

Toby nodded. "He's got a place in Finglas, on Mellowes Road."

Shauna waved a finger just under Toby's nose. "You'd better come through for us because I wasn't kidding. One fecking problem, one drop of blood on the upholstery of my car, and it won't be a finger we're cutting off," she said and pointed at his crotch. "Now let's go. We're headed to Dublin, and they've got the better part of a day on us already."

Toby continued to weep silently in the corner of the backseat. Fortunately, it appeared the wicked witch of Mullingar, Shauna Hanlon, had drifted off to sleep. The two knackers in the front seat were quiet, at least for the moment. His hands were still throbbing with constant pain. At least the bleeding seemed to have stopped, although he didn't dare remove the dishtowels. Damn his cousin, Crazy Brennan. If he ever got out of this, he'd make him pay.

FORTY-TWO

Megan sat at the kitchen table, shoveling in cornflakes and warm milk. She was ravenous. Brennan stood in front of the kitchen sink with his back to her, pouring more whiskey into his teacup. She noted the two empty bottles from yesterday on the counter. One of which was lying on its side. Brennan paid them no heed. Fortunately, Cormac, the strange one, was nowhere to be seen.

"Soon as you're finished with breakfast, we'll head out," Brennan said. He remained facing the kitchen sink, staring out the window as he took a hearty sip of his whiskey enhanced tea.

"Where are we going to go? If you don't mind my asking," Megan said.

He half-scoffed, took another sip, and said, "Don't you think it's about time you showed me where they stashed the rest of the delivery?"

Megan took a deep breath and tried to remain calm. "Yeah, if you can get me to where they were staying, I should be able to show you. Like I told you, I can't remember the street names. It was so crazy, all the partying. I can't even remember a lot of the time. It's just a great big blank."

"I just hope we're not too late, and the damn Guards haven't made off with it," he said and drained the teacup. He seemed to shudder visibly as he swallowed. Still facing the sink, he refilled his cup, this time ignoring the tea and simply filling the cup with whiskey.

"Yeah, I sure hope it's still there so we can party."

Brennan turned around, smiled in a weird way, and said, "Oh we're going to do a lot more than just party. We're gonna do things you'll never forget."

"Any more of those cornflakes?" Megan said, not wanting to hear any details.

"Figures, you're all the same," he said, shaking his head, and tossed the box of cornflakes at her.

She tried to catch the box, but it bounced off the edge of the table and landed on the floor. She quickly picked it up, filled her bowl, and started shoveling spoonfuls into her mouth. She focused on the bowl of cereal, afraid to look at him. Fortunately, he turned back around and returned to staring out the window, occasionally taking a sip.

After a few minutes, he drained his teacup, pushed it off to the side, and said, "It's time we got going."

"I think I had better use the bathroom before we go."

"Really?"

"It'll only take a minute."

"Jesus. Okay. Come on," he said and pointed toward the door. He followed her up the stairs, stopped at the top of the stairs, and watched as she walked down the short hallway into the bathroom.

"Be out in just a couple of minutes," she said and closed the door. She hurried to the window and peeked out, hoping she could see someone she could call to, but the street was quiet. She felt the sharpened spoon in her pocket, waited a few minutes until she thought she'd used up all the time she had, and flushed the toilet. She ran the sink for a half-minute and opened the bathroom door.

Brennan was nowhere to be seen.

She moved as quickly and quietly as possible toward the staircase. She was just about to turn and race down the stairs when he suddenly stepped out of the bedroom at the top of the stairs.

"Already done?"

"Yep. Ready to go," she said, smiled and made a quick glance past him. Cormac was lying face down on the bed. His left arm hung over the side of the bed with his hand resting on the floor. A broken table lamp lay on the floor alongside the bed.

Brennan saw her look, quickly reached over, and closed the door. "We better get going. Quiet now, we wouldn't want to wake Cormac."

Megan headed down the stairs, trying her best to move quietly. All the while, knowing it didn't make any difference, Cormac, the strange one, was dead.

As Brennan took hold of the doorknob on the front door, he lifted his shirt so Megan could see the butt of a gun tucked into his jeans. "Just so you know, if you try to run or call out to someone, I'll shoot you. And then I'll shoot whoever you yelled at, and it'll be all your fault. Understand?"

Megan could smell the whiskey on his breath and nodded.

"Good. Now when we get to the car, I'm going to open the door for you. I want you to climb in and get down on the floor just like you did when we drove here. Got it?"

"But I won't cause any problems. I promise I won't."

That seemed to make him smile for just a second or two. "Good. But then, I know you won't because you're going to be down on the floor. Any questions?"

Megan shook her head.

"Then let's go. Ladies first," he said and held the front door open.

He followed her out to his car parked on the sidewalk. The car was close enough to the small wall along the sidewalk that they stepped into the street. For just a nanosecond, she thought about running but knew she would never make it across the narrow street, let alone around the corner. She stopped at the door.

"Good," Brennan said as he pushed the button on his ignition key. The lights on the car blinked, the horn beeped softly, and he pulled the door open. "Hop in and down on the floor."

Megan did as she was told.

Brennan climbed into the front seat. A moment later, Megan heard something that sounded like fabric tearing. Brennan stuck his hand over the driver's seat, holding a length of grey tape. "I want you to wrap this around your ankles. Do it properly. You try to pull a fast one, and I'm going to mess up that pretty face of yours. Now take the tape and wrap those ankles."

Megan pulled the tape from his hands and wrapped it around her ankles. Just as she was finishing, she heard the tearing sound again, and Brennan held another length of tape. "Stick your hands up here," he said.

She placed her hands just above the back of the console.

"Okay, there, that should do it," he said, wrapping the tape around her wrists three times. "Now settle in down there. We've got a bit of a ride." With that, he placed the key in the ignition, buckled his seatbelt, and started the car.

Megan looked out the window from the floor of the backseat and watched the roofs on the houses as they passed. "Any chance you could maybe stop somewhere and get me some underwear and maybe a different t-shirt? My clothes are starting to get pretty gross."

"You behave and show me where they hid the rest of this stash and, hell, I'll buy you a fur coat," he said and laughed.

Megan took some comfort in reaching down and feeling the sharpened spoon in her pocket.

FORTY-THREE

illon and Suel entered Mountjoy prison through a side delivery door next to three loading docks. They'd driven to the main entrance just off North Circular Road only to find it was filled with a crowd of curious onlookers, not to mention news cameras and reporters holding microphones. The logical option seemed to be to drive around to the delivery area and enter out of sight.

"You think all these plonkers are standing around here because of the Sands brothers?" Suel asked as they traveled past the main entrance and down the street.

"That would seem to be the most obvious reason. I'd say, right about now, the powers that be are busy meeting in a closed room with the door locked. They're desperately trying to come up with a way to wipe the egg off their face and find some legitimate explanation. Problem is, there isn't one. Some poor bastard, probably a lowly guard, is going to end up paying for this. There'll be investigations and one hell of a lot of finger-pointing. The end result is, you and I are back to square one."

Suel pulled in next to the loading docks and parked. They got out of the car, walked up a set of metal stairs, and pushed an intercom button. A gruff voice answered, "State your business."

"An Garda Síochána, Special Branch," Suel said. "The main gate is filled with all sorts of reporters and knackers. We've got an appointment with the Warden's office."

A buzzer sounded, and Suel pushed the door open. He and Dillon walked into a caged area. A stone wall, maybe ten feet away with a window of bulletproof glass, was at the opposite end of the cage. Behind the bullet-proof window sat a guard, all three hundred plus pounds of him.

"Aw, Jesus I don't believe it," Suel mumbled under his breath as they headed toward the guard.

"Place your weapons in the drawer," the guard said over the microphone as a steel drawer off to the side slid open. Both Dillon and Suel placed their pistols in the drawer. The drawer was quickly retracted into the stone wall. "State your names."

"For feck's sake, Noel. You know who the hell I am," Suel shouted. "I was at your damn wedding."

"And damn near drank us out of beer," Noel shouted back. "Now state your names for the record. And let me remind you, Paddy, you're being recorded."

"Christ on a cross," Suel groaned and stated his name.

"US Marshal, Jack Dillon, with An Garda Síochána, Special Branch," Dillon said.

They were searched, patted down, and had a wand run over their bodies four separate times by guards who escorted them through a number of different security areas. Eventually, they were taken through a series of offices and into a conference room, where they were told to wait. They did just that, waited. For the better part of a half-hour. After twenty minutes or so, they were joined by a red-faced DCI McCabe, who looked like he was ready to explode. After his initial nod of acknowledgement, McCabe sat at the conference table drumming his fingers as his blood pressure continued to rise. Dillon crossed his fingers in the hope McCabe didn't go into cardiac arrest. He thought it best to sit quietly and look the other way.

Eventually, an assistant warden named Gilles arrived with two staff members. Dillon figured at least one, if not both, were more than likely department solicitors.

Suel, never one for subtlety, jumped to his feet as the three entered the room and asked the obvious. "What the feck happened?"

"Please, let's all just take a seat, and I'll tell you what we know thus far," Gilles said.

That seemed to light the short fuse on Suel's rant. "Weren't they supposed to be in isolation? Don't you have guards? After the attacks on them the other day, didn't it seem logical they should be placed in solitary confinement? They weren't even going to be sentenced until next week, for God's sake. Just in case you think we're overreacting, we were counting on their cooperation on a pending case. We were going to offer them a plea bargain today in return for that cooperation. Obviously, after this morning's fiasco, that's not going to happen now, is it?"

"Please, if you would just take a seat. We're in the midst of our investigation. I'm sure you can understand that—"

"I have to be honest. I'm having a very hard time understanding any of this. Is anyone in charge around here?" McCabe said, then, with a nod of his head, signaled Suel to sit down.

"Thank you," Gilles said as Suel sat down. Everyone seemed to take a deep breath, although the tension clearly remained.

"Here's what we know thus far. Both prisoners were—"

"You're talking the Americans, Kevin and Sean Sands," McCabe said.

"Yes, of course," Gilles said and nodded. "They were confined in separate cells in the CBU, the Controlled Behavioral Unit. Our residents refer to it as the block."

"And where is that unit located?" Dillon said.

"The CBU? It's located in the 'D' base, which is underneath the 'D' wing. They were under twenty-four-hour lock up with the exception of one hour of open-air exercise. They did not have any interaction with other inmates nor with one another."

"And yet they were both found hanging in their cells? How the hell did that happen?" Suel said.

"It appears to be a double suicide."

"Double suicide? Both of these knackers taking their own lives at essentially the same time, and yet they had no interaction?"

"It would appear that is the case, yes," Gilles said. He blinked a couple of times and McCabe, Dillon, and Suel all had the distinct impression he may have been reciting the company line. If so, it seemed apparent he didn't believe it.

"And what? They hung themselves from a bunk?" Dillon said.

"No. Both men were found on the floor of their cell with a t-shirt wrapped around their neck. At present, we're viewing it as self-administered strangulation."

McCabe and Suel looked wide-eyed and speechless.

"You can't really believe that," Dillon said. "Self-administered strangulation? On two men? Brothers. You're telling us, self-administered strangulation, done simultaneously, although they had no contact with one another. How is that even possible?"

"We're in the midst of investigating that aspect as we speak."

"Beyond ridiculous," McCabe said and rose from his chair. Assistant Warden Gilles looked at McCabe, not sure what he expected him to do. "You can rest assured I'll be filing a report with the Minister of Justice. After the violence and reports in 2016, you'd think you would have copped on. Obviously, that's not the case. You people are asleep at the switch. Self-administered strangulation. God save us. We've nothing more to say, except it's been enlightening. If you'd be so kind as to escort us out," Suel said.

Gilles stood, and as they stormed out of the conference room, he mumbled something about keeping McCabe informed on the latest developments. McCabe didn't respond. They were escorted out through the main entrance to Mountjoy, where they ran into the gauntlet of reporters and newscasters shouting questions and thrusting microphones in their faces. More than one individual shouted a question at McCabe by name.

"Sorry, no comment," he growled over a half-dozen times.

Someone recognized Dillon and shouted his name. Dillon kept his eyes focused on the back of McCabe's head and didn't acknowledge whoever it was that had recognized him. Eventually, they made their way far enough down the street that the media gave up and returned to their positions at the front entrance.

"Where are the two of you parked?" McCabe said.

"Around the back at the delivery entrance," Suel replied.

"I can give you a ride," McCabe said.

"Thank you, sir. But with all due respect, the walk might help to calm me, calm the both of us down. Once we get behind the wheel, we're off to Mullingar for the next day or two."

McCabe seemed to think about that for a long moment before he shook his head and pulled car keys from his pocket. "Safe journey. Keep me posted. I've had my fill of surprises for the week. Bloody hell. The cheek of them in there," he said and grew red-faced all over again.

Dillon and Suel walked to the end of the long block then around the corner and down another block. They turned and walked up to the lane marked 'Private Entrance' where their car was parked.

"God save us, I suppose we'd better go deal with numbskull Noel and get our weapons back. The things I do, God grant me patience," Suel said and headed up the metal stairs to the door.

FORTY-FOUR

Dillon and Suel had barely left the Dublin city limits and were still ranting about the brief meeting at the Joy when Dillon's phone rang. The screen on his cell read DI Turley, not that he needed to check. He answered the call with, "We're just now getting on our way, Eamon."

"The both of you sleeping in, are you's?"

"I wish. No, unfortunately, We got word early this morning that our friends Kevin and Sean Sands were found dead in their cells."

"What? The Sands brothers, dead? Both of them?"

"You heard me. It's been on RTE, still breaking news as far as I know. The staff at the Joy has no idea what in the hell happened, except that two prisoners, supposedly in isolation, were found dead."

"RTE, now there's a group that should be behind bars. But how in the bloody hell did this happen? Were they shot? Poisoned? Stabbed?"

"No. Get this, according to the staff briefing we just received, some poor bastard named Gilles had the pleasure of informing us, along with DCI McCabe, that both of them were the victims of a self-administered strangulation."

"Self-administered . . . What the bloody hell?"

"Yeah, I'd say that pretty much sums it up."

"But weren't they supposed to be in isolation?"

"We were told they were. Something called the Controlled Behavioral Unit. Twenty-four-hour lock up with one hour of open-air exercise, supposedly never simultaneous."

"What did DCI McCabe say?"

"Not much. The meeting was short and not sweet. Lasted no longer than two or three minutes tops. McCabe stormed out, making the promise he'd be filing a report with the Minister of Justice. He'll probably deliver it in person, just to ensure its looked at. I'm hard put to think of a time I've ever seen him this mad. From the look of him, he'll be lucky if he doesn't have a massive heart attack on this."

Suel glanced over at Dillon and shook his head, acknowledging he felt the same way.

"They promised to keep us posted with any new developments."

"Bloody hell. The pair of them? Self-administered strangulation?"

"That's what they told us."

"Bloody ridiculous."

"That's one of the words McCabe used," Dillon said, and half-laughed, although there was nothing funny about the event. "At some point, you'd think they'll have to arrive at the logical conclusion. They were murdered. Sooner or later, the truth will come out. A guard or two bribed, the cells unlocked. Maybe it was a guard who actually committed the murders. The longer they wait, the worse the reaction is going to be. It doesn't really matter now. We need to get back to the subject at hand, Kate Murray and Megan Gaffney. Did you learn anything on our man Toby?"

"I did, as a matter of fact. Tobias McDade, age 28. He's originally from Tralee, County Kerry. By the way, he drives a grey Nissan Juke. A 2018 model. Definitely your man on CCTV. I followed him to a home on the outskirts of Mullingar, to an older place that's seen better days. In a bit of a shambles based on what I saw."

"He's living there? Renting?"

"Not sure on that just yet. The place is owned by one Xavier Brennan McDade. Same surname. I'm guessing a relative of some sort, possibly even a brother, but I haven't had the chance to check that bit out yet. He's had the place for a few years, along with twenty hectares of land around the home. From what I could see, all the land lies fallow. I don't know, but if I had to hazard a guess, I would say the place was inherited and your man, this Xavier Brennan McDade, has something to do with the missing girls. Bit of a spotty record. Served six months some years back. Aggravated assault. No job or source of income that I could find for either one. I checked, and neither one of them are on the dole."

"And you're there now?"

"Just in the process of heading over to start watching."

"What if he's gone? What if we lose the bastard or he gets wind of us?" Dillon said and immediately regretted raising his voice.

Turley chuckled. "He'll not be going anywhere this morning. The small matter of two flat tires."

"Two?"

"Yes. I figured that way, even if he changes one, he's still stuck there."

"You're one clever bastard, Turley."

"I'll take that as a compliment," Turley said and chuckled again. "Call me when you're close to town. I'll give you directions to where I am. Drive safely."

"Always," Dillon said. "We should be there in the next forty minutes or so. Talk then."

FORTY-FIVE

Dillon was phoning DI Turley just as they drove past the Swordsman pub on the N42. The parking lot was empty, and the place wouldn't open until later in the morning. Turley's phone rang twice before he answered.

"Where are you guys?" He said by way of answering.

"Just passing the Swordsman. We'll be in town in another ten minutes. Anything on your man, Toby McDade?"

"Nothing. He's got the life, sleeping in until after ten in the morning. Out in a pub till the wee hours."

"He's still there?"

"Well, if he's not, he's on foot. His car is still back behind the house. No indication he's bothered to do anything. I'd say the plonker is still in bed. Let me give you the address. You've got GPS?"

"We do," Dillon said, pushing a button on the dash and bringing up the GPS. He punched in the address as Turley read it to him and then read it back to Turley just to double-check. "Great. It says we've got an ETA of twelve minutes."

"I'm in a squad car parked on the same side of the road, just past the entrance to the place in front of a clump of gorse bushes. If he somehow tries to leave, I can pull out and block him. Although, at this point, he'd have to be riding a bicycle."

"We'll be there shortly, Eamon. What are you thinking?"

"Once you get here, let's go in. He's had enough sleep. We can wake him up early, before noon."

Dillon laughed and disconnected.

"I just hope this bastard can tell us something," Suel said.

They drove for a few more minutes through an older section of Mullingar made up of large, two and three-story classic homes. The streets were tree-lined, and they followed the GPS directions, leading them out of the area and onto a country road. A minute or two later, Suel spotted Turley's squad car and flashed his headlights. Turley flashed back and drove into the McDade estate, stopping maybe ten feet inside the entrance, leaving just enough room for Suel to clear the entrance.

Turley stepped out of his car as Suel pulled alongside. Dillon and Suel hopped out of the car, and Turley said, "The rear door seems to be the entrance most used. Dillon, why don't you come back there with me. Paddy, you make your way to the front door. Anything happens, give us a yell. I'm thinking we'll knock on the back door as soon as we get there, so be prepared."

Suel headed across a field of weeds, following the semblance of a recent path. Dillon and Turley hurried toward the back of the house. As they came around the rear corner of the house, Turley nodded toward the grey Nissan Juke with the flat tires.

"Nice work," Dillon said and pulled his pistol from his belt.

They walked a half-dozen more steps when Turley suddenly said, "What the hell?"

Dillon looked at the back door standing wide open. "Did we just chase him back inside?"

Turley signaled with his hand that they spread apart. Dillon stepped over to the far side of the open door and moved up against the rear of the house. Turley did the same on the opposite side of the door.

They held that position for a minute or two. Turley signaled Dillon he was going in and moving to the left, Dillon was to follow him in and move to the right. Turley signaled with his fingers, one, two, three and hurried in through the open door in a crouched position. Dillon followed, moving to the right and using his pistol to cover the area. Fortunately, no one was in the room.

Turley put his fingers to his lips, signaling quiet, then pointed toward a chair at the far end of the kitchen table. A pool of blood covered the wooden floor around the chair and what looked like two fingers lay in the middle of the pool. Three partial footprints left the beginnings of a trail across the floor toward a couple of empty whiskey bottles and a cellphone on the kitchen counter. The kitchen sink was filled with dirty dishes.

Turley pointed toward the open doorway leading into the rest of the house, and they quietly made their way down the hallway, checking the rooms as they went. At the front of the house, just opposite the staircase leading up to the second floor, Turley opened the door and signaled Suel to remain quiet.

As Suel stepped in, Turley whispered in his ear, and Suel nodded. They moved up the creaking staircase, Turley looking straight ahead, Dillon covering the right, with Suel covering the left side of the staircase. Once upstairs, they began to clear one room after another. Dillon felt his heart pounding louder with every room they cleared, fearful that at the end of the hall it would be pounding so loud it was bound to alert whoever was waiting for them in the last room. Fortunately, the last room was just as empty as the others.

"What the hell?" Turley said as he stuffed his pistol back into his belt.

"You think someone picked him up last night? Maybe he saw the flat tires, snuck out the back, and high-tailed it out of town," Suel said.

"Bit of a surprise waiting for us down in the kitchen," Dillon said.

"He's dead?" Suel said.

Turley shook his head, "No, but I'm guessing right about now he wishes he was. A pool of blood and two fingers."

"Jesus Christ."

"No doubt self-administered finger amputation," Dillon said.

"I'm requesting the Technical section," Turley said, raising his phone to his ear.

"There's a little pantry room downstairs, just a line of cabinets against one wall. There was a blanket on the floor, along with a pink shoe and a white, ankle-length athletic sock. The shoe looked just like the one we saw at that abandoned place yesterday," Dillon said.

"They were here, that's for damn sure," Suel said.

"Sure as hell looks that way."

FORTY-SIX

Dillon, Suel, and Turley stood drinking bad tea next to the van. It was the same white paneled van labeled 'Technical Bureau' in blue letters on either side that had processed the dilapidated structure. Not surprisingly, it was also the same three-person crew at work in white hazmat suits that Dillon and Suel had been introduced to the other day.

"So they grab the American girls and cut a finger off each one. Why?" Suel said.

Dillon shook his head. "We don't even know if the fingers belong to the girls."

"Seems to me they grab the girls and either need some kind of information or they're of a mind to pay them back for testifying against the Sands brothers. Of course, the girls can't give them any information because they don't know what the hell these two idiots are talking about. The bollocks threaten to cut off a finger in order to prove they're not fooling around. And then to prove their point, well . . . Now the question is, where do they go from here?"

"Didn't really look like women's fingers," Dillon said as he dumped the remainder of his teacup into the weeds next to the van.

"Yeah, if you mean no fingernails with a French pedicure or whatever the hell you call that fancy treatment. But remember, these two women are working girls. One waited tables, and the other worked a cash register in a checkout lane when they weren't taking classes. So they probably, maybe, didn't have no fancy nails. You didn't like the tea?" Turley said.

"Just not sitting right. This whole thing, we've been grabbing at straws, and we still don't know shit," Dillon said.

"Well, I think we got about a ninety-nine percent chance that pink shoe is going to be a match to the one they found at that other site. We're bound to get some DNA and, with any luck, some hair from that blanket on the floor next to the shoe. The beds upstairs, along with that mattress on the floor, we're bound to get more clues from those as well."

"Yeah, but it's still grabbing at straws. Where the hell are they now? Still in this area? Out west? Dublin? Up into the north? Hell, by now, they could be on a ferry headed for the continent or over to the UK."

"Dillon, let's try to think a little more positive," Suel said.

One of the tech guys in a white hazmat suit came around the corner of the house and headed toward the van. He carried an armload of evidence bags. The fingers, along with blood samples from the kitchen floor, had been placed in a cooler earlier and were already in the van.

"How's it going, Colin?" Turley said.

"You lads are keeping us fully employed, Eamon," Colin said with a laugh as he approached.

"Any more fingers?" Suel asked.

"No, nothing like that. Hair fibers, the blankets. We'll wrap up that mattress that's on the floor upstairs and take it back to the lab. That shoe, the pink one, we'll know for sure when we run the tests, but I'm guessing it's a pretty safe bet it's a match to the one from the other day. Funny thing, we've just the one sock here. Hang on a minute." He set the evidence bags down in the rear of the van then rifled through the bags, there were easily a dozen or so.

"Yeah, here we go," he said, pulling out a bag with the white sock, just large enough to be even with the top of the shoe they'd found. "See this athletic sock. It's got that gold toe. We got one like this yesterday, came in from Midlands Regional. Seems some woman ended up there, no ID, just the one sock on her foot. Strangest thing."

"All she had on was one sock?" Suel said.

"Yeah, well, and she was dressed. Someone left her in a wheelchair just inside the ER at night. Just the one sock on her foot, no shoes. Craziest damn thing."

"What'd she say?" Dillon asked.

"Well, that was just it. I guess she was unconscious. In a coma or something and, hey, lads, where are you going?"

"Thanks, Colin. We owe you a pint," Turley called over his shoulder as he ran to his car. "You follow me to Midlands. It's just a couple of minutes. Flashers on," Turley yelled as he jumped into his car. A moment later, he shifted into reverse and sped out of the estate. He skidded to a stop and waited for Suel and Dillon to catch up just outside the entrance.

Suel jumped behind the wheel and shoved his key in the ignition. Dillon reached into the backseat and pulled the flashing lights apparatus from the floor. As Suel raced backward, almost striking the Technical van, Dillon slapped the flashing lights onto the top of the car then inserted the cord into the cigarette lighter. Turley took off down the road heading back into Mullingar with his lights flashing and his siren blaring. Dillon and Suel were right on his tail.

Less than ten minutes later, they raced past the white sign with blue letters that said Midlands Regional Hospital. The same sign Megan had seen from the floor of Brennan McDade's car the night they'd dropped off Kate and left Toby to fend for himself.

"Dear God, I'm praying it's one of those American girls," Dillon said.

"You're not alone, partner," Suel said as he screeched to a stop behind Turley's car, and they ran into the ER.

They hustled down a short hallway and into the ER waiting room as people stepped aside and shot strange looks their way. A reception desk stood against a wall on the right-hand side of the room. A young woman was just stepping away from the desk. She held a little boy by the hand. He looked to be maybe six. His eyes were swollen, and he kept a bloody tissue shoved up against his nose.

Turley had the leather holder with his badge and identification card out. The woman behind the reception counter was wide-eyed and visibly leaned back in her chair as the three men raced toward her, waving badges.

"An Garda Síochána. We need to see a woman who was brought in here last night with one sock," Turley half-shouted.

FORTY-SEVEN

The Sands brothers had spent the better part of two weeks partying and, in general making a nuisance of themselves in a two-story structure owned by Phoenix Properties. The firm was just one of a number of shell companies based in Malta that served as cover for Wee Timmy Bixby's businesses.

The building was located on North Circular Road, not too far from Dublin's Phoenix Park, hence the name Phoenix Properties. A two and a half story brick structure built in 1910, one of twenty attached to one another along North Circular Road. Brennan McDade slowed down and pulled to the curb in front of the property, double-checking the address, number one-seventy-eight.

All the units appeared more or less identical from the exterior. A wooden door with a glass panel mounted above the door, two tall main floor windows, one on either side of the front door and three windows on the second floor. All along the street, a set of nine granite steps led up to the front doors. From the exterior, the only apparent difference with the unit the Sands brothers had stayed in was there was only one doorbell.

It was, in fact, unique in that it was still a single unit consisting of all two and a half floors. Almost all the other units had been converted to multiple units years ago. Brennan counted four doorbells for the unit on the right and six for the unit on the left. It added up to a lot of people on either side phoning the Guards with noise complaints on the Sands brothers, which had eventually led to the Guards sending out a squad. Things had quickly gone downhill from there.

At this hour of the day, mid-afternoon, there was just the occasional person walking by. Usually, someone going to or coming from Phoenix Park or an older person invariably dragging a cart behind them on the way to the grocery store. There was no indication as to the police investigation that had taken place two months prior. No blue and white tape crisscrossed over the door with the words 'An Garda Síochána DO NOT CROSS' written every two feet. In fact, no apparent police presence appeared anywhere on the street. Brennan pulled away from the curb and drove to the end of the block. He made a right turn and almost immediately took another right, driving down the cobblestone alley heading back to number one-seventy-eight.

There was a parking space directly behind the unit, two spaces, actually. One of the spaces was empty. The other was occupied by a dark blue Mercedes. The front tire on the driver's side of the Mercedes was clamped. Brennan pulled in next to the car and climbed out. A Hertz sticker was in the corner of the windshield on the passenger side. The car was obviously a rental. More than likely, it was the car the Sands brothers had rented.

Megan partially raised herself from the floor of the backseat and peered out the window. Brennan stood with his back to her, looking at a dark blue car.

Brennan walked around the Mercedes, trying all the doors. They were locked. Based on the stains from the dust and the rain, the car had sat here for quite some time. Certainly weeks if not months. If he could get in touch with Toby, maybe they could somehow remove the clamp, open the door, and hotwire the Mercedes. He had a connection with a shop that, for the right price, might be able to install a new ignition switch and not ask any questions. He pulled out his cellphone and hit the speed dial number for Toby.

Back in Mullingar, Colin was just setting another batch of evidence bags into the box when he heard a cellphone ringing. He dug through the evidence box and pulled out the bag with the phone. The screen on the cellphone read 'Brennan.' Colin pulled out his cellphone and began typing a text message to DI Turley, alerting him to the call coming through from someone named Brennan. The ringing on the cellphone eventually stopped, and Colin heard a ding, indicating a voice message had been left. He added that information to his text message and sent it off to DI Turley.

Once he was finished leaving his voice message, Brennan silently swore and cursed his idiot cousin, Toby. Nothing to do, and all day to do it, and the knacker still can't answer his phone, he thought and shook his head. He glanced into the back of his car. Megan was still on the floor with her eyes closed pretending to be asleep. He hurried up the back steps to number one-seventy-eight and knocked on the back door. The door was painted white and had a window at about the five-foot level.

He noticed a small piece of blue and white Garda tape still stuck to a lower corner of the doorframe. With the Sands brothers behind bars and the tape removed from the front and back doors here, the chances were fairly good that the Guards had completed their investigation and wouldn't be back. He knocked on the door again.

After a minute or two, he went down the steps and stood at the back of his car. He pressed the unlock button on his car key twice and heard the locks click open. He opened the rear door, rummaged around and found a rag, grabbed the tire iron, and hurried back up the steps.

He took a quick look around and didn't see anyone. He wrapped the rag around the end of the tire iron, glanced once more for any curious onlookers, and hit the glass window with the tire iron. The panel cracked and formed a starburst pattern where he'd struck. He hit it twice more, the second time putting his all into it. The glass shattered into hundreds of tiny pieces. He ran the tire iron along the edge of the window frame, removing bits and chunks of glass, then stuck his head through the now open window, spotted a deadbolt lock, reached in, and pulled it open.

He stepped inside and quickly looked for a door alarm sensor or a security control panel. Fortunately, he didn't see either. He hurried back out to the car, opened the door, and said, "Time to wake up."

Megan opened her eyes, nodded, and said, "Everything okay?"

"You can tell me in just a minute. Come on," he said. He grabbed her by the ankles, moving her a couple of inches closer to the door. He lifted her ankles, fiddled with the tape, swore a couple of times, and said, "Finally." He unwrapped the tape around her ankles, crumpled it, and tossed it on the ground behind him. He helped her sit up on the backseat and undid the tape around her wrists.

"Come on. Let's go," he said, taking hold of her arm and half-pulling her out of the backseat.

"Oh, God, give me just half a minute to stretch," Megan said, spreading her legs to shoulder width and turning from left to right at her waist.

"Let's go. You can do that shite inside," Brennan said and pulled her ahead of him toward the back stairs.

Megan hurried up the stairs and in through the back door. Her feet crunched on the bits of glass scattered across the floor of the rear entrance.

"Well, what do you think? Welcome home, lady. Look familiar?" Brennan said as they stepped into the kitchen.

Megan took in the room. Wood grained cabinets, a center island, granite countertops, and a white porcelain sink. A number of the drawers had been pulled open and the contents piled on the countertops or dumped on the floor. She nodded and said, "Yeah, it's kind of coming back to me now. A bit hazy on the memory, but it looks kind of familiar. I don't remember it being this messy."

"You can thank the Guards for that. The paint cans were down on the lower level, supposedly. How do we get down there?"

Megan shook her head. "Um, they wouldn't let us go down there with them. So I'm not really sure. We were, you know, mostly upstairs in the bedroom."

"You said you could show me, damn it."

"I think I can, but it's going to take a few minutes to get my bearings. We were partying all the time, remember."

"Yeah, well, if you ever want to party again, you better start coming up with something and fast. The Guards have been through this place from top to bottom, at least twice."

"I think they said the rest wasn't here, exactly, but nearby."

"Nearby?"

"Yeah, the bigger one, he said it. God, I can't remember his name right now." She raised her eyebrows, pretending to look like she was trying to think.

"That would be, Kevin," Brennan said.

"Yeah, that's right. That's who it was, Kevin."

Brennan grabbed her by the arm and squeezed hard.

"Ouch, hey, what are you doing? Stop it, Brennan. You're hurting me. Stop it," Megan shouted and struggled to make him let go.

"Sean is taller than Kevin by a good six inches. What the hell are you trying to pull, you little bitch? You don't even know what the hell you're talking about."

"Let go of me, or I won't tell you a thing. I need some time to remember. Besides, if you have to know, I wasn't talking about who was taller."

"Well, then what—"

"Figure it out," Megan said and pulled her arm from his grip.

"Oh, yeah. You'd maybe know more about that than me, I guess."

"You think?"

FORTY-EIGHT

Suel suggested, "Maybe if we just gave her a gentle little shake."

"I've already told you, no. Apparently, you haven't been listening," the nurse said. She was an attractive, no-nonsense individual, wearing powder blue surgical scrubs with a stethoscope hanging around her neck. No more than five feet tall, she was not about to be intimidated by three cops, especially not DI Suel.

"I'm not sure you understand," Suel said.

"Please allow me to repeat myself yet again. No. Now, I've called the doctor. He will be here momentarily. Until then, I would like the three of you to move down to the end of the hall." She pointed to a small circular room with a couch, two chairs, and a coffee table in front of the couch. The room was maybe twenty feet beyond the nurse's station. "You'll wait there for the doctor who, I'm sure, will be more than happy to provide you with an update."

"We've got an individual who has been kidnapped and is in danger of losing her life. If we could just ask your patient one or two questions, we might be able to—"

"And I have a patient who is in a coma, which means she will be unable to answer any questions. She will not wake, even if you ask her nicely. Even if she did suddenly come out of her coma, she would be unable to answer any questions. I'm sorry, but unless you let this run its course, there is the possibility you would do serious, permanent damage. Let me repeat myself. Again. No, sir."

"We'll wait for the doctor at the end of the hall. Thank you," Dillon said and put his hand on Suel's shoulder, guiding him down the hall.

"Thank you, ma'am," Turley said and followed Dillon and Suel.

"God, can you believe the cheek of your woman?" Suel said.

"I think she had a thing for you, although God only knows why," Dillon joked.

Turley laughed and said, "It would serve you right. She'd be cracking the whip, literally." His phone suddenly alerted him to a text message coming in, and he pulled it out of his pocket. "Hmm, Colin. Says a call came through on that cellphone left in the kitchen. The call was from Brennan."

Turley input a number and placed the phone next to his ear.

"Brennan McDade?" Suel asked.

"Most likely. Hopefully, I'm about to find— Yeah, Colin, just got your text message."

Dillon pulled his cell out and began going through his contact list.

"Yeah, no, we don't have that kind of time. Listen to it and tell me what he says. No, it'll be my problem. I'm giving authorization. Can't you do it through the evidence bag? Just push the damn button and listen." He looked toward Dillon and Suel and rolled his eyes then pulled a pen from his pocket.

"Have him get the incoming number," Dillon said.

"Okay. Yeah. That's all?" Turley was writing notes on the cover of a fashion magazine resting on the coffee table. "Okay, click onto the contacts and see if you can get the phone number. Mmm-hmm, okay. Yeah. No, thanks, Colin, much appreciated. Any problem, you refer them to me, and I'll take full responsibility," Turley said and disconnected.

"Call was listed as coming from Brennan. I'm assuming it's Brennan McDade. Said he was at the Sands' place."

"That's most likely the place on North Circular Road, where they found the thirty kilos hidden in the paint cans."

Suel pulled out his phone and placed a call. "McCabe," he said to Dillon.

Dillon read the message Turley had written on the cover of the magazine. *"Toby, it's me. Get your ass over here. We're about to go into the Sands' place. Looks like Garda are finished here. Mercedes out back that looks prime for taking. It's clamped. Bring power saw & we can take it. We're going in. Hope coppers didn't find stash. Call me back."*

"DI Suel, sir, calling from Mullingar," Suel said into his phone. "Yes and no. We think one of the girls is in Midlands Regional Hospital. We're there now, but she's out cold, and we can't get in to see her. No sir, we're waiting on the doctor. I doubt they'll let us do that. Told us it wouldn't work, anyway. The reason for my call is we intercepted a phone message from Brennan McDade. We believe he has the other American woman in his custody. He is apparently about to go into the unit the Sands brothers occupied. Yes, sir, that's the one, North Circular Road. Came through just moments ago. It should be viewed as a hostage situation. He is armed and dangerous. Yes, sir. We're on our way. Thank you."

"We're out of here, Eamon," Suel said as he disconnected the phone and stood. "McCabe is sending the Emergency Response Unit. We might have this put to bed in the next thirty minutes or so. You've been a great help. You're welcome to join us."

"No, by all means, get back there. I'll wait here for a bit. See what the doctor has to say."

Everyone shook hands, promising to stay in touch. Dillon and Suel headed back down the hall. Suel stopped at the nurse's station. The nurse who denied them access just minutes before was seated at a desk next to a foot-high stack of files.

"Gentlemen?"

"Sorry to interrupt," Suel said. "We have to head back to Dublin. Our friend DI Turley is still waiting to talk with the doctor. I neglected to mention we believe the woman's name is Kathleen Murray, American. She goes by the name Kate."

"The two girls missing for the last few days?" the nurse said.

"She'd be one of them. We're heading back to Dublin. The other girl might be held there."

She actually smiled and said, "Be careful and stay safe. Please feel free to contact me for an update on our patient."

"Would you have a card?" Suel said.

"I do," she said and smiled. She pulled open the center drawer in the desk, pulled out a card, wrote her name across the front, and handed it to Suel. "Like I said, feel free to call."

Suel handed his card to her and said, "And you do the same. Call anytime. Thank you."

They hurried down the hallway to the elevators. When they stepped onto the elevator, they were the only ones.

"You're going to call her?"

"Only to get an update." Dillon shot him a look. "What?" Suel said.

"Nothing, I shouldn't even be surprised."

Once in the car, Dillon placed a call to Tommy Walsh in the computer forensics branch back in Dublin. He answered after the third ring.

"Hi Tommy, Jack Dillon. I'm calling for a favor."

"Now there's a surprise. What do you need?"

Dillon went on to explain their situation and the Emergency Response Unit being activated. "I'm heading back to Dublin from Mullingar. We're an hour out at best. Suel is driving."

"I'll say a prayer for the both of you."

"Thanks, that was one of the two reasons I called. The other is, can you run a trace on that number again for me? With any luck, this will be over in the next forty-five minutes, but in the event it's not, I'd like to be ready."

"You thinking a standoff or something?"

"Could be anything, certainly that, negotiations, who knows? Be good to know exactly where he is."

"I can do that. I'm guessing that means you didn't bother to download that free app. You came in on the department line, so I don't have your number. Give me your number again, so I'll be able to contact you."

Dillon gave him his number and disconnected. Suel was just turning onto the N42 and picking up speed. He glanced at the clock on the dash. "With any luck, the Emergency Response Team should be there in the next ten minutes or so. Let's keep our fingers crossed and hope this ends on a positive note."

They raced past the Swordsman pub, continued on the N4 for another twenty-five minutes to where it changed to the M4, Suel racing past every vehicle on the road.

"You'd think we would have heard something by now," Dillon said.

Suel shook his head. "You know how these things go down. You plan everything down to the final second, and it all goes out the window the moment you step out of the van and face the problem head-on."

FORTY-NINE

Megan was in the process of walking through the upstairs bedrooms, telling Brennan things were beginning to come back to her, hopefully calming him down while she tried to think of what her next move might be. She made up a couple of stories, hoping to convince Brennan she knew what she was talking about and had actually been there before. Just now they were standing at the base of a four-poster bed. The contents of a chest of drawers, mostly sheets, pillowcases, and a white duvet, had been dumped on the floor. The empty drawers were piled haphazardly off to the side. The doors to a mahogany wardrobe were open, and a pile of trousers and shirts, still on the hangers, was heaped on the floor.

There was a wingback chair next to an end table on the far side of the bed just in front of two windows. A crystal carafe, maybe half-full of a brown liquid, rested on the end table, along with two glasses.

"I don't need to hear any more about the pillow fight or the whipped cream, okay," Brennan said. "We've been here long enough. You should have an idea where the hell this stash is. That's why we came here in the first place, so get on with it. Cut the bullshit and let's get down to business."

He walked around to the far side of the bed, pulled the stopper from the carafe, and sniffed. What do you know? It smelled like whiskey. He filled one of the glasses with a healthy amount and took a sip. Not bad. "Okay, so where is this stash?" he said. As he took another sip, he glanced out the window just in time to see a Garda van pull to a stop across the street. The double doors on the rear of the van flew open, and eight heavily armed men jumped out into the street. They were dressed all in black, wearing helmets and balaclavas. They immediately formed two teams of four men and hurried down the street in a crouched position with weapons at the ready.

Brennan spit out his whiskey and half-shouted, "What the bloody hell?"

Megan didn't know what to say.

"Come on. We're out of here. How in the hell?" he said, grabbing her wrist and hurrying down the stairs. Megan attempted to keep up, but between the speed he was moving and him swinging her arm back and forth, she tripped and began to fall, taking Brennan with her. They stumbled and tumbled down the last half-dozen steps, coming to rest on the entryway floor.

Brennan groaned to his feet and limped over to a front window. He pulled the drapes back no more than an inch and looked out onto the street. The van was painted black with no markings, which made it look all the more sinister. The two teams had hurried down the street and seemed to be stationed around the front wall of a place maybe a half-dozen units away.

Megan was still lying on the floor, groaning.

"Come on. We're getting out of here, now," Brennan said and pulled the gun from his belt.

"My ankle, it really hurts. I think I broke it when we fell. I don't think I can walk."

Brennan glanced at her right ankle. It was already red and definitely in the process of swelling. The right knee on her jeans was torn, and both elbows were scraped raw and bleeding.

"Come on. Let me help you up," he said. He reached down and began to pull her up.

"Ouch, God, ahh, stop, stop. Oh, give me a minute," she said and hobbled a half-step or two.

"There, see, it's not broken you can walk, I think. Come on. Let's go."

"Can you just wait a minute? It really hurts."

"No, as a matter of fact, I can't. I don't know what's going on out there, but we're not going to wait here to find out. Now come on. Get moving."

He waved the gun at her as an incentive. They limped and groaned down the hall, into the kitchen, and to the back door. Brennan peeked out through the broken window, didn't see anyone, and opened the door. He pulled Megan along, holding tightly onto her upper arm.

"Not so fast, not so fast. Please," Megan pleaded as they made their way down the steps. Megan hung onto the railing with both hands. Brennan pulled her along. Somehow, they made it down without falling again. Brennan dragged her around to the passenger side of the car and opened the front door.

"Get your bum in there, but I'm warning you. You try anything, and I'll shoot you without a second thought. I'm not fecking kidding."

Megan slid onto the passenger seat, then carefully turned and lifted her right leg into the car. No sooner had her foot cleared the frame than Brennan slammed the door shut and hurried around to the driver's side, glancing left and right as he did so. He slid in behind the wheel, shoved the key into the ignition, and fired up the engine. He threw the car in reverse and shouted, "Buckle up."

He backed out of his parking space and into the alley. He looked in his rearview mirror and counted four squad cars in the alley. Two of the cars were no more than fifteen feet from him, both parked bumper to bumper, blocking the alley. Four heavily armed men, all dressed in black with helmets and balaclavas, knelt behind the two cars with weapons at the ready. One of them turned and stared for a moment at Brennan's car. He raised his arm and motioned to Brennan to drive away. Brennan headed down the alley at a moderate pace. He took a left onto the street and drove away, staying just under the speed limit.

FIFTY

Petey asked, "We're just about to head into Finglas. Another two kilometers, what's your man's address?"

"His address? How the hell should I know?" Toby said and felt a wave of pain surge down his arms and up through his hands.

"Listen, you worthless little gobshite. If you want to live long enough to see the end of the day, you damn well better drop the attitude and give us the fecking address."

"I just told you I don't know the address. Honest. But, I'll know the house as soon as I see it, and I can give you the directions."

"That's better, much better, now watch the damn attitude. We've enough to deal with right now."

Shauna came awake and stretched. "How much longer will it be?"

"We're almost in Finglas now, ma'am, and in just a moment, your man will be giving us directions to the house," Mickey said.

"And do we know if he's there, Crazy Brennan?"

"No, we don't," Mickey said. "But then it's not like we can give him a call and tell him we're coming over for a tea now, can we?"

"You'd best watch the attitude, Mickey. I'm not liking the tone."

"Sorry, ma'am."

Petey took the Finglas exit off the M50 and followed Toby's directions. He took a left at the second light, past the Spar and Hickey's pharmacy, and merged onto Mellowes Road. Two-story attached houses were on the right-hand side of the street and an industrial center, behind a ten-foot cyclone fence with razor wire strung across the top, ran all along the opposite side. The low garden walls in front of every house were embellished with various forms of graffiti, none of it legible. As they approached a bend in the road, Toby said, "Slow down. It's one of these coming up. He studied the structures for a moment then said. "That's it there, the one with the green Opel parked in the drive. I recognize it. I'm sure that's Cormac's car."

The rear of the Opel was dented along the right corner. The brake lights had been shattered and were currently replaced by red plastic that looked like it came from a cup cut in half. The plastic had been taped to the car as a temporary substitute for the brake lights. Petey pulled up on the sidewalk and parked across the drive, effectively blocking any attempt to enter or exit.

"Find a way in. I'll wait for you here," Shauna said.

Petey climbed out of the car and opened the rear door for Toby.

"Wait a minute. I showed you where he lived. You didn't say a thing about having to go in there. This wasn't part of the bargain. Besides, I wouldn't be any good to you." He held up both hands with the dishtowels wrapped around them to emphasize his point.

"There never was a bargain, shite for brains. Now get your ass out here," Petey said.

Mickey opened his door, turned slowly in the passenger seat, extended his legs out and onto the pavement. He placed one hand on the dash, the other on the doorframe, and groaned as he rose to his feet. He shuffled toward the front door, bent forward at almost a forty-five-degree angle. A rangy, untrimmed bush stood on either side of the entrance.

"You gonna make it, Mick?" Petey said.

"Just get that pain-in-the-ass up to the door and see who's home. I'll catch up. I'm just fine."

Petey grabbed Toby by the arm and headed toward the front door. "Careful, careful," Toby cried out, keeping his hands raised as Petey grabbed his arm.

They stepped up onto the front stoop. Petey pounded on the door then quickly stepped behind Toby as the door swung open about a foot. He shoved his pistol into Toby's back and whispered, "Say something, damn it."

"Hey, umm, Cormac, surprise, it's me, Toby. Cormac? You there, mate? Cormac?"

"Well, looks like you're welcome to go in. Might as well see what the place looks like," Petey said and pushed Toby in the door with his pistol.

Mickey followed them in, groaning as he slowly took the two steps on the front stoop and groaned. Once inside, he looked at the sparse furnishing and said, "So, where is this knacker, Cormac?"

"Beats me," Toby said.

"You two check upstairs. I need to find a seat," Mickey said and made his way into the sitting room. He backed up in front of the couch and slowly settled in, groaning and gasping as he lowered himself.

Petey grabbed Toby by the collar of his shirt and pushed him up the staircase.

"Easy, easy. Fragile, handle with care," Toby said as Petey shoved the barrel in his rear end.

"Just get a move on," Petey growled.

They climbed to the top of the stairs and stepped into the first bedroom. There was Cormac, face down on the bed with his left arm hanging over the side of the bed and his hand resting on the floor. The broken lamp lay on the floor, right where Brennan had left it.

"I think he might be asleep," Toby whispered.

"Get out of the way, you bollocks," Petey said as he shoved Toby off to the side. He took a step closer to the bed and bent over to have a look. The back of Cormac's skull had a large dent. "Saints preserve us. Okay, don't touch anything. Come on."

"Aren't you going to wake him up?" Toby said in a tone that suggested he knew that wouldn't work but just in case.

"I don't think that's going to help. Now come on. Let's check the other rooms," Petey said. He took hold of Toby's collar and pulled him out into the hallway. They checked the other two bedrooms and the bathroom, all empty, and hurried back down the stairs.

Mickey was seated on the couch with his eyes closed. A wingback chair was opposite him, faded orange with a bit of stuffing hanging out of either arm on the chair. "No one up here?"

"That Cormac bollocks is upstairs in bed, but he's not going anywhere."

"Not going—"

"Someone took a lamp to the back of his head. Deader than your man Elvis."

"Dead?"

"I'd say it might have been Crazy Brennan."

"Any sign of the girl?"

Petey shook his head.

"This should be interesting," Mickey said to Toby. "You'd better do some fast thinking between here and the car because herself is going to be wanting some answers."

"But I don't have any idea where Brennan—"

Mickey held his hand up, silencing Toby. "She's going to want answers from you. Now I'm going to sit here for a bit and rest my weary bones. Meanwhile, it would be the wise man who thought long and hard about where we're going to find Crazy Brennan. Just a little reminder, you've got six more fingers and two thumbs. Now I don't want to hear another word. Just sit there and try to think for once." Mickey groaned as he settled back on the couch and closed his eyes for a couple of minutes.

Eventually, he took a deep breath and slowly groaned to his feet. "All right now, we'll make our way out to herself. You had better come up with an idea by the time we're settled in the car. Now follow me." Mickey shuffled out the door and focused on the two steps as he gingerly made his way off the stoop. He groaned with each step he took. Petey and Toby were right behind him.

They hadn't moved five feet from the stoop when a voice called from behind. "I'd say that's far enough, lads." Two muscular individuals, each holding a very large pistol, stepped away from the bushes on either side of the front door. The man who spoke had a shaved head and massive biceps. He took the pistol from Petey's hand while his partner reached over and pulled the gun from Mickey's belt. "Back inside," the shaved head said and gave a nod toward the car. The door suddenly opened, and Shauna stepped out, looking very unhappy.

The car rocked from side to side as a massive figure gradually made his way out of the backseat and stood behind Shauna. He was at least six and a half feet tall, had to weigh close to four hundred pounds, and looked like a giant bear standing behind her. Wee Timmy Bixby.

"What say we join the lads inside, darling," Wee Timmy said and slapped Shauna Hanlon across her rear to get her moving.

FIFTY-ONE

They had just merged onto the M50, the six-lane highway that ringed Dublin. It had been close to an hour since they'd heard anything regarding the Emergency Response Unit. "We damn well should have heard something by now," Dillon said.

"Maybe it's a hostage situation," Suel said.

"Yeah, maybe."

"Or worse, shots fired, there's wounded, or God forbid, dead."

"Stay on the M50 to the Ballymun exit. We can take Ballymun into Phibsboro and get on the North Circular Road. Twenty minutes tops," Dillon said.

"Soon as we get off the M50, you put those flashing lights on the roof. That'll make up some time," Suel said.

Five minutes later, with the flashing lights on the roof of the car, Dillon squinted through mostly closed eyes as Suel wove in and out of traffic, swearing up a storm and leaning on the horn in an effort to get those not paying attention out of their way. Dillon prayed they didn't crash. They raced down Ballymun, which eventually merged into Mobhi Road and then Phibsboro road, all the while with Suel swearing at every second car on the road. As he took a right onto North Circular Drive, they were nearly broadsided at the intersection by a Dublin city bus. Suel fishtailed out of the way and raced down North Circular Drive toward number one-seventy-eight. A minute or two later, they could see the Emergency Response Unit's van parked just across the street from one-seventy-eight. Several officers, all dressed in black, two or three still wearing helmets and balaclavas, loitered casually along the front sidewalk. Some apparently sipping tea. Two news vans, RTE, and Virgin Media were parked on the street. The news crews appeared to be standing off to the side with a uniformed officer, probably the Garda Public Relations officer.

"Looks like it's over. I don't see any ambulances, thank God," Suel said. He pulled to the curb behind two squad cars and stopped. They climbed out of the car just as DCI McCabe stepped out the front door of one-seventy-eight and hurried down the steps. He stopped and said something to one of the men on the Emergency Response Team. The man shook his head and pointed down the street to where three squad cars were parked. McCabe didn't look happy. He spotted Dillon and Suel heading up the sidewalk toward him. He held his hand up, suggesting they wait a moment while he finished his conversation. He and the officer he was talking with seemed to be in a bit of a heated discussion for another minute or two before McCabe made his way toward Dillon and Suel.

"This isn't looking good," Suel said under his breath as a red-faced McCabe headed toward them.

"Everything okay, Sir?" Dillon asked as McCabe approached, wishing he'd kept his mouth shut before he'd even finished the question.

"Bloody hell. The bastards hit the wrong house."

"What?"

"You heard me. They hit the wrong bloody house. Someone, somewhere transposed the address number and instead of here at one-seventy-eight, they kicked in the door of one-eighty-seven. There'll be a hell of a re-pair bill, not to mention a lawsuit and all of it no doubt on the bloody news tonight," McCabe groaned and stared down the street at the news crews who seemed to be having a good laugh. Another news van was pulling to the curb, this one labeled BBC One. "Oh for the love of God," McCabe growled as he read the side of the van.

"You've got to be kidding," Suel said and nodded at the steps McCabe had just come down. "We went through this place top to bottom for three or four days just eight weeks ago. No one noticed that when they pulled up today?"

"Oh, not to worry. It gets worse."

"Worse?"

"The teams stationed in the alley were guarding the back of one-eighty-seven to make sure the innocent fam-ily, a mother and three little ones, didn't escape. Did I mention it's the home of the local council rep? I guess he's in there now asking what in God's name is going on and who's in charge. Who can blame him? Anyway, the team waved a car off and down the alley. A silver Range Rover, maybe a 2014. They got a brief look at the occupants. Sounds like the couple in the car was likely your man Brennan McDade and a woman, maybe the other American. The window in the back door to one-seventy-eight had been smashed in. I'm back to thinking thirty kilos confiscated two months ago was only a portion of the stash. They're in there doing a search now. They'll be lucky if they can find their own ass with both hands. Damn it. I'd be willing to bet that crazy bastard McDade just made off with the rest of the stash right from under our noses. Meanwhile, we've got our lads knocking in the door and storming a home a half-dozen doors down the way. Saint's preserve us."

Suel stood speechless.

"I don't believe this," Dillon said and pinched himself just to make sure he wasn't dreaming.

McCabe shook his head and growled through clenched teeth, "Bloody hell. I just thank God it was the ERU and not our lads. Some days, you can't make it up fast enough."

FIFTY-TWO

Brennan glanced in the rearview mirror for about the thousandth time to make sure they weren't being followed. He had stopped briefly in a roadside rest and put Megan back on the floor of the backseat. At least with the damaged ankle, now easily swollen to twice the size, and in the process of turning purple, he didn't have to worry about taping her legs together. He'd just had to bind her wrists with the tape. "I still don't understand how they knew. Your damn girlfriend must have told them. I knew leaving her at the hospital was a bad idea. This changes things completely."

Megan wasn't sure what his next move was going to be, but she certainly didn't like the sound of that last bit. "What could she tell them? She was unconscious the entire time. So, unless you left a note in her pocket with exact directions, there was nothing she would know. I was with you, and I'm still in the dark as to where we were. And that's another thing. The police obviously weren't even interested in where we were. They were going in that place a few doors away. I think it was just an unfortunate coincidence."

"But there were Garda all around. Did you even bother to look?"

"Yeah, and none of them were going to where we were. In fact, you said that one of them in the alley even waved at you to go the other way. They weren't after you, I mean us. They were going after someone else, and I think it was just an unfortunate coincidence we were there. Probably a good idea you left, you know, just to play it safe. But I don't think they were looking for you."

He seemed to think about that, and Megan figured it must have made some kind of sense to him because she could feel the car gradually slow back down closer to whatever the speed limit was. They drove on for an interminable amount of time. At some point, Megan drifted off to sleep despite her throbbing ankle. When she woke, she glanced out the side window and stared at what looked like the top of a gas pump. The sign above the convenience store read 'Topaz.' He must be filling up the car, she thought and figured this might be the best place to try and make a break for it. There were people around. If she could run into the station, she could cry for help. Maybe it would be enough to frighten Brennan, and he would flee the scene in the car.

She gritted her teeth. Since her wrists were taped, she half-turned and placed both arms on the backseat. Excruciating pain shot through her ankle and up her leg. She bit her lower lip to quiet her groan. She attempted to lift herself onto the backseat and was halfway up when her arms gave way, and she slipped back to the floor.

This time, the pain nearly caused her to vomit, and she laid back down, taking in deep breaths to settle her stomach.

The driver's door suddenly opened, and Brennan slid in behind the wheel. "Here, thought you might need something to eat," he said. His hand reached over the seat and dropped a white paper bag onto her thighs. She opened the bag and looked inside. There was a sandwich, possibly chicken salad on white bread. The sandwich was cut in half and sat in a little triangular plastic package. Next to it was what looked like a candy bar in a red and yellow striped foil wrapper. The words 'Chocolate Carmel Wafer Bar' were printed across the front.

"Oh, thanks," she said.

"My pleasure," he said and started the car.

She couldn't tell if he was joking, and frankly, she was so hungry she didn't care. Under normal circumstances, she would have never, ever taken even a bite out of the sandwich. God only knew how long it had sat on the shelf in the convenience store, but then, these were not normal times. She devoured both halves of the sandwich in about six bites. She tore open the foil wrapper on the candy bar using her teeth and devoured that in two bites.

"Oh, thank you. I was starving."

"Well, like I said, you help me find where they hid the rest of that stash, and I'll put you up in the fanciest hotel, buy you an expensive car, and we'll celebrate with a steak dinner. As much as you can eat."

"Sounds wonderful," she said and rubbed the front pocket of her jeans to make sure the sharpened spoon was still there.

FIFTY-THREE

Wee Timmy said, "So, what you're telling me is you don't have the money to pay me. Now, according to my calculations, that means I'm out six million euros. And apparently, I'm simply supposed to grab my ankles and be patient and understanding. Is that about right?"

"Well, actually, sir, it's not quite six million. I think the estimate for your share was closer to just three million. If you don't mind me saying," Mickey said.

They were all arranged in Cormac's sitting room. Well, almost all of them. Wee Timmy sat in the faded orange wingback chair. The chair with the stuffing coming out on both arms. Shauna Hanlon, Petey, Mickey, and Toby were all crammed together on the couch facing Wee Timmy and not looking very happy. Cormac remained face down on the bed directly above the sitting room. He was still dead. Wee Timmy's two thugs stood on either side of the couch, holding their pistols and looking rather pissed off.

"You know, Mickey, you're right, and good for you for setting the example." Wee Timmy nodded at the thug with the shaved head and the massive biceps. "Mickey's setting the example for the others, Dermot. Perhaps you might be able to help him out."

Dermot didn't blink, smile, or nod. He simply aimed his pistol and fired, sending a round through Mickey's left foot. Mickey screamed as he fell off the couch, grabbed his foot, and rolled from side to side.

"Excellent," Wee Timmy said. "I have to say, much better than I expected. Now, would anyone else care to set an example? Good, I didn't think so. Sit that bollocks back up."

Dermot tucked his pistol into his belt, reached down, effortlessly pulled Mickey up off the floor, and half-tossed him on top of Toby.

"Now, Mickey," Wee Timmy continued. "best to quiet down. I hate to be interrupted. Shauna, I believe we were discussing exactly how you intend to pay me six million euros. I'm still waiting for any ideas."

Toby continued to sob silently. Petey frowned but didn't say anything. Mickey bit his tongue and tried to breathe through his nose, hoping he could remain quiet.

Shauna said, "That's exactly what we were in the process of trying to do, Mr. Bixby. Get you paid, in full, I hasten to add."

"And pray tell, how did you intend to come up with the funds? Don't tell me a personal check from your man upstairs in the bedroom."

"No, sir. Cormac was simply an intermediate connection. Unfortunately, crazy Brennan McDade killed him before we had the opportunity to discuss any of this

with him. Crazy Brennan has been making things diffi-
cult all along, and he's the real reason we've been unable
to pay you."

Wee Timmy turned his attention to Toby. "Is that
true? Your cousin killed our man upstairs, and in doing
so, eliminated the opportunity to find out where, exactly,
Crazy Brennan was going to take possession of my product?"

"Well, maybe not exactly, sir."

"Tell me more," Wee Timmy said and leaned forward. The wingback chair creaked but fortunately continued to hold Wee Timmy's four hundred pounds.

"See, he brought this girl, um, two girls. Yeah, two
American girls. They were the ones what testified
against the Sands brothers. The ones who partied with
them and then told the Guards everything. Anyway, they
showed up in Mullingar, and I got in touch with Brennan.
We thought, if we could grab them, and you know, bring
them to you or find out what they knew, then we could
tell you, right away like. Then you'd be able to get at
least some of your product back, and things would be
just fine. Kind of. Maybe."

"And where are they now? The two American girls
who are supposed to know where the product is."

"See that's just it. We don't really know. I mean
they're both with Brennan, I think. But we don't have
any idea where he is, and Cormac, your man upstairs, he
probably knew. But as you said, it's not like he's going
to be doing any talking, you know," Toby said and

started to laugh. He stopped laughing almost immediately when no one else joined in, especially Wee Timmy.

"Um, sir, I think he was going to go to the Dublin house the Sands brothers stayed in because one of the girls said they knew where the stash was, but being Americans, they didn't know street names or anything. But if he got 'em back to the house, they could probably show him where everything was hidden."

"All right. Thank you. Now there, was that so hard? So, Crazy Brennan is going to where the Sands brothers stayed, and he's going to find the remainder of the product and turn it over to me, correct?"

Toby nodded vigorously. "Yes, sir. At least I hope so."

"He's going to the house where they partied themselves right into Mountjoy. And of course, we all know what happened to them in Mountjoy, now don't we?" Wee Timmy said.

"I'll take credit for that, sir," Shauna said. "Since they were the ones who caused this whole disaster in the first place. Getting caught. Having some of your product confiscated. I thought it only fitting we put the word out. That type of behavior simply won't be tolerated."

"I see. So, in other words, you made sure they wouldn't try to cop a plea bargain with the Garda by telling anyone where the rest of the stash was hidden."

"That's right. I made the decision, and I take full responsibility."

Wee Timmy nodded. "So if I'm understanding what you just said, you gave the order to make sure the Sands brothers didn't tell anyone, especially the Garda, where the rest of the product was hidden."

"I knew they planned to use that information to get their sentences reduced, maybe even time off for good behavior if they talked to the right people." Shauna grinned, having laid out the scenario where she'd saved the day.

"I see, and the end result is?"

"The end result? Well, I just told you. The stash is still out there."

"True. Somewhere. Of course, the two individuals who could have told us aren't talking. Compliments of you putting out the word. And Crazy Brendan McDade has two women with him who might know where it's hidden. And unfortunately, I still come back to the same bottom line. I'm out six million euros."

"But I—"

"Shauna, do you have six million euros for me?"

"Well no, not yet, but I—"

"Please, stop. Mickey do you have six million euros for me?"

Mickey just stared down at his bloody foot. He could hear his shoe squish as he moved his foot, and he simply groaned.

"Petey, I don't suppose you—"

"Now wait a minute, sir. Please, I'm just the damn driver here."

"Yeah, I suppose you're right. Toby," Wee Timmy sighed. "I'm not even going to ask." The chair creaked loudly as he rose to his feet. He looked to his two henchmen and shook his head. "All right, they don't know anything else. Might as well send them on their way. I'll be out in the car."

The four on the couch all seemed to breathe a sigh of relief. Dermot took a step forward and waited for Wee Timmy to close the door behind him. Once the door slammed shut, he nodded at his partner, and they both raised their pistols.

FIFTY-FOUR

When McCabe finally drove off, Dillon and Suel climbed the steps up to one-seventy-eight and went inside. Five officers were standing in the front hallway, two dressed in Emergency Response Unit black, none of the five looked to be doing anything.

It had been the better part of two months since Dillon and Suel had been in the place, and nothing much had changed, other than various piles of items pulled off bookshelves or dumped out of drawers and spread around. They knew their way and quickly hurried into the kitchen, nodding at various officers as they passed and getting blank stares in response.

Once in the kitchen, they took in the room with a quick glance, ignored the two officers leaning against the center island sipping tea, and walked toward the back door. There wasn't much to see other than the broken window in the back door and the bits of glass on the floor.

Dillon looked at the door. "I'm presuming it's a safe bet this is the work of Crazy Brennan McDade. Break the window, reach in, turn the lock, and step inside. Maybe took him all of about thirty seconds."

"If even that long," Suel said, looking around the back hall. "It still surprises me there isn't an alarm system in here. Expensive books, nice kitchen, if I remember, the bedrooms upstairs were pretty high class."

"They ever determine who owns it?" Dillon asked.

"Seems to me, during the investigation, they tried to check into whoever owned the place but ran into all sorts of shell companies across eastern Europe and Russia or someplace. I don't believe they've ever determined who it is, leastways not yet. Rest assured, it's some rich bastard who's got enough money not to have to pay any bleedin' taxes."

"You know, if it was McDade they waved down the alley—"

"I'd say that's a pretty sure bet," Suel said, shaking his head.

"So maybe he's staying here, sees the activity outside, gets in his car and hightails it down the alley."

"Why the hell would he come back here in the first place? Why not just get a hotel, and what's up with bringing the woman along?"

"He brought her because he still thinks she's one of the women who were with the Sands brothers."

"But she's not."

"Yeah, we know that, but he doesn't."

"But why wouldn't . . ." Suel seemed to think for a moment.

"Yeah," Dillon said. "She's somehow convinced him she's one of those girls. She's American. They have the same first names. A redhead and a blonde. The only thing that's keeping her alive is convincing him she's one of those two women."

"But why? Isn't there a price on their head? The Americans."

"Maybe, but like McCabe said. He's thinking there's another stash somewhere. Maybe here. Maybe she's convinced Crazy Brennan she knows where. They're here to find it when the ERU shows up. Just luck of the draw they end up going to the wrong house. Crazy Brennan runs out of time here and drives away empty-handed."

"Meaning he's liable to come back," Suel said.

"That's exactly what I'm thinking."

FIFTY-FIVE

Dillon and Suel were seated in McCabe's office. McCabe sat behind his desk with his tie loosened and his sleeves rolled up to his elbows. His tea mug was partially filled with water, and there was a bottle of Ibuprofen standing next to it. The cap was off the bottle of Ibuprofen.

McCabe was leaning back in his chair, rubbing his face with both hands. He looked exhausted. "So let me get this straight. Your plan is to stake out this place on North Circular Road in the hopes that this Crazy Brennan McDade character will, at some point, return. At which time, you can place him under arrest and rescue the American girl. Exactly how many individuals do you plan on using? And just how long do you think it will be before he decides to return?"

"Actually sir, we weren't planning on using anyone but ourselves," Dillon said.

"Yourselves? Just the two of ye?"

"Yes, sir."

"One out front and one in back? You planning to close your eyes at any time or is the idea to simply to go without sleep for seventy-two hours?"

"We were planning to remain inside the unit, sir. We can establish a temporary alarm at the front and back doors, maybe another on the staircase, and we'll remain out of sight upstairs in one of the bedrooms. Unless I'm mistaken, Brennan McDade has no other option but to return to the unit and seek out the remainder of that stash. He can't return to Mullingar. They're looking for him. He's bypassed the Hanlon organization, tried to pull a fast one on them, which hasn't worked. I'm guessing he's not at the top of the list with Wee Timmy Bixby. It would seem he's quickly running out of options. He's basically living on borrowed time unless he finds this stash and offers to get it to Wee Timmy Bixby in return for protection."

McCabe drummed his fingers on the desk. "And you'd remain inside the unit?"

"Yes, sir."

"When would you start?"

"Just as soon as the ERU and the investigators are ready to clear out. Ideally, I'd like to go in just as they're about to leave. In the event Brennan McDade somehow has his eyes on the place, hopefully he'd lose the likes of us in the shuffle of people leaving."

"Just the two of you?"

"Yes, sir."

"Let me make a call. Suel, I'll list you as the point of contact. I'll have them contact you one hour before they're ready to depart, which means you'd better prepare to receive that call shortly. I suggest you hurry and get ready," McCabe said and picked up his phone. He dialed a number and nodded at the office door, indicating they were dismissed.

"I'm home to pack a quick bag," Suel said.

"Likewise. We'll drive our own cars over." Dillon said. "No point in alerting anyone with a squad parked down the block."

Dillon raced home and quickly packed a small bag. He hurried across the street and rang Tara's doorbell. She answered dressed in short shorts and a small bikini top. She smiled when she saw it was Dillon. "Well, Mr. Dillon, perfect timing. I was just about to open a bottle of wine. Care to come in?"

"Thank you, Tara. God knows I'd love to, but I'm going to be working through the night and possibly the next few days. I'm wondering if I could ask a favor."

"Sure, you need a lift back to the station."

"No, not that I wouldn't like it. I'm wondering if you wouldn't mind letting Lucifer out over the next couple of days and just making sure he has food and water. I can leave everything out for you. You can just let him out once in the morning and again in the evening. Toss a biscuit out the door to get him outside. You don't have to clean up any mess he makes in the house and just leave the pooh in the front garden. I'll deal with it when I'm home."

"Well, um, yes, I suppose I can. You sure it wouldn't be better if you brought him over here and I could just watch him?"

"That's very nice of you, but believe me, you don't want that."

"Well, yeah, I guess I can. Morning and night, you're sure that's all?"

Dillon nodded and handed her the spare key to his front door. "Thank you so much. Twice a day is all he needs. Saves me the trouble of having to ask next door. I owe you a dinner out."

"Ask next door? You don't mean, Deitora do you?"

"Yeah, 'fraid so."

"Good lord, she'd have the poor little thing cooked in a stew and feed him to you. No, don't be asking her for anything."

"Thanks so much. I really appreciate the help."

"Not a problem. You just mind yourself and stay safe. Feel free to call anytime to check on him. On the both of us, for that matter."

"Thanks so much, Tara."

"Go on now, get. You said enough thanks for one day."

He hurried home, set Lucifer's food and water dish alongside the front door. He carried a kitchen chair into the front entry and placed the bag of dog food on the chair. He double-checked the lock on the doors leading out to the patio in the back, pulled the shade halfway down over the doors, and hurried out to his car.

He was back at the station in twenty minutes and up in the Special Branch office. A toll booth report from twenty-four hours earlier had come through. The silver

Range Rover registered to Brennan McDade had passed through the toll booth on the M50, which meant Brennan's credit card account would be debited for the toll payment of six euros fifty.

"Just in case we had any questions, for sure, the plonker is up here in Dublin," Suel said.

"I know it's going to take some time, but let's start the paperwork to have that credit card account frozen. We can use the kidnapping of Kate Murray and Megan Gaffney, add on the attempted murder of Kate. Hopefully, we'll be able to freeze all his assets."

"Only until now we really didn't have enough evidence, certainly just hearsay. I'm not even sure we've enough solid evidence now," Suel said. "Other than he paid a toll on the M50, it's largely speculation."

Dillon's cellphone rang, and he pulled it out of his pocket. "It's Turley," he said and answered. "Hi Eamon, what's the news?"

"She's awake, the Murray woman. Not much to remember other than she thought they met your man Toby McDade at the Swordsman Pub. He bought them drinks, no indication they were drugged. She thought they were following him to McGovern's Guest House B&B, but they ended up in some abandoned, rundown place. No doubt where we found that first shoe. At least at this time, she doesn't recall anything else. There's a chance it may come back to her over the next while. I only got a minute or two with her. She asked about her friend Megan Gaffney. She's no recollection of how she got to the hospital."

"She never mentioned Brennan McDade?"

"No. I asked her, and she had no idea who I was talking about. Gave her a brief description, hoping it might trigger something but no luck. Any luck in Dublin?"

"Unfortunately, it looks like we're back to grasping at straws." Dillon went on to describe the botched ERU action.

"Say it ain't so. The wrong damn address? Who the hell did that? On second thought, best not to tell me. It's better I don't know. So what's the plan?"

"We're going to stake out the house. Hope maybe Crazy Brennan will make another try to search the place for the rest of the stash, and we can nab him. Be interesting if he does. There are teams in there now turning the place inside out."

"Well, let me know if there's anything we can do from here. We've got the McDade estate locked down, literally. Your man heads back this way, and we'll know. Oh, one other bit of information. The blood on the kitchen floor and the fingers."

"What about them?"

"DNA results say they belong to a male."

"A male?"

"Yeah, so I guess the good news is the other American woman, Megan Gaffney, at least seems to still be in possession of all her fingers."

"A male? Who could that be? And then the next question would be, why? You think they could belong to Crazy Brennan?"

"They're looking into that as we speak. I hear anything, I'll pass it on. We've been lucky so far, the media hasn't jumped on this yet, but I don't see our luck holding for another twenty-four hours. They'll be all over this sooner rather than later."

"Well, they were lining up on North Circular Road when we left. That fiasco is bound to be all over the news, probably is already. I just haven't had the heart to look. We can only hope they report on the wrong address fiasco and not the fact they should have been a few doors down. That part comes out, and it will pretty much end the slim chance we have."

Suel's desk phone rang. "It's McCabe," he said to Dillon before he picked up the phone. "Yes, sir."

"I think the alert just came through. We have to get back down to North Circular Road. Keep us in loop. Anything comes up, let us know. Gotta go," Dillon said and disconnected with Turley.

"Sounds like they're just finishing up, so we'd better get over there," Suel said.

"They find anything?"

"No. They tore the hell out of the place and managed to come up empty-handed."

"I guess we'll see soon enough," Dillon said, and they headed out the door.

FIFTY-SIX

McCabe informed them that a unit just four doors down from one-seventy-eight was up for sale and unoccupied at the moment. Suel pulled around back, parked behind that unit then made his way over to one-seventy-eight, up the steps and in through the back door. Dillon parked a couple of doors down and out on the street. He headed for the front door. He was carrying a small backpack with a change of clothes and toiletries. Experience had taught him to bring a roll of toilet paper just in case. As he climbed the stairs, two uniformed officers he recognized but forgot their names stepped out the front door and headed down the stairs.

"Enjoy yourself," one of them said.

"Charming place," the other said, and they both laughed.

Dillon headed inside. The first thing he noticed was a length of floorboards pulled up in the hall from the front door all the way back to the kitchen. Obviously, the word had gone out to search the place for the suspected kilos. There was a room on either side of the hallway. Both rooms had a fireplace and an elaborate mantel with a beveled glass mirror above the fireplace. Floorboards had been pulled up along the length of both rooms. The smaller of the two rooms had a built-in floor to ceiling bookcase against the end wall. The books were now piled on the floor, not neatly stacked but dumped in three separate mounds. The paneled back of the bookcase featured a large, recently cut hole in it maybe every ten inches or so. A doorway next to the bookcase led into the dining room. Once again, floorboards along the length of the room had been torn up. An antique dining room table sat in the middle of the room. It appeared to be mahogany, but Dillon was too busy focusing on the dusty footprints across the surface of the table. A crystal chandelier that had been torn out of the ceiling now rested on the table.

He walked back out to the hallway and entered the kitchen. Suel stood in the middle of the kitchen, taking in the damage. The dishwasher had been disconnected, and along with the stove and refrigerator, had been pulled out and away from the wall. Cabinet doors hung at odd angles, and the countertops were covered with stacks of china plates, dishes, and cups. The remnants of three or four plates lay in a pile on the floor along with what used to be three stemmed crystal glasses.

"They've absolutely destroyed this place," Suel said, slowly turning around and taking it all in.

"You should see the front rooms, same thing. Someone's going to end up on the hook for this, and heads are bound to roll."

Suel pulled out his cellphone and started taking pictures.

"What are you doing?" Dillon asked.

"Making sure you and I aren't the ones who catch the blame for this."

FIFTY-SEVEN

It was well after midnight when Brennan pulled to the curb across the street from one-seventy-eight. From the floor of the rear seat, Megan could see the second story windows of the house but didn't know where they were exactly. This was the third or fourth place they'd stopped and then sat for maybe thirty minutes before driving off.

Brennan sat and studied the house for the next ten minutes, no police tape, no lights on, no squad cars on the street. He wondered what all the fuss had been earlier in the day then decided it didn't make any difference. He had to find the remaining kilos before anyone else did. He turned the engine back on, headed down the block, and took a right. He turned into the alley and slowly cruised down toward one-seventy-eight.

Most of the lights were off in the houses he passed. If a light was on, invariably it was the kitchen light. The two houses before one-seventy-eight were completely dark. The clamped Mercedes was the only vehicle parked behind one-seventy-eight. Brennan turned off his lights and pulled into the open space next to the Mercedes. He sat and studied the back door and the windows for a good five minutes. The door appeared just as he had left it, a gaping open window where the glass used to be. He reached into the glove compartment, took out a small flashlight, and climbed out of the car. He opened the back door and reached down to pull Megan.

"No wait, please don't," Megan said and kicked with her good foot. "My ankle, it really hurts. If you can just help me up onto the seat, I can get out. I think I can walk, but I'm not sure."

Brennan mumbled something and hurried around to the other side of the car.

Megan was sitting up on the floor when he opened the door. "Just help me up onto the seat."

Brennan placed his hands under her arms and lifted her up. Megan placed her arms on the backseat and pushed, at the same time using her good leg to lift her body. She shuffled across the seat and was finally able to sit.

"Oh, God, that hurts. My ankle is killing me."

"Well, come on. We have to hurry and get inside."

"I don't know if I can make it. It would be a lot easier with this tape off my wrists."

He seemed to think about that for a moment and then struggled with the tape before unwrapping it and tossing it on the ground behind him. He took hold of Megan's legs and swung them out of the rear door and helped her up onto her feet.

She took a half-step and nearly fell. "Oh, God, that hurts. I don't know," she said, looking at the staircase leading up to the back door.

"Put your arm over my shoulder, and I'll help you up. We have to get inside."

She wrapped her arm around his shoulder, thought for just a second about choking him but realized she couldn't. They stepped off together and slowly made it to the steps leading up to the back door.

"Okay, you hang onto the railing with your free hand. We'll take the steps one at a time."

They finally made it up to the top of the staircase. Brennan tried the door, but it was locked. "Damn it. Okay, hold onto the railing. I'm going to unlock the door," he said. Once Megan had both hands clutching the railing, he reached in through the broken window, unsnapped the lock, and pulled the back door open. He took hold of Megan's arm, draped it over his shoulder, and together they hobbled into the back entrance. Brennan let the door slam closed behind them.

FIFTY-EIGHT

Dillon whispered, "Did you hear that?"

Suel nodded and pulled his pistol out of his belt. They had been sitting on the floor upstairs in the master bedroom reading internet articles on their cellphones. The bed had been torn apart, and the upholstered chair sitting in front of the window had been slit open by the previous crew's vain attempt to find drugs.

"Check it out?" Suel said.

Dillon placed a finger to his lips, signaling to be quiet, and picked up the pistol lying next to him on the floor. They sat there with their ears perked for a minute. It seemed like an hour.

Downstairs, Brennan and Megan stood in the kitchen. Megan had both hands on the kitchen counter for support as she balanced the majority of her weight on her left leg. Her right ankle was throbbing after the climb up the back steps.

Brennan was slowly running the flashlight over torn cabinet doors, broken plates and glasses, and the floorboards pulled up. "What the hell?"

"It looks a lot different than the last time we were here. Who did this? Who trashed the place?" Megan said.

"It had to be the Guards. They're the only ones who could have done this. It's a good thing we left when we did."

"But why?" Megan said.

"Why? Same reason we're here. They were looking for the kilos. They know there's more to that shipment besides what they already confiscated. The difference is they obviously don't know where it is, and you do. So let's get going. The sooner you show me where it is, the sooner we can get the hell out of here."

"I can't remember where exactly. But it was a room, painted white. Somewhere upstairs, and it was all hidden in the ceiling," Megan said, hoping her story sounded somewhat credible.

"A room upstairs painted white?"

"Yeah, yeah, upstairs."

"They're all white, bitch," Brennan yelled and slapped her hard.

"But this was a small room," she screamed back. "A little room and the ceiling had tiles or something, so it was easy to stash things above the ceiling."

"Show me where it is now or so help me," Brennan shouted.

"I told you I can't walk because I think I've got a broken ankle. It's broken because you pulled me down the stairs."

"I didn't pull you. You were dragging your ass, and I just helped you along. You wouldn't have fallen if you weren't such a clumsy cow. Now you're gonna—"

"I think we've heard just about enough from you, McDade," Dillon said and stepped into the kitchen with his pistol aimed between Crazy Brennan's eyes. Suel stepped out from behind Dillon and moved to the left.

"You can put the gun down, McDade. Just lay it on the counter, nice and easy like."

Crazy Brennan seemed to be thinking as he glanced at Dillon and then Suel.

"You heard your man, Brennan. Put the gun down, so no one gets hurt. We've got a team outside, front and back," Suel lied.

Brennan suddenly grabbed Megan by the hair, pulling her in front of him.

"Aww, my ankle, my ankle. Stop it, Brennan, stop it, please."

Brennan pressed his pistol up against Megan's neck. "Okay, who wants to be first. Which one of you's is gonna make me pull this trigger? Which one of you's is going to get the blame for making me kill this American slapper."

"Brennan, just calm down. No one needs to get hurt here. But we can't let you go, and you're safer here with us than with all the lads outside. So why don't you just put your gun down and we can make sure everything is okay. Brennan, you listening? We want to help you."

"Yeah, I'm listening, and I got news for the likes of you two. Why don't you's put your guns down and tell everyone else to do the same before your woman here gets killed, and it'll be your damn fault. And you know what else?"

Megan had slowly reached inside her pocket and taken hold of the sharpened spoon. She cautiously pulled it out, shot her arm up, knocking Brennan's pistol off her neck. As she dropped to the floor, she raised her arm to stab him in the thigh with the spoon, but Brennan moved and instead, she stabbed him in the crotch.

Brennan got off half a scream before Dillon shot him in the head, and Suel pumped two rounds into his chest. All three shots were kill shots.

Dillon lifted Megan up off the floor and carried her into the dining room. As he hurried out of the kitchen, he kept telling her, "You're all right. Everything is okay. You're okay, Megan. You're okay."

"Is Kate all right? I want to see, Kate. Where is Kate?" Was all she kept saying.

FIFTY-NINE

It was after two in the morning before Dillon and Suel had finished giving their statements. DCI McCabe congratulated them and suggested it might be a good idea if they went back to Special Branch, filled out their reports, and went home. They'd be on administrative leave with pay pending the standard follow-up investigation.

By four in the morning, the last of the technical team had left one-seventy-eight.

At five, Dermot knocked on the car window. Wee Timmy Bixby lowered the window and said, "Anyone?"

"No, sir. They've all cleared out. I checked the front and back, not a soul around. Tow truck left fifteen minutes ago with the Range Rover. Neighbors are all still asleep."

"And the Mercedes?"

Dermot grinned and said, "Still clamped and resting peacefully."

"All right. Hop in and let's go."

Dermot climbed into the front passenger seat, and they drove down the block, took a right, and then another right heading down the alley. They backed partway into the empty space where Crazy Brennan's Range Rover had been parked. Dermot hopped out of the passenger seat and walked over to the back of the Mercedes. He gave a quick look around before he pushed the button on the Sawzall, a tool that did just that, sawed through everything. He slipped the blade beneath the lid on the trunk of the Mercedes. His partner stepped out from behind the wheel, holding a pry bar. As soon as Dermot finished with the Sawzall, the pry bar was inserted, and after three or four forceful tugs, the lid on the trunk flew up revealing thirty-five kilos of cocaine. Dermot quickly loaded the kilos into the trunk of Wee Timmy's vehicle, closed the lid on the trunk, and the moment he hopped back in they drove off down the alley. None of the neighbors ever woke.

SIXTY

Dillon arrived home at a little after six in the morning. He made his way around three piles, compliments of Lucifer, and unlocked the front door. The bag of dog food he'd placed on the chair had been knocked down onto the floor. Dog food was scattered from one end of the front entry to the other. The chair lay on its side. He cleared a path through the dog food to the kitchen using his foot and pulled a biscuit from the cookie jar.

He stood at the landing heading upstairs and called to Lucifer. On the third call, he heard him jump off the bed and land on the floor. A moment later, Lucifer peeked around the upstairs newel post.

"Come on, boy, treat. Outside. Treat. Outside."

Lucifer seemed to consider his options for a moment then hurried down the stairs and waited at the door. Dillon tossed the biscuit out the door then headed into the kitchen for the broom.

Once Lucifer was back inside, Dillon set his alarm for two hours and went to bed. When the alarm went off, he headed into the shower. He shaved and splashed on some aftershave. He pulled on a clean pair of jeans and a sport shirt, checked himself in the mirror, grabbed a bottle of Prosecco, and headed across the street to Tara's.

He rang the doorbell and waited. Her car sat in the drive, and after a couple of minutes, he was about to knock when the door opened. Tara stood before him with two black eyes, a bandage over the bridge of her nose and a gauze bandage wrapped around her ankle.

"Tara?"

She glared at him. "You have the meanest little dog I've ever met. He bit me," she said and lifted her ankle. "I fell onto that chair and broke my nose. No thanks to you. This will do nicely," she said, grabbed the bottle of Prosecco from his hands, and slammed the door.

SIXTY-ONE

The following morning Eric Bergman, pulled to a stop in front of St. James hospital. "You ready for this?" Dillon said to Bergman.

"Yeah, let me grab that stuff out of the backseat," Bergman said. He climbed out of the car, opened the rear door, and pulled out a small black suitcase.

"Maybe take the price tag off the handle," Dillon said.

"Huh? Oh yeah. The wife went out and got all this. If you or I did it, they probably wouldn't be seen in public with whatever we picked out."

They walked into the hospital and took the elevator up to the third floor then followed a maze of hallways to a nurse's desk. "An Garda Síochána, Special Branch," Dillon said. He smiled and flashed his badge and ID.

"Eric Bergman, American Embassy," Bergman said. He didn't show any ID.

"Is it all right to go in?" Dillon asked. He indicated the closed door to the hospital room.

"I'm sure it is, but let me just check," the nurse said. Her name tag said Nora. She was wearing powder blue hospital scrubs. Dillon had met her the day before. She walked around the counter and opened the door, poking her head in. "Megan? You've visitors, honey. Your man from An Garda Síochána. You doing okay? Good. Okay, I'll send them in." She left the door partially open. "Yes, lads. You can go on in," she said, walking back behind the nurse's station.

"How's she doing?" Dillon asked.

"After all's she's been through, I'd say very well. Long phone conversation with her friend down in Mullingar."

"Kate Murray," Dillon said.

"Yes, that's the one."

"She need to fill out some paperwork or anything?"

"No, I'll have to get your signature on some forms, and I need to burn a copy of your ID, both of you's. Then we'll get a wheelchair, and you can take her out."

"A wheelchair? Is she—"

"Not to worry. Technically, she doesn't need one, but it's policy. Go on in, she's eager to get out of here, and who can blame her?"

Dillon knocked on the door and opened it a little further. "Hi Megan, you ready to escape?"

Her red hair was pulled back in a ponytail. She was dressed in jeans with a torn knee and a wrinkled, stained top. She wore a grey plastic support boot on her right ankle. "You kidding? I've been waiting since sunrise. Yeah, let's go."

Dillon stepped into the room. Bergman followed. Megan immediately focused on Bergman and the black suitcase.

"Megan, this is Eric Bergman. He's with the American Embassy."

"Hi, Megan. I brought a suitcase for you. My wife picked out some outfits for you and Kate. She said you might not want to be traveling in the same things you've been wearing for the past week."

Megan's eyes grew wide, and she smiled. "Oh, thank you. That's wonderful. They're in the suitcase? The outfits?"

"Yeah," Bergman said. He set the suitcase on a visitor's chair and opened it. "I don't know what belongs to who, but you've got first choice."

"Can you give me just a minute while I change?"

"Not a problem. We've got some forms to sign out at the nurse's station. Take your time," Dillon said.

They stepped back into the hall, and Bergman closed the door behind them. They signed the hospital forms while the nurse burned copies of their ID's. When Megan stepped out of the room, her hair was freshly brushed and hung down to her shoulders. She had makeup on, and there was the slightest hint of perfume.

"All set?" the nurse asked.

"Yes. No offense, but I can't wait to get outside. Thank you for everything you've . . . ." Megan's voice cracked, and a tear began to run down her cheek.

"Oh, sweetie, we're all just glad you're safe. You go and give a big hug to your friend Kate from all of us," Nora said as she wrapped her arms around Megan. Two other nurses suddenly appeared and hugged Megan.

"Now, hospital policy. You hop in this wheelchair, and the lads will take you out. We're all saying a prayer for you and Kate. Safe journey, darling."

"Thank you. Thanks to all of you," Megan said. She hopped into the wheelchair and looked up at Dillon. "Come on. Let's go."

Dillon laughed and pushed her down to the elevator. Bergman followed carrying the suitcase.

The ride out to Mullingar was mostly quiet. Megan stared out the window, apparently deep in thought, and didn't say much. Dillon caught her staring as they passed the Swordsman pub. She turned in the seat as they drove past and stared out the rear window until it disappeared from sight.

"We'll be at Midlands Regional in just a few minutes," Dillon said.

They drove past the white sign with the blue letters. Megan turned her head so she wouldn't have to look at it. They parked in front of Midlands Regional Hospital, at the opposite end from the ER. Dillon hopped out and opened the door for Megan while Bergman grabbed the suitcase. They headed toward the same door Toby McDade had exited from a few nights earlier. They moved through the revolving door and met DI Turley on the other side. He shook hands with Dillon, introduced himself to Megan and then introduced Mullingar Chief of Police, Niall O'Donnell.

Megan smiled, nodded, and looked past O'Donnell, obviously anxious to link up with Kate for the first time in almost a week.

"Megan." O'Donnell smiled, picking up on her anticipation. "If you'll follow me, I've got an elevator standing by, and we can rush you up to see Miss Murray. She's doing very well, by the way, and is just as anxious to see you." He extended his hand in the direction of the hall heading off the reception area. Megan grinned and hurried around the corner. Sure enough, there was a uniformed officer holding an elevator for them. They took the elevator up to the second floor. O'Donnell stepped off and pointed Megan in the right direction. "Room 206," he said. "You go ahead."

Megan looked at him for a brief moment and said a quick, "Thank you." She took four or five quick steps before she started quickly hobbling wearing the boot. "Kate. Kate. Kate," she kept calling until she disappeared into a room. Shrieks and squeals followed.

They spent a total of forty minutes in the room, Kate and Megan. O'Donnell managed to get two photos of him with both girls before the men were shooed from the room, so Kate could slip into new clothes. The girls finally exited the room, smiling. Kate looked good, considering the split lip still healing and the eye, no longer swollen but still discolored with a brownish tone fading to yellow. The fresh makeup more or less covered it.

They were both wheeled out of the hospital by O'Donnell and a uniformed officer. Dillon, Turley, and Bergman, carrying the suitcase, followed closely behind along with three doctors and a handful of nurses. Local media were there filming, taking pictures, and asking for comments. Everyone shared polite goodbyes and thank you's for a couple of minutes. O'Donnell managed to scam two more photos before they drove off. Once they departed, he turned to address the media.

With Bergman behind the wheel, driving close to twenty miles over the speed limit, Dillon and the girls made it to Dublin airport in record time. The girls never stopped hugging one another the entire way.

Bergman parked behind Terminal Two, and they took the girls through a secure entrance to a private room where security simply gave them a nod. Dillon escorted the girls onto the plane and their first-class seats, compliments of Aer Lingus airlines. Once they were settled, he took his seat back in the coach section.

It was an eight-hour, direct flight to Minneapolis-St. Paul. At the captain's instruction, the passengers remained seated so Dillon and the girls would be the first ones off the flight. Dillon delivered them to smiling, tear-stained families.

"You're the American, the one who saved Megan's life. I can't tell you how much . . . ." Megan's father started to say but quickly choked up, began crying, and never did finish.

SIXTY-TWO

Dillon remained in the airport. He phoned two friends and a cousin but ended up leaving a voice message on all three calls. He sat at the gate for the next three hours before boarding his return flight once they called rows twenty-nine and above in the coach section. It was nearly an eight-hour return flight back to Dublin, and he drifted off to sleep twice, only to wake himself with his snoring. The flight arrived in Dublin at 7:45 in the morning. He was able to clear passport control by flashing his IDs after being led past a line of a few hundred people in the process of queuing up for passport control.

Suel was waiting for him outside the airport. Twenty minutes later, they were sitting in DCI McCabe's office. Both of them had just been taken off administrative leave and restored to full status, standard procedure after the shooting of Crazy Brennan McDade.

"Tired?" McCabe said, looking at Dillon. His eyes were puffy, he was in need of a shave, and his suit was wrinkled from the past twenty-four hours.

"I'll be fine, sir," Dillon said.

"Yes, you will because once we're finished here, I'm sending you home to get some sleep. Over to the States and back in less than twenty-four hours. God save us."

Suel was in the process of reading through a copy of the pending lawsuit that had been placed on McCabe's desk.

"Bloody hell. A million-euro lawsuit for emotional stress to the young family when their doors were battered in. Seems a bit much."

"Well, her husband sits on the Dublin council. A million euros, compared to the threatened media coverage, sounds like we might be getting off easy," McCabe said.

"And five hundred thousand euros for the damage to one-seventy-eight? Christ on a cross. They were searching for drugs," Suel groaned.

"They tore the place apart looking for the drugs. Pulled up the floors, unhooked appliances, tore light fixtures from the ceiling. And after all that, they didn't find a damn thing. Once again, more potential for a lot of bad publicity. It'll be interesting to see, but I wouldn't be at all surprised if they pay up and pray everything remains more or less quiet. Now you two weren't involved in any of that damage, were you?" McCabe said.

"No sir, well, other than a small hole in the wall," Suel said.

"Actually, three holes, sir," Dillon replied.

EPILOGUE

D illon pulled into the parking area next to his front door and thought, with any luck, he could be in bed within the next ten minutes. He climbed out of the car, careful not to step in any of the piles Lucifer left behind. To his amazement, there weren't any. The way his luck had been running that could only mean one thing, his neighbor Deitora had gotten fed up. Not what he needed right now.

He unlocked the door and stepped inside. The place appeared unusually clean, and there even seemed to be the hint of a pleasant scent. Lucifer bounded down the steps and peeked around the corner.

"Lucifer?" Dillon said and noticed a shiny new red collar around the dog's neck. "Outside?" Dillon asked, wondering where the collar came from. Deitora was more the type to put a noose around Lucifer's neck. The dog hurried out the open door and jumped off the stoop.

Dillon left the door open and walked into the kitchen. A vase of fresh-cut flowers sat on the counter. An envelope rested against the vase. Dillon opened the envelope and pulled out a condolence card, the kind you'd send upon someone's death. He opened the card and read the short note:

'Sorry I was such a pain. Saw you on the news. Call me so I can cook you dinner. I still have a chilled bottle of Prosecco. Tara'

THE END

Thank you for taking the time to read <u>Mistaken Identity</u>. If you enjoyed the read please consider leaving a review on Amazon. Even if it's just a sentence or two it really, really helps.

Check out the sample of the next book in the Jack Dillon Dublin Tales series, <u>Picture Perfect</u>.

PROLOGUE

It was a sunny Dublin morning when Killian Graham attempted to hit the snooze alarm for the third time. He missed and knocked the clock radio onto the floor. Pulling the pillow over his head didn't help, and he reluctantly slid out of bed and turned off the alarm with his foot. He took a couple of deep breaths, stretched, and cleared his throat on the way to the bathroom.

After shaving and a shower, he dressed and wandered into his kitchen area to make breakfast. He put the kettle on, took some black pudding (actually blood sausage) and streaky bacon (strips of bacon instead of a rasher) from the refrigerator, and tossed them into the frying pan. Once the kettle had boiled, he poured a tea and tossed two eggs into the frying pan.

Today was the first of the month, which meant the American would deposit two hundred euros in his account. The deposits had been going on for the past four years. He'd had his doubts initially, but they were legitimate and arrived like clockwork, not to mention the credit card he'd received. On the first of every month, he also received an email telling him where to go. There'd be a hotel reservation, a dinner reservation, a list of two or three pubs to stop for a pint, and some fool over in the states he'd never met was picking up the tab. It was crazy, but why look a gift horse in the mouth?

He dished up breakfast, sat down at the dining room table, and turned on his laptop. By the time the laptop was working, Killian had finished his eggs and streaky bacon and was about to dive into the black pudding. He logged into his bank account. Sure enough, the two hundred euro deposit was there waiting for him.

He cut into the black pudding, stuffed a piece in his mouth, and checked his cellphone. There were two text messages. The American wanted him to travel down to Wexford and spend the night in the Riverbank House Hotel. He'd made reservations for Killian and a guest at the Emerald Gardens restaurant. Perfect. A two-hour drive on the M11, and he knew someone who would make the night enjoyable. He quickly finished the blood pudding and tossed his plate in the sink.

He poured a fresh tea, grabbed his phone, and settled onto the couch in the sitting room. He hit speed dial and waited. Ciara answered on the fourth ring.

"Killian? Is that you?"

"Who else, darling? Say, my business has me down your way later today. I'll be staying at the Riverbank. Wondered if you'd be able to join me for dinner." He checked his laptop screen. "I've got an 8:00 reservation at the Emerald Gardens."

"Today? Mmm-mmm, something planned with me mum, but, well you know… Let me cancel, and if there's a problem, I'll get back to you."

"Perfect, I'll swing by to pick you up at 7:00. We can have a glass or two before dinner. Looking forward to seeing you, darling." He disconnected and sent a short two-sentence response to the text messages.

Thank you, more than happy to make my presence known. Standard procedure, leaving tips and will forward photos.

It always struck him as odd that the tour company wouldn't use stock photos, but for two hundred euros and an all-expenses paid weekend, who was he to argue? Three hours later, he had packed a bag and was on the road down to Wexford.

Part of the arrangement with the American was he couldn't tell anyone the circumstances. That was just fine with Killian. Just keep the money and the hotel stays coming, and he'd be more than happy to keep his mouth shut.

ONE

US Marshal Jack Dillon turned the corner and walked down the lane toward his house. He held onto the leash attached to Lucifer's dog collar. They were returning from making two rounds of Albert Park, just a few blocks away. Two rounds added up to two point four miles, and the walk, plus twenty minutes of chasing a tennis ball, hopefully, added up to enough exercise to keep Lucifer from causing any major damage today.

They passed Tara's house, across the lane and two units up from Dillon's. He turned to look for a moment, but only a moment, not wanting to be caught staring. Things were off and on with her, hot or cold. The last interlude had slowed to a halt when she'd told him she was interested in an older gentleman. Just now, there was a black Mercedes in the drive, the same one that had been there an hour ago at 7:00. Someone had spent the night.

He hurried down the lane, hoping his next-door neighbor Deitora wouldn't see him. No doubt, she'd open the door and rain on what was shaping up to be a sunny day. They made it safely into the house without Deitora's negative greeting. He wandered into the kitchen, tossed a biscuit to Lucifer, and then hurried upstairs to get ready for work. He showered, shaved, and pulled on pressed gray trousers and an open-collar white shirt. He strapped on his shoulder holster, shoved his nine-millimeter pistol into the holster, and covered it with a black sport coat. He draped the lanyard with his An Garda Síochána ID around his neck and headed downstairs.

Lucifer had settled into his pillow next to the fireplace in the sitting room. Dillon checked the locks on the backdoor then glanced out the window to see if Deitora was working in her front garden. Fortunately, she wasn't. He hurried outside, locked the front door, hopped in his car, and backed out onto the lane.

He was about to head up the lane when the black Mercedes suddenly pulled out of Tara's driveway. Tara was in the front passenger seat, saying something to the older gentleman driving. She glanced over at Dillon, obviously saw him, but didn't acknowledge him, and they drove up the lane. Dillon waited until they'd turned left and disappeared before he followed up the lane. He waited for a car to pass and then turned right.

Fifteen minutes later, he nodded at Dermot checking vehicles pulling in and out of the headquarters parking lot. He was able to grab a spot close to the door just as a car backed out. At the back door he waved his ID over the keypad and heard the door lock snap. He pulled the door open and walked down the hall to the elevator. He stepped inside, pressed the button for the fourth floor, and rode up by himself.

The door to the Special Branch was just down the hall on the fourth floor. Dillon waved his ID over the keypad then stepped into the office. It was a large room with too many desks and the constant hum of chatter coming from officers on the phone. Dillon headed for his desk up toward the front of the room. Prior to his being assigned to An Garda Síochána, his desk had been a collection spot for empty tea mugs, dirty plates, and the occasional sandwich wrap, along with a variety of silverware.

Nothing had changed, and Dillon started his day like every day, stacking up dirty plates and tea mugs. This morning he had the added treat of a Yorkie candy bar wrapper. He carried everything into the break room, tossed the wrapper in the trash, and set the plates, mugs, and silverware in the sink. He went back to his desk, grabbed his coffee mug, and hurried back into the break room to fill it.

There was maybe an inch of coffee remaining in the pot, which suggested it had been on the burner since yesterday. He filled his mug anyway, dumped the small amount remaining into the sink, and turned off the burner. He built up the courage to take a sip, which only served to convince him that, indeed, it had been on the burner since yesterday.

He went back out to his desk, settled in, and began reviewing his file, actually two files— both concerning missing American girls. The girls were students at DCU, Dublin City University, which coincidently was only two blocks from Dillon's home. As a matter of fact, he'd driven past it just this morning on his way to work.

The girls, Gretchen Malden from Big Falls, Montana, and Mary Ellen Schneider from Chicago, were studying for master's degrees in the International Business program at DCU for the next two semesters. Their disappearance was concerning but not alarming.

He'd been through a number of these cases where the individuals simply neglected to inform anyone of their travel plans. Usually, the travel amounted to a week or two on the continent, oftentimes with a new boyfriend. Upon their return, the girls would have to deal not only with the school but with parents who hadn't slept for a week, worried about their daughters. Over the past four years, two fathers and one couple had traveled to Dublin to aid in the search. Fortunately, in all three cases, the girls had returned to Dublin, surprised to see a parent and having to do a bit of explaining.

The odd thing with this situation was the anonymous tip that had been phoned in suggesting there may have been a kidnapping. Even stranger was the fact that the recording sounded as though whoever made it had been cut off in mid-sentence. The number had been traced to a payphone on the DCU Campus. Dillon figured he could probably count on one hand the number of existing pay phones in the city. Ten-year-old children had their own cellphone in today's world.

"Anything on those two?" a voice asked, and Dillon looked up to see Detective Inspector (DI) Paddy Suel, his partner.

Dillon shook his head and said, "Nothing, yet. I've got a call into Eric Bergman at the embassy along with Delta, Aer Lingus, and Ryan Air. Hopefully, someone will have a flight record. DCU is checking for cellphone numbers."

Suel shook his head. "Probably dragged some poor knacker off to Paris for a romantic interlude, and they broke up after the first night."

"Oh, these are smart girls, working on master's degrees in International Business. They wouldn't end up with guys like you or me."

That brought a smile to Suel's face. "Well, one can only hope."

Dillon sipped from his mug and made a face.

"Oh, bad coffee is it? I'm heading into the break room for a tea. I'll do up a fresh pot for youse."

"No, no, don't do that, Paddy. I'll make it. I thought I could get this down, but it's God awful. I'll make a pot."

"You don't like the way I make a coffee?" Suel asked and laughed.

"Right, and I'll get you a tea while I'm at it."

"Perfect. Much appreciated, Dillon. I take back some of the awful things folks around here have been saying about you."

"Yeah, right," Dillon said and carried his mug back to the break room. He put a fresh pot of coffee on, made a tea for Suel, and waited four or five minutes for the coffee to finish. He'd just brought the mugs out, set Suel's on his desk, and was heading back to do follow-up calls on the missing girls when Detective Chief Inspector (DCI) McCabe stepped to the door of his office and called, "Suel, Dillon, if you wouldn't mind."

Suel stood, shaking his head, and together, they hurried into McCabe's office.

DCI McCabe headed up the Special Branch. Not a man to spend time with fools, he ran a tight ship. He was highly respected by the force, the members of special branch in particular, and by the citizens at large. As they entered his office, he remained focused on a file and said, "Take a seat." He signed the top sheet in front of him and then placed the file on top of a stack of maybe a dozen other files.

"What's the word on the two girls?"

Dillon gave him a rundown, such as it was. They'd only received the case yesterday afternoon. "We should have a better handle on it in a couple of hours. Give the school, the airlines, and the embassy a chance to check things."

"DI Suel, you were looking into a group of women?"

"Yes, sir, the usual. They were transported here with promises of a job. Unfortunately, the job is in the sex trade. Beatings, drugs, the usual. It looks like eight women from the information we have, but they're being moved around, so it's been impossible to get a fix on them. Lots of rumors but nothing we can really act on."

"Dance clubs?" McCabe asked.

"That would be the usual route, but nothings turned up there, at least locally. I've got calls into Cork, Limerick, Sligo Town, Galway, and Waterford. So far, a big fat zero. It may be some faction of the Smirnov group but nothing definite so far."

McCabe drummed his fingers on his desk for a moment. "Okay, see if you can't yank some chains and get things moving one way or another. Thank you for the update, gentlemen. Keep me posted."

TWO

It was close to five when Killian Graham pulled in front of the Riverbank House Hotel. He'd never been there before, but that was no surprise since it was way out of his league. This was one of the great things about the arrangement. Killian stayed in the finest hotels, ate at the best restaurants, not to mention receiving favors from a number of very talented women, and it didn't cost him a cent.

The Riverbank House Hotel was located across the bridge from Wexford town, on the Slaney River estuary with a view of Wexford Harbor. The hotel was a two-story white stucco structure at least a hundred and fifty years old. Killian parked in the guest parking lot and wheeled his suitcase into the hotel. The receptionist counter was built of dark wood paneling with a black marble countertop. A smiling, uniformed receptionist stood behind the counter. Her name tag read Maureen.

"Welcome to the Riverbank House Hotel, sir. How are you?"

"Fine, just fine, I have a reservation. Killian Graham is the name," Killian said and proceeded to spell out his last name.

She clicked some keys on the computer and a moment later said, "Oh, yes, sir. Here it is. Paid in advance and you're in one of our deluxe suites. All I'll need is your signature, just here," she said, setting a 4X5 card down on the counter and pointing to the signature line.

"Perfect," he replied as he signed. "I'd like to leave a twenty percent tip to the final bill. I'm not carrying any cash, but I would like the staff to be taken care of upon my departure. If you would just add an amount to my bill, that would be fine with me."

"Only too happy to oblige, Mr. Graham. We'll debit your card. Conrad, two-oh-seven," she called.

A uniformed man suddenly appeared from seemingly out of nowhere. He took hold of Killian's suitcase and led the way to the antique elevator. After a twenty-second ride, they stepped out of the elevator into a hallway covered with thick plush carpet. Conrad led the way down the quiet hall. Occasional oil paintings in gilt frames hung on the wall. Conrad stopped at the third door labeled 207 in brass numerals. He inserted the key card into the lock, a green light flashed, and he opened the door.

Killian stepped into a paneled room with a massive, four-poster canopy bed. Red and gold velvet curtains hung from the window behind an antique red velvet couch. An elegant white fireplace was centered on the wall opposite the bed.

"Will there be anything else, sir?" Conrad asked as he rolled Killian's suitcase next to the upholstered bench at the end of the bed.

"No, thank you, much appreciated. I left my tip information with Maureen down at reception."

"Very good, sir. Enjoy your stay," Conrad said. He smiled, gave a slight nod, and pulled the door closed behind him.

Killian's brief inspection revealed the switch for the gas-fueled fireplace which he turned on. Bottles of red and white wine rested in the refrigerator. The bathroom sported a shower and a Jacuzzi. Killian walked back into the bedroom and stretched out on the four-poster bed. He snuggled into the fluffy pillows and opened his eyes only to discover a mirror across the top of the massive bed canopy. He gave himself a little wave, chuckled and thought, *Oh, this is going to be a very interesting evening.*

He pulled in front of Ciara's home a few minutes after 7:00. He grabbed the bouquet of flowers off the passenger seat and hurried up to her front door. She opened the door while the doorbell was still chiming.

"Well, look what the cat dragged in," she said. She was wearing a short black leather skirt with a large silver zipper down the front. Her blouse was black, apparently devoid of buttons, and tucked into her skirt, displaying her wonderfully deep cleavage.

"Hello, darling," he said and thrust the bouquet toward her after a quick kiss.

"Look at you, Killian, all decked out. Oh, the flowers, you always remember how much I love them. Let's go to the kitchen, and I'll place these in some water. I've got a glass of wine poured. I hope you're partial to the Sauvignon Blanc, nicely chilled," she said and gave him another kiss. This time, the kiss lasted twice as long as the previous one.

"Whatever wine you've got is just fine with me. So how are you? It's been too long."

"I'll say," she said, entering the kitchen. Two glasses of chilled wine sat on the counter, and a small plate held a half-dozen crackers with cheese and some sort of sauce on top of the cheese.

Killian stared as she arranged the flowers in a cut-glass vase. When finished, she pushed the vase off to the side and handed a wine glass to him. She raised her glass, they clinked, and each took a healthy sip.

"So what have you been up to, darling?" he asked.

"Well, mostly working. Keeping my head above water, thank God. But business is tough."

"You're still doing the handmade jewelry thing?"

She nodded and took another sip. "More or less. I've expanded it to some knitted items and gift cards. I've taken on a line of crystal from a guy out in Carrick on Shannon. That's doing rather well. Being self-employed, I've never worked harder for less money," she said and laughed. "Now, what about you? What brings you down this way?"

"Meeting with some people tomorrow afternoon. I've done some online marketing work for them and hope to make that a little more permanent. We'll see what happens," he lied.

"Well," she said, raising her glass. "Here's to the both of us. Let's hope this year will be better than the last."

"Always," he said as they clinked glasses once more. They chatted for another ten minutes until their glasses were empty, then climbed into his car and headed to the Emerald Gardens restaurant.

"I thought you were going to get rid of this thing," Ciara said as Killian pulled his black Peugeot away from the curb.

"You know how it goes. You make all sorts of plans, and then life happens. A couple of bumps in the road, and the next thing you know, I'm driving it for another year."

Ten minutes later, he pulled in front of the Emerald Gardens. He hurried out from behind the wheel and ran around the front of the car to open the door for Ciara.

"Thank you," she said. Once she climbed out of the Peugeot, she stood on the sidewalk and examined the front of the restaurant. "Mmm, oriental food. I am so ready."

Killian glanced across the street at Flanagan's pub, where the email instructed him to have an after-dinner drink. "Well then, let's not waste a minute," he said and held the door for her.

The restaurant wasn't large, and it projected the sense of a private setting. They settled in at a table with a red linen tablecloth and napkins. Killian gave a quick look at the wine list and ordered the most expensive white at sixty-five euros a bottle. They sipped wine, had a starter, and lingered over their meal. He ordered a glass of dessert wine for each of them, and when the waiter returned with the wine, Killian said, "Say, would you mind taking a couple of pictures?" He held out his cellphone, and the waiter took three photos.

"Thank you. I think just the check when you have a moment," Killian said.

"Why do you always do that?"

"Do what, ask for the check?"

"No, have them take pictures. Everywhere we go, you always do that."

"Could it be because I want to remember my wonderful evening with you?"

"Oh, stop," she said and laughed.

Once they finished, they headed across the street to Flanagan's pub. Killian promised they'd stay for just one. They left after two drinks and more pictures. They had a goodnight cocktail at the bar in the Riverbank House, had two more pictures taken, and then staggered up to Killian's suite.

While Ciara hurried into the bathroom, Killian sent his text message with the photos.

THREE

Sarah Halloran called through the closed office door. "You ready to go, Jimmy? I don't want to be late."

"Just finishing up. We'll be done in a minute," Jimmy Dugan called and then looked at the two men seated across from him. He was Jimmy Dugan to them and a handful of others. Outside in the world he went by Sarah's name, Halloran. "You tell that fat sack of shit that he either pays or an unfortunate accident is liable to happen. Got it?"

Both men nodded. There was no point in arguing or attempting to explain. Jimmy Dugan wasn't the type to listen. "You enjoy your evening," Freddy said. "We'll take care of this."

"Yeah, well, see that you do. Otherwise, we'll use him as an example of what happens when you don't fol-low directions," Jimmy said.

The two men opened the door and headed down the hall. Jimmy heard them call goodbye to Sarah in the kitchen. He shut down his computer, checked the desk to make sure nothing was out of place, and then stood. Just as he was about to head out, he heard the burner phone vibrate in the desk drawer. He quickly unlocked the drawer and ran his finger across the screen. Perfect, a text message from Killian Graham, three messages actually, all with photos. Well worth the investment. He glanced at the time, 7:30, which meant it was 12:30 over in Ireland.

'Hope you enjoyed your evening, Killian'

"Jimmy, I'm ready to go. I don't want to be late," Sarah said as she appeared in the doorway, placing the clip onto the back of a diamond earring.

"Just locking up. You look lovely. Look even better if you smiled."

"I'll smile when we're on our way."

"Well then, let's be off," he said dropping the burner phone back in the desk drawer and locking the drawer. He pulled on his sport coat and stepped out from behind the desk.

Sarah's eyes moved up and down, examining his attire.

"That's what you're wearing?"

"Yeah, this is what I'm wearing. I'm a guy, honey. No one cares what I wear, and no one will remember. You, on the other hand, look like a million bucks. Everyone is gonna remember how great you look."

She shook her head. "Cowboy boots?"

"I'm telling ya, no one is gonna care, let alone notice," he said, failing to mention they also covered his ankle holster and switchblade.

"All right, let's go, but one of these days…"

It was a fifteen-minute drive to the Venice Country Club. As Jimmy pulled up to the front door, an attendant appeared, pasted on a smile, and opened the door for Sarah. "Oh, Mr. and Mrs. Halloran, nice to see you again. Are you here for the Becker event?"

"Yes," Sarah said.

"They're in the Beach Room," he said as Sarah stepped out of the car. He closed the car door and hurried over to the driver's side.

"No scratches, Sean," Jimmy said and didn't smile.

"Of course not, sir. Have a pleasant evening."

Jimmy and Sarah headed into the country club as Sean pulled the car into the parking lot. He held his right hand out over the console and extended his middle finger. "Screw you, you pain in the ass," he said to Jimmy's back, as he cautiously drove into the parking lot. He debated peeing into the gas tank or in the back seat, all the while knowing for certain he'd be caught if he ever dared. He'd love to screw that prick Halloran, but he'd never be able to work up the courage. He'd get a five-dollar tip at the end of the night and then have to watch as Halloran walked around the entire car checking for scratches and dents.

He pulled into the parking lot, climbed out, locked the Mercedes, and placed an orange valet tag beneath the windshield wiper on the driver's side. He glanced around for anyone watching. The lot was empty, and he hurried to the back of the car and unlocked the trunk. He looked around once more then raised the lid. The trunk was spotless. He'd hoped to find a briefcase full of money or, God forbid, a body, but no such luck. Lights from a car pulling in front of the clubhouse suddenly lit up the short drive down to the parking lot, and Sean closed the trunk and hurried back to the clubhouse.

Jimmy leaned against the bar in the Beach room, sipping from his glass of sparkling water with a twist. Sarah was busy mingling and making the rounds, laughing and telling stories. Jimmy was content to stand at the bar until they moved to the dinner tables. He got a few nods from other guys ordering drinks. Two even said, "Hello," but didn't wait for a response. That was just fine with Jimmy. What the hell would they ever do for him? Besides, the last thing he needed was a new friend.

FOUR

Dillon was on his morning walk with Lucifer. They'd circled around Albert Park twice, and he'd been throwing the tennis ball for maybe ten minutes when his phone rang. "Dillon," was how he answered as he tossed the ball halfway across the field, and Lucifer took off after it.

"Good morning, my precious," DI Paddy Suel said. "I hope I'm interrupting something."

"Not at all, just getting out of the church service," Dillon said.

Suel paused for a second or two. "Really?"

"What do you think? What the hell do you want, Paddy? If it's bail money, I'll have to think about it."

"No, thankfully. Got a tip on where the Russian girls might be. It's early enough, they haven't been moved and probably won't be for the next hour or two. Care to pay a visit with me?"

"Yeah, I can meet you at the station in fifteen."

"Make it thirty. I'll meet you in the parking lot. We'll take my car."

"See you there," Dillon said as Lucifer headed toward him, holding the tennis ball in his mouth. He dropped the ball at Dillon's feet. Dillon picked up the ball, then turned around and made two fake throws across the walking path toward the field closer to the exit. Lucifer took off across the path then stopped maybe ten feet into the field. He turned around to look at Dillon, walking toward him. Dillon tossed the ball over Lucifer's head, and the dog took off, catching it in mid-air after the second bounce. Dillon tossed the ball two more times, each time drawing closer to the exit. After the second toss, he clipped the leash onto Lucifer's collar, and they jogged the rest of the way home. Jogging down his lane, Dillon noticed the black Mercedes wasn't parked in Tara's drive this morning.

He quickly shaved, pulled on jeans and a sweater before slipping on his shoulder holster and a leather jacket. He checked Lucifer who had settled onto his pillow, and hurried out the door. He was backing into a parking place in the Headquarters parking lot when Suel arrived. As Suel pulled in front of Dillon's car, he unlocked the car doors. Dillon had barely climbed into the passenger seat when Suel pulled away. Two paper cups with white plastic tops rested in the console of the car. One of the cups had the letter 'C' written on it with a marker.

"Please tell me that's a coffee for me," Dillon said.

"It is, and good morning to you," Suel replied.

"How'd you hear about this?"

"Where they're staying? I've got a snitch with a court appearance coming up. He's eager to help just now."

Dillon pulled the coffee out of the console and took a sip. It wasn't bad.

"Meet with your approval?" Suel asked.

"Yeah, very nice. You get this at Kennedy's or Bang Bang?"

"Bang Bang, Danny says hi, by the way."

"Thanks for this."

"You link up with Tara last night?"

"Nope, she seems to be taking a bit of a break, and I'm okay with that."

Suel glanced over for a second then said, "Yeah, but if she'd knocked on the door and wanted to spend the night, you wouldn't have turned her away."

"Hell no, I'm not crazy," Dillon said and changed the subject. "So where are we headed and tell me again who gave you the information."

"We're headed into the Liberties. The address is forty-four Reginald Street. Billy the Butler called me about six this morning with the tip."

"Isn't he the guy who worked at the hotel and was breaking into all the rooms?"

"Yeah, that's him, ended up serving three years."

"But you said he has a court appearance in a couple of weeks."

"Apparently, he didn't quite learn his lesson. If this tip works out, it could go a long way in reducing any sentence, maybe even tossing the case out."

The Liberties is a famous Dublin working-class area along the Liffey River. The area was a part of the city of Dublin but preserved its own jurisdiction from back in the twelfth century. Among other things, it's home to the Guinness Brewery.

Suel took Queen Street across the Liffey to Thomas Court and then a number of twists and turns until they finally arrived at Reginald street. They had to wait for a paneled plumbing van to turn off of the street. The truck was light blue with an image of a white sink, tub, and toilet on the side. The company name and phone number ran beneath the images of the plumbing fixtures. As the truck turned, the driver gave a friendly nod, and his pal in the passenger seat seemed to slink down.

"Come on, move, you plonker," Suel said then finished up with a colorful bit of swearing. They pulled in front of number forty-eight Reginald Street and parked. The block-long two-story brick structures shared common walls and looked to be at least two hundred years old. Each unit appeared to be about ten feet wide.

"You think they've got eight women stashed in number forty-four?" Dillon asked as he climbed out of the passenger seat.

"Probably have them sleeping on the floor," Suel said.

"Or in line for the bathroom."

"You think there's a bathroom in these places?" Suel said, laughed, and headed twenty feet down the street to number forty-four. There was a front window, maybe two feet wide, centered between the door and the shared wall. A yellowed shade, curled along the sides, was pulled down, covering the window. A sign resting on the windowsill read 'Unit For Sale.'

They stood on either side of the door. Suel nodded at Dillon and knocked on the door. They waited, and nothing happened. He knocked again and tried the doorknob. The knob turned, and the door drifted open maybe six inches. Suel pushed the door with his foot and looked in. "Hello, anyone home?" he called.

Dillon peeked into the empty front room with a small, coal-burning fireplace. A soiled pillow and a worn gray blanket rested on the floor in front of the fireplace. A steep staircase maybe six feet from the front door led up to the second floor.

"Nice of you to invite us in, thank you," Suel said louder than normal and stepped inside. Dillon followed and closed the door behind them. "Jesus Christ," Suel said and shook his head. A doorway led to a back room, and Suel walked toward it while Dillon stood at the base of the staircase. Suel peeked in the room and stepped back to Dillon. "Nothing but a broken window and an empty whiskey bottle. Let's check upstairs."

Dillon grabbed hold of the wooden railing, which was surprisingly sturdy, and headed up the staircase. A small, empty room was at the top of the stairs, no hall-way, just the room. Another coal-burning fireplace was positioned roughly above the fireplace on the first floor. Pieces of newspaper were scattered around the floor. A bathtub, sink, and toilet were in a far corner. The card-board tube to a roll of toilet paper lay on the floor next to the toilet. Lengths of heavy twine and what looked like bits of duct tape were piled in a corner.

"You think they were given that newspaper to cover themselves?" Dillon asked.

"Maybe. I'd guess they were tied up and probably gagged," Suel said, nodding at the twine and duct tape as he walked over to the sink. He turned one of the worn handles. Rust-colored water sputtered out of the fixture and a moment later ran onto the floor. He quickly turned off the water, glanced at the toilet, and recoiled. "Christ almighty, don't get any nearer to that. Nothing here to see, and if we stay any longer, we're liable to catch some dreadful disease. I'd say they were here, but we missed them. For all I can tell, they could have been here last week."

They headed back down the stairs, and Dillon stepped over to the entrance to the back room. A drain-pipe stood where there must have been a sink at one time. A strip of wood ran across the wall against the ceiling for maybe four feet where a cabinet or shelves had hung.

Suel was already outside when Dillon stepped out and closed the door behind him. "You want to try the neighbors?"

"I don't see any point, but we can try," Suel said. They knocked on a half-dozen doors but never got an answer.

"I'm going back to that place for a minute. Pick me up there," Dillon said and hurried up the street. He pulled out a pocket notebook and wrote down the phone number listed on the 'For Rent' sign. Suel pulled up a half-minute later, and Dillon climbed in.

"You leaving a note?" Suel asked.

"No, but I'd like to talk to whoever is renting the place out. See if they gave the key to anyone."

"That broken window in what used to be the kitchen is probably how they got in and then opened the front door from the inside. Damn it. I wonder when they were actually in the place."

"I'm guessing last night," Dillon said.

"Care to share with me what you're basing that assumption on?"

"Well, based on your reaction to whatever you saw in the toilet, the fact that that room didn't reek to high heaven yet, might suggest that the toilet had been recently filled."

"By a lot more than one," Suel added.

Dillon nodded. "Plus, you know what else I'm thinking? What if we just missed them and that plumbing van with the two guys actually had the women in the back? Now I'm thinking that guy sort of ducking down in the passenger seat might make a lot more sense."

"You recall the name on that truck?"

"No, I was too busy listening to you bitch at the driver to pay any attention."

"I was doing that to keep him occupied so you could memorize the name and phone number," Suel said. He turned onto the main road and headed back to the station. "Hopefully, there aren't a lot of companies with a van like that. We can check it out when we get back."

Once back in the Special Branch office, Suel headed to the restroom. Dillon gathered up the plates, mugs, and spoons from his desk and deposited them in the break room sink. Fortunately, the lights were off in DCI McCabe's office, which gave them some time to try to identify the plumbing van they suspected of transporting the women.

TO BE CONTINUED . . .

Thanks for taking the time to check out <u>Picture Perfect</u>, the ninth book in the Jack Dillon Dublin Tales series. Things are bound to get absolutely crazy, grab a copy and enjoy!

Check out the list of books by Mike Faricy on the following page!

BOOKS BY MIKE FARICY
CRIME FICTION FIRSTS

A boxset of the first four books in four crime fiction series:

Russian Roulette; Dev Haskell series
Welcome; Jack Dillon Dublin Tales series
Corridor Man; Corridor Man series
Reduced Ransom! Hot Shot series

The following titles comprise the Dev Haskell series:

Russian Roulette: Case 1
Mr. Swirlee: Case 2
Bite Me: Case 3
Bombshell: Case 4
Tutti Frutti: Case 5
Last Shot: Case 6
Ting-A-Ling: Case 7
Crickett: Case 8
Bulldog: Case 9
Double Trouble: Case 10
Yellow Ribbon: Case 11
Dog Gone: Case 12
Scam Man: Case 13
Foiled: Case 14
What Happens in Vegas… Case 15
Art Hound: Case 16
The Office: Case 17

Star Struck: Case 18

International Incident: Case 19

Guest From Hell: Case 20

Art Attack: Case 21

Mystery Man: Case 22

Bow-Wow Rescue: Case 23

Cold Case: Case 24

Cash Up Front: Case 25

Dream House: Case 26

Alley Katz: Case 27

The Big Gamble: Case 28

Bad to the Bone: Case 29

Silencio!: Case 30

Surprise, Surprise: Case 31

Hit & Run: Case 32

Suspect Santa: Case 33

P.I. Apprentice: Case 34

Rebel Without a Clue: Case 35

Puppy Love: Case 36

The following titles are Dev Haskell novellas:
Dollhouse
The Dance
Pixie
Fore!
Twinkle Toes
(*a Dev Haskell short story*)

The following are Dev Haskell Boxsets:
Dev Haskell Boxset 1-3
Dev Haskell Boxset 4-6
Dev Haskell Boxset 7-9
Dev Haskell Boxset 10-12
Dev Haskell Boxset 13-15
Dev Haskell Boxset 16-18
Dev Haskell Boxset 19-21
Dev Haskell Boxset 22-24
Dev Haskell Boxset 25-27
Dev Haskell Boxset 28-30
Dev Haskell Boxset 1-7
Dev Haskell Boxset 8-14
Dev Haskell Boxset 15-19
Dev Haskell Boxset 20-24
Dev Haskell Boxset 25-29

The following titles comprise the Jack Dillon Dublin Tales series:
Welcome
Jack Dillon Dublin Tale 1
Sweet Dreams
Jack Dillon Dublin Tale 2
Mirror Mirror
Jack Dillon Dublin Tale 3
Silver Bullet
Jack Dillon Dublin Tale 4
Fair City Blues

Jack Dillon Dublin Tale 5
Spade Work
Jack Dillon Dublin Tale 6
Madeline Missing
Jack Dillon Dublin Tale 7
Mistaken Identity
Jack Dillon Dublin Tale 8
Picture Perfect
Jack Dillon Dublin Tale 9
Dublin Moon
Jack Dillon Dublin Tale 10
Mystery Woman
Jack Dillon Dublin Tale 11
Second Chance
Jack Dillon Dublin Tale 12
Payback Brother
Jack Dillon Dublin Tale 13
The Heist
Jack Dillon Dublin Tale 14
Jewels To Kill For
Jack Dillon Dublin Tale 15
Retirement Scheme
Jack Dillon Dublin Tale 16
The Collector
Jack Dillon Dublin Tale 17

Jack Dillon Dublin Tales Boxsets:
Jack Dillon Dublin Tales 1-3
Jack Dillon Dublin Tales 4-6

Jack Dillon Dublin Tales 1-5
Jack Dillon Dublin Tales 1-7
Jack Dillon Dublin Tales 6-10

The following titles comprise the Hotshot series;
Reduced Ransom! Second Edition
Finders Keepers! Second Edition
Bankers Hours Second Edition
Chow Down Second Edition
Moonlight Dance Academy Second Edition
Irish Dukes (Fight Card Series)
written under the pseudonym Jack Tunney

The following titles comprise the Corridor Man series:
Corridor Man
Corridor Man 2: Opportunity knocks
Corridor Man 3: The Dungeon
Corridor Man 4: Dead End
Corridor Man 5: Finger
Corridor Man 6: Exit Strategy
Corridor Man 7: Trunk Music
Corridor Man 8: Birthday Boy
Corridor Man 9: Boss Man
Corridor Man 10: Bye Bye Bobby

Corridor Man novellas:
Corridor Man: Valentine
Corridor Man: Auditor

Corridor Man: Howling
Corridor Man: Spa Day

The following are Corridor Man Boxsets:
Corridor Man Boxset 1-3
Corridor Man Boxset 1-5
Corridor Man Boxset 6-9

THANK YOU!

Contact the author:
- Email: mikefaricyauthor@gmail.com
- Twitter: @Mikefaricybooks
- Facebook: Mike Faricy Author
- Website: http://www.mikefaricybooks.com

Published by

MJF Publishing